By George Baxt:

The Pharoah Love Trilogy

A QUEER KIND OF DEATH*
SWING LOW, SWEET HARRIET*
TOPSY AND EVIL**

The Van Larsen/Plotkin Series

A PARADE OF COCKEYED CREATURES*
"I!" SAID THE DEMON*
SATAN IS A WOMAN**

The Celebrity Series

THE DOROTHY PARKER MURDER CASE*
THE ALFRED HITCHCOCK MURDER CASE*

Non-Series Novels

THE AFFAIR AT ROYALTIES
BURNING SAPHO
THE NEON GRAVEYARD
PROCESS OF ELIMINATION

*now available in a Crime Classic® edition.
**forthcoming from the IPL Library of Crime Classics®

GEORGE BAXT

THE
ALFRED HITCHCOCK
MURDER CASE

INTERNATIONAL POLYGONICS, LTD.
NEW YORK CITY

THE ALFRED HITCHCOCK MURDER CASE

This novel has not been authorized or endorsed by Alfred Hitchcock, his estate, or any of the individuals or companies that may be licensed to use the name "Alfred Hitchcock." It is simply a historical novel, a work of fiction that includes Alfred Hitchcock as a character.

With the exception of a few film people of the era and, of course, Alfred Hitchcock and his family (all whose real names are used), the characters in this novel are fictitious and are not intended to be based on any actual persons. Similarly, the novel's story and the incidents depicted in the novel (including those involving real people) are fictitious, although some of the places and historical events mentioned in the novel are real.

Library of Congress Card Catalog No. 87-80312
ISBN 0-930330-55-2

Printed and manufactured in the United States of America
by Guinn Printing.
First IPL printing April 1987.
10 9 8 7 6 5 4 3 2 1

For Fred Terman, Barbara Ferris,
John Quested, Madge Ryan,

and also starring
Sally Ann Howes and Douglas Rae

THE
ALFRED HITCHCOCK
MURDER CASE

BOOK ONE

Munich,
June 1925

One

The Furies were gaining on him. He couldn't run fast enough; he was too fat. His fiancée, Alma Reville, was shouting a warning.

"Back!" he screamed. "Back! you sons of bitches!"

But still they came laughing maniacally, grabbing for him with fingers like steel talons.

"Why don't you love me?" Hitch shrieked at his father, but the pudgy greengrocer brandishing a bunch of celery like a weapon continued to gain on him. The police constable at his side was huffing and puffing, waving his billy club, threatening Hitch with jail. Hitch had no idea where he was leading them. "I have no ideas!" he yelled.

"What do you mean, you have no ideas?" The voice was familiar. Hitch looked to the right, and there was Michael Balcon, his film producer, pacing him. "What the bloody hell do you mean by no ideas? I stick my neck across the chopping block convincing them you're the perfect man to direct this film, your first bloody film ever, and you tell me you have no ideas? I arrange to have the film shot here in Munich so the money people won't be breathing down your neck and you have no ideas? Really, Hitch!"

"Pay us what you owe us!" screamed Hitch's creditors. Now how the hell did they get into this scene? Hitch wondered as he heard their heels pounding the pavement behind him.

"Go away!" Hitch shouted at them over his shoulder, "You're not in this scene! I'll have no improvisations on this film! Get out of this scene! Get out! Get out! Get the bloody hell out!"

"Hitch, Hitch," said Alma softly. "Wake up, Hitch, you're screaming the house down." She shook him gently, and the bed wobbled.

"Herr Hitchcock, waking zie up!" That was Frau Schumann, the landlady of the guest house; unlike those other Schumanns, terribly unmusical and terribly loud. She jingled her key ring over Hitchcock's face. "Waking zie up, Herr Hitchcock!"

His eyes flew open. "What the bloody hell!"

"You were having a nightmare," explained Alma, "and Frau Schumann unlocked your door."

"That sounds obscene." Hitch struggled into a sitting position and greeted the landlady and his fiancée. "Good morning," he said solemnly. "I have had a most disturbing nightmare."

"We heard it," said Alma. Frau Schumann said something about coffee and rolls and left them, slamming the door behind her. Hitch took Alma's hand and recited as much of the nightmare as he could remember. After a few minutes of the litany, Alma said, "This is where I came in. You've been having this nightmare ever since we arrived in Munich."

"Well, I can't help it," said Hitchcock mournfully. "I'd just as soon shift to a different reel, but it's out of my hands. I wish my father would get his apron washed, and the rakish tilt of his straw hat is most unbecoming. That horse's ass of a police constable with him is the same monster who locked me up in a cell for quarter of an hour at my father's request when I was a child. And as for Mickey Balcon accusing me of having no ideas, why, that's treason!"

"Hitch, dear." Alma was standing, tightening the belt of her slightly tatty bathrobe. "Mickey believes in you, he fought for you."

"Well, he was most disconcerting in my nightmare!" Hitch was out of bed, looking like a week-old muffin in his crumpled pajamas as he struggled into a bathrobe Alma recognized as the one she had given him for his birthday last year. "And as for those creditors with their deadly fingers reaching out for me . . ." He shuddered and Alma went to him and put her arms around his neck.

"My dear, you shall bring this film in on schedule and on budget. It may not be the most memorable film debut—"

"You have no confidence in me! I knew it! I could tell it on your face from the first day we saw rushes!"

"The first day we saw rushes I knew, I very proudly knew, that my intended was a man of great talent and great promise but sadly lacked a great script."

"It *is* a shoddy piece of merchandise, isn't it?"

"As long as you recognize that. But what I also see in the rushes is a beautiful ability to camouflage mediocrity with some lovely film work."

Hitchcock smiled. "I knew I chose well when I asked

5

you to marry me." He kissed her lightly on her cheek. "Now get out of here while I shave, bathe, get dressed, and try to conjure up some flashy new camera angles. Oh, my God, what a deadly plot!"

The Pleasure Garden, Alfred Hitchcock's debut as a film director, was the story of two girlfriends who danced in the chorus of a music hall called, of course, The Pleasure Garden. Two American film actresses, Virginia Valli and Carmelita Geraghty, had been imported to Germany to co-star in hopes that their names would encourage a distribution deal in America. Their co-stars were British actors, Miles Mander and John Stuart, known mostly to their own families. Somehow, the climax of the film occurred in one of those sordid Indian Ocean island villages usually favored by W. Somerset Maugham. Unfortunately, Maugham had nothing to do with the plot of this film, and neither did the scriptwriter, as far as Hitchcock was concerned, so Alma was busy doing some clandestine rewriting, displaying a marvelous talent for scripting.

An hour later, in a taxi taking them to the Emelka Studios, Hitchcock thumbed through the script and found the scenes he'd scheduled for filming that day. After a few moments he sighed and said, "We need a rape scene." The taxi driver studied his passengers through his rearview mirror with a slight look of shock and distaste.

"Who gets raped and why?" asked Alma while attacking a fingernail with an emery board.

"I think Miles Mander should attempt to rape Carmelita."

"When? Where? Why?"

"How do I know? Think about it."

"How soon do you want it?"

"I don't know. I don't even know if we need it. Maybe

6

the film will hang together without it once it's been edited. I wonder if childbirth is as painful as filmbirth."

"I wouldn't know. I hope to someday, but at the moment I can't much help with an opinion."

Hitchcock was staring out the window. "What a lovely city this is."

"I find it disturbing."

"Why, for heaven's sake?"

"I don't mean Munich, I mean Germany. I find Germany disturbing. The economy's a disaster. The mark is worth bloody nothing or next to that."

"Thank God for that where we're concerned."

The taxi driver was looking hostile.

"Then there's the rioting, those awful fascist groups and their menace. I can feel it at the studio."

"Oh? Have you uncovered menace in our midst?"

"It's nothing I can name or put my finger on, but I have this feeling that the smiles that greet us aren't genuine smiles. I know they're all glad to be working, what with so many of their major talents drifting off to Hollywood. . . ."

Hitchcock shifted and tried unsuccessfully to cross his legs. He gave up the effort with a sigh and said, "Who can blame them? Lubitsch was the first to go and sent back such glowing messages about gold in the streets that soon F. W. Murnau and Paul Leni and a whole raft of actors followed suit—and what have they got left?" He sighed again. "Me and some second-raters of their own."

"Oh, come now! Fritz Lang's not a second-rater, and neither is Pabst. They're doing marvelous work. You haven't forgotten we're dining with the Langs tonight."

"That dreadful wife. Thea's a fascist. Fritz is fascinating, but Thea's something else. Promise me when we're married that you won't be dreadful."

7

"I'll try my best not to be, but I do have my quixotic moments. I don't think the film needs a rape."

"It needs something." Hitch stared out the window as they passed St. Peter's Church, which dated from the eleventh century. Alma waited. She was soon rewarded. His face lit up. "I know what we need. We need a marvelous, brutal, bloody murder! The gorier, the better." The taxi driver cringed and narrowly avoided hitting a pedestrian.

Alma's shoulders sagged. "Now how do I work a murder into a story of two chorus girls in a music hall? Have you a clue?"

"If I had a clue, we'd have a murder." He folded his hands across his stomach. "I ought to be doing thrillers. That's what I ought to be doing."

"Well, my darling, if you pull off this one even halfway successfully, Mickey Balcon's bound to listen sympathetically to anything you propose."

"Let me break this to you gently. Mickey's sent me a letter, it came yesterday, and my next film is already settled."

"Oh, Hitch, how marvelous! Why didn't you tell me!"

"It's too depressing. It's called *The Mountain Eagle*."

"Set where?"

"On a mountain, where else?"

"Have you read the script?"

"Yes. Mickey's letter accompanied the script. I think it's what brought on my nightmare again. To be perfectly kind, the script is dreadful. And it's to star another American actress. Nita Naldi."

"The vamp? Is this one about a vamp? Aren't vamps a bit passé?"

"Oh, vamps are terribly passé. That's why Miss Naldi has so agreeably agreed to do a film in Munich."

8

Alma's chin dropped. "You mean we're to do another film here in Munich?" Hitchcock nodded his head solemnly. Alma looked unhappy. So did the taxi driver.

Ten minutes later, they were walking arm in arm toward the stage housing their project. The sky was overcast, and the grayness of the day gave the studio the look of a prison compound. Alma was thinking it was too bleak and damp for a day in June and longed for the sunshine and warmth of Italy, where they had earlier done some location shooting.

"I thought our taxi driver was sinister," said Hitchcock.

"Really? I never even noticed what he looked like."

"He looked sinister. He was listening to every word we said. I could catch him reacting every so often. His reactions were terribly unfriendly. I wonder if he's a spy."

"What would anyone be doing spying on us?"

"Why shouldn't they be spying on us? We're Britons making a film in their godforsaken country with American actresses and a partially British crew. They're probably wondering why we didn't stay at home where we belong."

"Surely they realize we're here because it's cheaper to film here. The rate of exchange from pounds to marks is so great it's embarrassing."

"I don't know if they realize anything of the sort. For all they know, we've been set up as a project by British Intelligence to come over here for a firsthand study of this rise of incipient fascism. It's an absolutely marvelous idea. Why hasn't anyone thought of it before?"

"You're thinking about it now. Do something with it."

"What an odd-looking man."

"Don't change the subject."

"What a magnificently ugly face he has."

Alma looked at the man. He was over six feet tall, terribly thin and gaunt, and his face looked as though it had once been shattered and then badly reconstructed. It was a frightening face, the chin and cheeks pitted with deep scars. She wondered if his tragedy had befallen him in the war. Surely no one could be unfortunate enough to be born with that face. He was probably younger than he looked, possibly not yet thirty. They knew the person he was chatting with, Fredrick Regner, a scriptwriter. Alma and Hitchcock liked Regner. He was in his mid-twenties and very good-looking, a Viennese by birth. The two men stood near the entrance to the sound stage.

"I must find out if he's an actor. Someday, when I do my first thriller, I want an actor with a face like that."

"He'd be a marvelous-looking murderer."

"Oh, no. Not with a face like that. It would be too obvious he's the murderer. I would use him as a red herring."

Alma smiled. "Your MacGuffin."

"Oh yes, he's a perfectly delicious MacGuffin." In Hitchcock's parlance, a MacGuffin was the device used to fool the audience away from the truth of the story, something he had invented for several original screenplay ideas he'd been nursing but had been unable to sell. Alma had come to love Hitchcock's MacGuffins. There wasn't one in *The Pleasure Garden*. It wasn't that kind of story. It wasn't very much of a story. It was just a wonderful opportunity for Hitchcock to get his foot in the door of directing. He was a good director, she knew this from working with him and comparing his early results to those of the hacks with whom she had worked as continuity girl in England. Hitchcock had a magnificent imagination, a wonderfully creative eye, a deliciously sly sense of humor, and she knew that if opportunities continued to open up for him, Hitch would mature into one of the finest directing talents of the cinema. (And

God bless Mickey Balcon, Hitch's senior by only three years, for his faith in Hitch, who was only twenty-six.)

"Where did he go?" Hitch's voice snapped Alma out of her reverie.

"Where did *who* go?"

"My MacGuffin. I blinked my eyes and he's disappeared! Hey, there! Freddy!"

Fredrick Regner recognized Hitchcock and Alma, and his face brightened. "Halloo, Hitch! Alma!"

"Where did he go?" Hitch was annoyed and frustrated.

"Where did *who* go?" asked Regner, almost managing to look as innocent as a newborn babe.

"The man you were talking to!"

"Oh, *that* man."

"That face! That absolutely unique face. Is he an actor?"

"I haven't the vaguest idea."

"But you were talking to him!"

"He was looking for Stage Three. I sent him off in the right direction."

"Well, go reclaim him!" ordered Hitchcock, the others recognizing the irritation in his voice. "I want to know him and file him for future use."

"Is this a joke?" Regner, along with just about everybody else at the studio, was familiar with Hitchcock's practical jokes.

"Of course it's not a joke. It's a face. A wonderful face. A perfect MacGuffin."

Regner looked as though he might be contemplating suicide. Alma came to his rescue and explained the Mac-Guffin. Regner laughed. "I'll go look for him."

"You'd better find him," growled Hitchcock, "or I shall reveal the shame of your birth." Alma followed him into the sound stage while Regner reached into his jacket breast pocket for his pipe, placed it in his mouth, his face a deep study.

The Hitchcock stage was a beehive of activity. Carpenters were hammering away at the stage of The Pleasure Garden music hall, reinforcing it for the dance number Hitch was planning to shoot that morning. Electricians were climbing high in the flies like monkeys gone berserk, adjusting the arc lights and replacing burned-out gelatins. The stage manager was barking orders at invisible recipients, and in an isolated corner a three-piece orchestra, hired to provide mood music for the American actresses, was tuning up. There were a pianist and two violinists. The pianist, Rudolf Wagner, was improvising a melody that immediately caught Alma's fancy. While Hitch went to consult with the camera operator, Alma crossed to the musicians and stood next to the pianist. "That's so beautiful," she told Wagner the pianist, "it's so touching, so elegiac, so . . ."

"So mournful," said Wagner.

"No, not really mournful. Not mournful in the sense of death or tragedy."

"Mournful can mean other things." His English was remarkably good; in fact, Alma and Hitch and the others who were not German were amazed at the perfect English spoken by so many Germans. Wagner repeated the melody. "Mournful can mean the memory of a happiness in the past that will never again be recaptured; it can allude to a loss of innocence." Alma was humming along with the pianist. "I am pleased that you like my little melody."

"It's your own?"

"My very own. Just these few bars. I have no idea how it will develop, if it will develop. This may be all there is."

"Well, I think it's exquisite. Oh, dear. Here's your daughter frowning in our direction."

12

There was a slight trace of a smile on Wagner's lips. "Rosie is very much her mother's child. Her mother was always frowning. She frowned when I asked her to marry me. She frowned on our wedding night. She frowned when Rosie was born, and she died with a frown on her face last winter."

"I'm so sorry to hear she's dead."

"I'm not. She was an absolute bore. I only miss her frowns. Rosie's frowns aren't as inventive as my wife's frowns were. My wife had a frown for every occasion, and no two frowns were alike. Rosie's frowns are lazy frowns. Rosie disapproves of me. She is only seventeen years of age. . . ."

"Really? I thought she was much older."

"That's because she is so dough-faced and pudgy and her hair is so stringy and brown. Rosie disapproved of me from birth. Her birth, not my birth."

"Is she an only child?"

"*Gott*, yes. After Rosie, all further procreation was discouraged. When I was away in the war and I heard Munich was bombed, I had this wonderful fantasy that my wife and Rosie had disappeared. No such luck. I came home, every house on the street was in devastating ruins. But not ours. There it stood, with my wife and Rosie in the doorway, frowning." Alma laughed. "Shall I tell you why Rosie is frowning now? I don't even have to turn and look at her. I can tell you what she is doing. She is holding her pad and pencil trying to look less unimportant; she doesn't like being a script girl's assistant. Rosie does not like unimportance. So she doesn't like me. I am unimportant. I play atmosphere music for actresses who could use a lot of atmosphere, instead of being a world-famous musician and composer. Rosie once said to me when she was still a child and I couldn't find

13

a job, 'Better your hands should have been blown off in the war than to waste your talent as a lowly pianist.'"

"How awful!" Alma hoped Rosie couldn't overhear her father.

"Oh, she's very awful. Just this morning she was crossing the street ahead of me and she didn't see a truck bearing down on her. For the first time in weeks, I smiled. Then some damn fool shouted at her and she leapt out of the truck's path and now she stands behind me frowning. She's also a virgin."

Rosie joined them. "Must you keep repeating this melody over and over again, Father?"

"It's such a lovely melody," remonstrated Alma.

"You do not find it boring that he repeats it over and over again?" Rosie stared at Alma as though she had just arrived from outer space.

"Not at all. I've memorized it." She la-la-la'd along with Wagner, who was immensely pleased, not noticing the strange expression on Rosie's face. It was no longer a frown; it looked more like a suspicion.

"Alma!" Hitchcock sounded annoyed.

"My master's voice," said Alma, and left them to join Hitch, who seemed to be in the midst of a problem with the camera operator.

"Miss Reville is very pretty." Coming from Rosie's mouth, the statement sounded like a death sentence.

"Very," agreed her father, now having switched to a Viennese waltz.

"You fancy her?"

"She's not so fancy. She's quite down to earth."

"You know what I mean. You would like to sleep with her."

His hands crashed down on the keyboard. Heads

turned, and he quickly resumed playing the waltz. "Go away, Rosie. I see enough of you at home." They were joined by Anna Grieban, the script girl.

"Rosie, I have some changes for Miss Valli." She held out a sheet of paper to the girl. "Would you please give them to her?" Rosie took the paper and began reading it. Anna said to Wagner, "What was that lovely melody you were playing a few minutes ago? It's enchanting." Smiling, Wagner returned to his original composition. Frowning, Rosie went in search of Virginia Valli.

"Rosie doesn't like this melody," Wagner told Anna.

"There isn't very much that Rosie seems to like." She began to hum along with Wagner. "How lovely. How really lovely."

"Miss Reville likes it too. She memorized it."

"Has she really."

"Yes."

La-la-la-la . . . la-la-la . . .

Fifteen minutes later, Hitchcock was ready for his first setup. The camera was placed exactly where he wanted it, and Virginia Valli and Carmelita Geraghty were summoned to the set. Though neither was a major film star, both had enviable reputations for beauty and acting ability, Virginia Valli being especially gifted. In their chorus-girl costumes, they were provocatively sexy. They greeted everyone with a warm friendliness, and Hitchcock was grateful the ladies were liked by the crew and the other members of the acting company. Hitchcock embraced both women and then began to explain the action. He led them onto The Pleasure Garden stage where, with the choreographer, he began to line them up and illustrate where the camera would follow the simple dance routine devised for them.

As Hitch dealt with his principals and the chorus line,

the assistant director gave instructions to the extras and supporting players at the tables portraying music-hall patrons. Many were smoking, and the air was growing heavy with cigar and cigarette smoke. Alma began to wonder if their meager film budget could cover the cost of a gas mask. She asked one of the assistants if it was possible to find an electric fan, and as he went off in search of one, she heard Rosie Wagner say to her, "You think my father has talent for composing melodies?"

"He does. And you shouldn't be so pessimistic about him. He's a very nice and a very gifted man."

"You think this, yes?"

"I think this, yes."

"That is why you memorize his melody?"

"Is there something wrong with wanting to learn it by heart?" She hummed it. "I wish it had words."

"Perhaps it has words." They heard Anna Grieban shouting for Rosie, who, before leaving Alma, favored her with an enigmatic expression.

What a strange, unattractive, po-faced little creature she is, thought Alma. Then her face lit up. Rudolf Wagner was playing his composition again. Alma turned toward the trio and saw Hitch's MacGuffin half concealed behind a scenery flat just past where the trio was situated. She hurried to Hitchcock.

"Hitch, he's here on the stage."

Hitch was not in the mood to be interrupted. "Not now, Alma. This is a very difficult shot. . . ." He added under his breath, ". . . considering that none of these ladies knows the first thing about chorus dancing."

"Your MacGuffin is here."

Hitch turned to her. "That face? Here? Where?"

She pointed past the trio. "Over there, just behind . . ." He wasn't there. "He's gone."

"Yes, dear. Of course, dear." He returned to the problem of filming the movie.

"I saw him," said Alma to no one in particular, and would remember the chill that suddenly overtook her in the smoke-filled and overheated stage.

Two

In her sadly furnished bedroom in Frau Schumann's guest house, Alma sat at the dressing table staring at her image in the mirror. The face was attractive, but it was also pale and troubled. Her mind was as overcast as the skies had been all day, and she did not like this feeling of uneasiness that had enveloped her like a dark shroud at the studio that morning and continued to worry her. She could not stop thinking about the man with the strange face, the mutual hatred of Rudolf Wagner and his odd daughter, Rosie, or the lovely melody Wagner had presumably composed that morning and kept playing and playing throughout the day. She was now humming it under her breath and wished she could stop, but it had captured and possessed her.

"Alma!" Hitchcock was banging on their communal wall. "We'll be late!"

"Almost ready!" shouted Alma as she hastily rouged her lips lightly and then dusted her face with powder. She heard him leave his bedroom and lock the door. He tapped lightly on her door. When she told him it was open, he came in, shut the door, and leaned against it with his arms folded.

La-la-la-la . . . la-la-la . . .

"Oh, for God's sake, Alma, have done with it! That tune's becoming as boring as 'Yes, We Have No Bananas.'"

"I fell in love with it this morning, but falling out of love with it is twice as difficult." She was examining the contents of her handbag. "It is pretty, though, isn't it? He should be composing film scores and operettas, don't you think?"

"I think we're going to be late for dinner with the Langs if you don't stop ferreting about in that handbag."

She snapped the bag shut, stood up. "Ready."

"What's troubling you?"

"Oh, dear, is it all that obvious?"

"You're whistling between your teeth. That always sets me on edge. That means Miss Alma Reville is on edge. Did something happen today to upset the balance of your usually admirable equanimity?"

"Oh, stop being so pompous!" She sat down again. He sat on her bed, which was uncomfortable and lumpy. "My uneasiness is absolutely unexplainable, but it's there and I'm not quite sure how to cope with it. Maybe after a glass or two of wine . . ."

"You'll still be uneasy, and in addition tipsy, and then ill. Was it the man with the face? The fact that he wasn't there when you insisted he was there?"

"Oh, he was there all right. I don't hallucinate. Half

hidden behind a piece of scenery, staring at Rudolf Wagner at the piano repeating that lovely melody. I'm sure he noticed me trying to draw your attention to him and did his flit."

Hitchcock shrugged. "Well, so what? It isn't as though we're in the midst of some spy melodrama, you know."

"Then there's Wagner's daughter, Rosie. She said something very strange to me."

"Rosie is a very strange child."

"Her father detests her."

"Full marks for Wagner. She's perfectly detestable. She looks like an unbaked pudding."

Alma told him about her conversation with Wagner, his detestation of both wife and daughter. "And then later, when Rosie heard me humming Wagner's melody, she challenged me."

"To a duel?"

"Can we skip the asides, Hitch, and let me get on with it?" He looked as though he was about to fall asleep, which he wished he could do instead of going out to dinner with Fritz Lang, the director, and his wife, Thea von Harbou, a talented scriptwriter. He heard Alma say, "Rosie asked me if I thought the melody was all that good, and I said of course I did and it was too bad it didn't have words. And then she said the strangest thing. She said, 'Perhaps it has words.' Then she gave me a very strange look and then Anna Grieban called her away and—oh, the hell with it—let's not keep the Langs waiting." She was standing and stealing one last look at herself in the mirror. Hitchcock was at the door holding it open.

"And all this is what's been disturbing you?" She motioned him to precede her out the room so she could lock the door.

"It isn't so much disturbing as nagging, you know what I mean?"

He took her arm and led her to the staircase. "Of course I do."

A wicked smile appeared. "Somewhere in all that there lies a MacGuffin."

"Oh, Hitch, for crying out loud, you and your bloody MacGuffins!"

Anybody who was anybody in films and theater in Munich frequented the Altes Hackerhaus on Sendlinger Strasse, one of the oldest restaurants in the city. Hitchcock loved it for its generous servings of its heavy German cuisine. Alma liked it because the string quartet had a large repertoire of American and British popular songs. The Langs were already sitting at the table when Hitchcock and Alma arrived.

"Sorry we're late," said Alma, as the maître d' assisted her onto her chair. "It's been one of those days." Hitchcock ordered a bottle of wine and felt Thea von Harbou's penetrating eyes.

Hitch looked at Thea, "Yes?"

"Something about you puzzles me, Alfred." She was jamming a cigarette into a holder, and Lang held a match which he was poised to strike the moment his wife was ready to light up. Alma studied Thea's almost attractive face and waited for the verbal shells to explode. She didn't like the woman and hadn't liked her from the moment they had met a few weeks earlier at a studio cocktail party to welcome the visiting company. At the party she and Hitchcock had been subjected to von Harbou's perorations on the political and economic future of Germany, which she believed lay in the hands of the burgeoning National Socialist party under the

21

leadership of someone named Adolf Hitler. Alma hadn't liked the sound of any of it then and hoped they weren't in for more of the same at dinner.

"What puzzles you?" asked Hitchcock with his perennially benign expression.

"Your lack of political commitment." Alma groaned inwardly. Lang heard it and smiled as he struck the match to ignite his wife's cigarette.

"Oh, but I *am* politically committed."

"Ah so?" With her head cocked, von Harbou looked more like an inquisitive sparrow rather than a menacing vulture.

"Oh, yes. In England, I always vote for the monarchy." The wine steward arrived and held the bottle under Hitchcock's face for his approval. Hitchcock studied the label while von Harbou blew a smoke ring and composed herself. Hitchcock approved the wine, which the steward proceeded to uncork and decant.

"You are pulling my leg," announced von Harbou in a voice that belonged at the Munich Station announcing train departures.

"I wouldn't dream of it, certainly not in your husband's presence."

"My wife," said Lang, "is an incredibly good scriptwriter, but somehow I believe she has missed her true calling." His wife was staring with narrowed eyes at her husband. "She belongs astride a white horse bearing a huge shield and a dangerous spear, the true Wagnerian heroine, bellowing her Yo-ho-te-os across the countryside to awaken it to a future of . . ."

"Enough!" Von Harbou's hand banged the table, and Hitchcock's wine slopped over the edge of the glass. Alma didn't miss his pained expression and contemplated fainting, but thought better of it when her rumbling stomach reminded her she was hungry.

"Why enough?" asked Lang as he placed a monocle in his right eye. "We are gathered here tonight as fellow artists, not as pamphleteers for a presumptuous little popinjay who thinks Germany would once again prosper if it was rid of its Jews."

"What a lovely wine," trilled Alma. "So dry and so natural!"

"I did not know you are a connoisseur," commented Lang.

"She isn't," said Hitchcock with a wicked glint in his eye, "but she's a past master at diverting troublesome conversations."

Von Harbou held her hands up like a traffic policeman. "All right! All right! No politics! So tell me, my dears, what shall I give Fritz for his birthday?"

"His freedom," suggested Hitchcock. Lang exploded with laughter. Von Harbou glared at Hitchcock, and Alma waited for a devastating reply, but none was forthcoming. Instead, von Harbou turned to Alma, putting her hand on Alma's hand.

"So tell me my dear, how do you like Munich?"

"Oh, it's quite lovely."

"Have you seen the sights? Have you visited our wonderful gardens and St. Peter's Church?"

"Well," said Alma weakly, "we've been so busy with the film."

"We're on a very tight budget," said Hitchcock. "There's not a moment to spare."

"That's one thing we film directors can understand," said Lang, as he lit a small, narrow black cigar, "tight budgets. But now, on my latest film, *Metropolis,* I can be very expansive. . . ."

"And very expensive," interjected his wife.

"That's how you wrote it, my darling." He explained to the others. "*Metropolis* is about the future, a very dark, very grim, very foreboding future where machines and robots rule the world and men and women are enslaved in underground warrens. . . ."

"Good God!" exclaimed Alma. "Are there any laughs?"

"Oh, no! Not in Thea's future! There is no laughter in Thea's future!" And Lang roared with laughter while Alma thought, and no laughs in Thea's present either.

"I'm terrible hungry," Hitchcock announced, "and I would like to see a menu. Isn't anybody else hungry?"

Lang signaled the waiter for menus, and five minutes later, choices had been designated and the waiter bowed himself away to the kitchen. Lang was waving at a familiar face across the room.

"Isn't that Conrad Veidt?" asked Hitchcock. "He's such a good actor."

"Connie is quite wonderful," agreed Lang. "He's leaving us for Hollywood."

"Doesn't everybody," grumbled von Harbou.

Lang ignored her. "He's been captured by Papa Laemmle at Universal Pictures. He takes with him his new wife, Lily."

"She's very pretty," said Alma.

"She's a Jew," said von Harbou.

"She's a very clever woman," said Lang, glaring at his wife. "Connie found her in a tearoom where she was the hostess."

"I find her terribly manipulative," said von Harbou in a

24

voice studded with nettles. "She has taken over Connie's life completely."

"For the better, I should say," added Lang. "At least he no longer puts on lipstick and rouge and frequents decadent homosexual bars. Lily has changed all that."

Hitchcock stirred. "I assume she accomplished that with her Lily Veidt hands." Alma nudged him gently under the table with her leg.

"My, my, my," said Lang with mock amusement, "just about everybody seems to be here tonight and it's only Thursday. There's Hans Albers with Lil Dagover. Perhaps you remember her from *The Cabinet of Doctor Caligari*."

"Isn't she lovely," commented Alma with her usual generosity.

"Who's the pretty blonde at the corner table?" asked Hitchcock.

"Hitch has a passion for blondes," explained Alma.

"How does that explain you?" asked von Harbou.

"She needs no explanation," said Hitchcock, "only a good dinner and more wine." He signaled the steward for refills.

"The pretty blonde at the corner table," said Fritz Lang, grabbing his opportunity to identify her with a display of exaggerated patience, "is named Anny Ondra. She's not a bad actress."

"She's not a good one, either," interjected von Harbou.

"She'll improve," said Lang. "You see the brunette sitting across from Ondra and her escort? I read her for a part in my next film. Her name is Marlene Dietrich."

"She needs to lose weight," said Hitchcock, unmindful of his own increasing obesity.

Lang smiled. "She's deliciously *zaftig*. She's all wrong

25

for my movie, but I think there's a place for her in films. Ah! Here are the appetizers!"

"At last," said Hitchcock with a purr of contentment. He smiled at Alma, but her attention was diverted elsewhere. "Alma? The food's here."

"So's Anna Grieban." Her voice was so low, Hitchcock had to bend his head to hear her.

"Where?"

"Over there. The secluded corner next to the violinists."

"She's with *him*," said Hitchcock. The Langs were intrigued.

"*O mein Gott!*" exclaimed von Harbou, "that terrible face! It should not be permitted in public!"

"Thea, for God's sake," growled Lang," the poor man must have suffered something awful in the war."

"I think it's a wonderful face," said Hitchcock, "don't you agree, Fritz? Wouldn't he make a marvelous red herring in a . . ." he smiled at Thea, ". . . political thriller. I'm so glad he's a friend of Anna Grieban's. Now I can meet him."

"And who is this Anna Grieban?" inquired von Harbou as she dissected a herring.

"She's our script girl," said Alma.

"That is all she is? A script girl? And she comes to *this* restaurant?"

Alma felt her face flush with anger, and she clenched her hands together under the table. What political repercussions would there be between England and Germany, she wondered, if she grabbed Thea von Harbou by the shoulders and tried to shake some sense into the arrogant, bigoted bitch.

"*Ach!*" exclaimed Lang. "They are arguing!"

Anna Grieban and the man were undoubtedly arguing, their pantomime exquisitely eloquent to the table where

26

Hitchcock's group sat. The man threw his napkin on the table, as Anna Grieban pushed her chair back, grabbed her handbag, and went hurrying out of the restaurant.

"Now you shall not meet him," said Lang with mocking sadness.

"There's always tomorrow," said Hitchcock.

The man put a pile of marks on the table and then hurried out of the restaurant.

"You see what I mean?" von Harbou asked Alma. "Underpeople like this script girl of yours are always making scenes."

"But this one," said Hitchcock, "wasn't terribly well directed."

Outside the restaurant, the man emerged just as Anna Grieban entered a taxi and it drove away. He cursed and then hailed a taxi for himself.

Back in the restaurant, as the main course was being served, Lang exclaimed, "But that is *wunderbar*, Hitchcock! I'm delighted you're going to make another film here."

"I'm not," said Hitchcock as he examined his plate of *Schweinshaxe* and *Knödel* (pork shank and potato dumplings) and then attacked it with unrestrained relish.

"Ah so?" asked von Harbou. "You do not like our working conditions here?"

"My dear Thea," explained Hitchcock, beginning to understand why Alma disliked the woman, "working conditions here are perfectly adequate, but these films I'm being assigned, though I am most grateful for the opportunity they present for me to learn my craft, are little more than mediocre potboilers. I wish to get on to better things."

"You must not be so impatient," admonished von Harbou. "You should stay here in Germany. Your talent could replace that of the swine who are defecting to Hollywood, whores seduced by Jewish millions. A word in the right ear, and I could help you set up as a director right here in Germany. I've heard good things about you!" Alma loathed people who spoke while they chewed food. Chalk up another demerit against Thea von Harbou. "What you call a potboiler my friends at the studio tell me you are directing with great flair and imagination. Is that not so, Fritz?" Fritz nodded as he ate, and Alma wondered if Fritz wasn't secretly praying for an opportunity to be seduced by Hollywood's Jewish millions. "What do you say, Alfred?" Thea's voice was growing anxious and shrill, like a recruiting officer who'd heard the enemy had arrived at the outskirts of the city.

"I want to go home," said Alfred with the simplicity of a small boy, and Alma wanted to lean over and kiss him.

"*Ach!*" Thea dropped her knife and fork with disgust.

"What displeases you, dear?" inquired Lang, "Hitchcock or the food?"

"They are both indigestible," snapped von Harbou. She turned to Alma. "Tell me, Alma, what do you plan this weekend?"

"I plan to rest." Is there no escape? she thought; is there no escape from this awful woman? She and Hitchcock exchanged glances.

Hitchcock asked swiftly, "What about your next picture, Fritz? Is it set after *Metropolis*?"

"I have been offered a thriller located somewhere in India. I don't think I wish to travel to India."

"Oh, I would!" said Alma. "I'd love to travel the world."

"Well, not me," said Lang, "this location is so obscurely placed geographically, the Russians don't have spies there."

"And what is this tune you are humming?" Thea asked Alma.

"Oh, dear, forgive me."

"But why? It is so charming. I've never heard it before." Alma explained its origin. "Ah so? This Rudolf Wagner is a piano player, and he composes such a charming melody? Isn't it charming, Fritz?"

"Very nice."

"Perhaps we should meet this Wagner. He might be a discovery, a real find. He might be the person to compose the score for *Metropolis*." She explained to Hitchcock and Alma. "We are most anxious to provide the cinemas with our own suggested scoring for *Metropolis*. It needs the right atmospheric music, doesn't it, Fritz?"

"It does, but it won't get it. *Ach*, Hitchcock. Wouldn't it be wonderful if the motion picture could talk and sing and then we could control everything?"

Anna Grieban climbed the stairs to her apartment in the attic of a building located on the street along which the Isar River flowed. She could smell boiled cabbage and boiled turnips and stale urine from the communal bathrooms on each floor. She was tired and troubled and hungry and cursed herself for the fool she was for not having eaten before arguing with the Man. That Man. That face. It had once been so handsome, so beautiful. She paused on the landing outside her door and listened. Was someone coming up the stairs behind her? She looked over the handrailing into the void below, but there was nobody. She strained her ears, but she heard nothing, only the drip-drip-drip of the leaky shower stall that adjoined the door to her apartment. She found the key to her door in her handbag and let herself into her untidy bed-sitter. She shut the door, tossed her handbag and her hat on the bed, and then realized the lamp next to her bed was glowing. Had she left it on all day? God, the electric bill! She must have. Because the room was dimly aglow when she entered, she hadn't reached for the light switch. Oh, the hell with it. She crossed to a chair while removing her jacket. She sat and removed her shoes and stockings. She stood up and removed her blouse and skirt, making an untidy pile on the floor. She wiggled out of her girdle and, with a contented sigh, let her stomach sag. She scratched herself gently and then yawned and stretched. From a hook on the door she removed a gaudy silk bathrobe festooned with a design of oversized flowers. a gift from an old admirer, her mother. From another hook she grabbed a towel and a bath cap. In a drawer she found soap and a washcloth. Had she really left the contents of the drawer this disorganized? She opened another drawer and then another.

Someone had been in her room. Someone who had switched on the lamp and left it on when he fled from the room upon hearing her come up the stairs. She crossed to the closet and on tiptoe reached for the shoe box on the shelf. She placed it on the dresser table, removed the top, and then examined the contents carefully. Nothing was missing. Nothing was touched, not even the pearl earrings Herbert had given her before going off to war. The intruder had had no time to invade the privacy of her closet and the shoe box. She replaced it in the closet, shut the door, and smiled. Whoever the damn fool was, he was an amateur. What did he expect to find in such mean and impoverished surroundings? Who steals from the poor? She was humming to herself as she found a jar of cold cream and sloppily removed her makeup.

The poor. Poor me. Poor Herbert. Poor pearl earrings that Herbert must have scraped for months to afford to buy for me. Poor Germany. This damned tune of Wagner's, but still, it was important.

La-la-la-la . . . la-la-la . . .

*   *   *

"A perfectly awful woman!" Alma and Hitchcock were in a taxi returning to the guest house. Hitchcock was stifling a yawn. "You do realize, don't you, Hitch, that she's a fascist sympathizer?"

"You don't say."

"Oh, *you*."

"But still, she's written all his hits."

"He doesn't like her. I could tell. Don't you agree?"

"I think Fritz is biding his time, waiting for the right moment."

"To do what?"

"Decamp."

"To Hollywood? And . . ." Alma mimicked von Harbou brutally: ". . . 'all der filthy Jewish millions.' How can he let her talk that way?"

"I don't know. Especially since I've been told he's Jewish."

"Oh, no!"

"Fancy seeing Grieban at the restaurant, and with my MacGuffin, of all people. Do you suppose that's why he was hanging around the studio yesterday?"

"Well, if that was his reason, why did Freddy Regner tell us he'd given him directions to Stage Three? We're on Stage One."

"That's so, isn't it? Well, m'dear"—he patted her hand—"and there we have another MacGuffin!"

Anna Grieban covered her hair with the cap and tried once again to shut the door of the shower stall. Damned fool, whoever it was, that broke the lock. There was a wooden stool in the stall, which she propped against the door. At least she would hear if one of the other tenants attempted to

31

enter while she was showering, not that many of them took advantage of the shower facility, she supposed, if she could trust her nose. She stepped into the stall and drew the curtain, then, steeling herself for the first blast of cold water, turned the knobs. The water hit her, and she suppressed a shriek; no need to frighten the neighbors. Then the warm water began to flow, and she soaped herself vigorously. She began la-la-la'ing Wagner's melody at the top of her lungs. Poor little Wagner. Poor downtrodden little man with that awful daughter Rosie. Why had she let that actor, Hans Meyer, talk her into hiring Rosie? Meyer was another misbegotten soul. Oh well. Maybe he was screwing her. But who in God's name would screw anything as unappetizing as Rosie Wagner?

She hadn't heard the door being pushed open quietly, a hand reaching in and carefully, gently moving the stool to one side so as not to give the intruder away. Anna stood with her face into the gushing stream of water and could hear nothing. She didn't even feel the first time the knife blade entered her body. Or perhaps not even the second. And by the third thrust of the blade, she was paralyzed by shock.

Blood began to flow from her wounds, and soon she was beginning to crumple to the stall floor in a sea of water and red. Would the knife never stop? Again and again and again the blade plunged into her, until she lay on the floor, her eyes open in death, her hands open in supplication, and of no avail.

Three

The next morning the streets of Munich were curtained with a bone-chilling drizzle. It reminded the British contingent of London, and they were smiling as they arrived at Sound Stage One for the day's filming. Hitchcock was at the refreshment cart ordering a coffee and a sweet roll when a handsome young man with a head of thick black curly hair and a pencil-thin mustache approached him.

"This is Herr Hitchcock?" asked the young man in a voice coated with butterscotch.

Hitchcock was busy examining the tray of sweet rolls and pastries. German bakers and chefs were his downfall, and he was falling with a smile of content. Abstractedly, Hitchcock replied, "This is."

The young man clicked his heels and bowed from the

waist. Hitchcock winced. German formalities unnerved him. "Please, I may introduce myself?"

"Oh, by all means do." Hitchcock wondered if a pastry that appealed to him had a fruit filling.

"My name is Hans Meyer. I am an actor."

Hitchcock's eyes rolled up. "Oh please. Not before breakfast."

"I hear your next film is to be in the mountains, yes?"

Hitchcock selected a pastry and bit into it. "Damn. It's cheese."

"In the mountains, yes?"

Hitchcock showed him the contents of the pastry. "It's cheese."

"You do not like cheese?"

"I also loathe mountains."

"I am very good with mountains." A trace of perspiration appeared on the nervous young man's brow. "I have climbed many times."

"I do not need mountain climbers. I need actors."

"I am an actor who only sometime climbs. You understand?"

Hitchcock caught the eye of the middle-aged woman in charge of the refreshment cart who he'd described as being built like an avenging Carpathian peasant. "This cheese is off," announced Hitchcock in a sad stentorian voice.

"Where off?" asked the woman, whose English was as inadequate as her pastries.

"It's rancid." Hans Meyer translated into German and the woman stood back in horror and clutching her breast. To Hitchcock she looked like an inflated Lillian Gish. The woman remonstrated, but Hitchcock persisted. "Take this pastry back to the baker and demand a refund." He dropped the pastry back on the tray, and the woman scooped it up

34

and bit into it. Hitchcock watched her ruminating with distaste.

"Is good!" said the woman. "Is good, you I tell!"

Hitchcock snorted and said to Hans Meyer, "The woman suffers from an inferior palate." To her he said, "Is bloody awful and I shall select something else." Which he did with a gesture befitting royalty, paid the woman, and then slowly walked to his director's chair, with the young actor trailing in his wake. He saw Fredrick Regner, the scriptwriter, approaching him carrying a script.

"Good morning, Herr Hitchcock," said Regner, his smile displaying what appeared to be a perfect set of teeth.

"Good morning. In fact, I'm glad you're here. That strange-looking man—"

"Which one? There are so many here."

Hitchcock settled into his director's chair while Regner and Meyer stood staring down at him.

"The one you said you directed to Stage Three yesterday. Surely you remember him. Nobody could forget that face once they've seen it, the poor bugger."

"Oh, *him*. Of course. What about him?"

"Well, if you directed him to Stage Three, what was he doing slinking around ours?"

"I have no idea."

"Alma Reville saw him peeping from behind a piece of scenery. Skulking, I suppose, is more like it. Do you know if he's an actor?"

"I don't know him at all. I've never seen him before yesterday, and I haven't seen him since."

"Most peculiar." He turned to Meyer. "Do you know as much about actors as you do about mountains? What did you say your name was? This is Freddy Regner. . . ."

"We've met before," said Regner.

35

Hitchcock bit into his pastry and munched with a preoccupied expression. He swallowed and asked Meyer, "Have you run into a person with a magnificently disfigured face?"

"I do not recall, no."

"No," echoed Hitchcock.

"Herr Hitchcock," said Regner anxiously, "this script . . ." Hitchcock looked at it suspiciously, as though the script might be wired to explode. "I wonder if you could find the time to read it."

Hitchcock sighed. Rudolf Wagner and the violinists were halfheartedly playing "I Dreamt I Dwelt in Marble Halls" and Hitchcock wished he dwelt among them too. "I could find the time to read it," said Hitchcock, "but if I like it, I don't know when I'll find the time to direct it. You see, I'm set to do this blasted mountain picture. . . ."

"Very majestic, mountains." Which won Hans Meyer a look of distaste from Hitchcock and one of irritation from Regner.

"I would be content just to have your opinion," persisted Regner.

"Aren't you under contract here?" asked Hitchcock.

"Oh, no. Not at all. I am a free lance."

"But I always see you about on the lot, dancing attendance on no one in particular." Hitchcock was bored with his pastry and flung it into a convenient wastebasket.

"Please, but they are filming a scenario of mine on Stage Two. It is a spy thriller."

Hitchcock's face lit up. "A spy thriller! I'd love to do a spy film, one with lots of MacGuffins!"

"Please?" asked the perplexed writer.

"Oh, yes, I'd be pleased." He took the script from Regner and flipped through it. "Is this a spy thriller?"

"It is a thriller, yes. You will read it?"

"I will read it. Now go away and take this mountain actor with you. I have work to do." He was looking around for Alma and Anna Grieban.

"Please, Herr Hitchcock. You will consider me for your mountain film?" Hans Meyer sounded desperate enough to make Hitchcock suspect he was being pursued by the police.

"I will consider you. Leave your name, your phone number, and your credits with my script girl, Miss Grieban—that is, if you can locate her. And if you do, please tell her I would like to see her at my side ready to begin a day's shooting on this misbegotten mess I'm involved in. Alma!" He had spotted Alma chatting with Miles Mander, one of the film's leading men. Alma acknowledged Hitchcock with a wave of her hand and crossed to him as Hans Meyer and Fredrick Regner departed in separate directions.

"The actors are getting restless," said Alma. "When do you start your first setup?"

"The actors are fortunate they are employed, and you may quote me." Hitchcock made no effort to disguise his annoyance. "And as for getting started, I'm not ready for that until the bloody script girl arrives to confer with me so I can confer with the bloody camera operator. The bloody pastries were bloody awful this morning."

"Other than that, dear, what's your mood?"

"My mood is one of gratitude that you are here with me"—his voice was softening—"helping to make this ill-starred adventure bearable. And if your good behavior continues, I shall demand we set a date for our wedding, at which point I'm sure we'll both be delighted to rid ourselves of our virginity."

"Oh, hush up, Hitch. Rosie! You there, Rosie!"

Rosie Wagner was looking more than usually unattractive that morning. She had been chatting with the actor

Hans Meyer when Alma hailed her, and she turned with a start like a child caught raiding a biscuit box. Rosie hurried to Alma and Hitchcock. "Good morning, Miss Reville. Herr Hitchcock. Is something?"

"Is something indeed," said Alma briskly. "Where's Anna Grieban this morning?"

"Oh? She is not here?" She looked like a fawn at bay.

"She is not. Don't you report to her first thing in the morning?"

"This morning I am typing script revisions." She was holding the sheets of paper behind her back and now displayed them as though they were a cache of fine jewels.

"Well, go find her. We'll be late getting started this morning, and we can't afford that."

"And who is *this*?" asked Hitchcock, as a tall man in his mid-forties wearing a raincoat and a bowler hat approached. "Not another mountain actor, I pray."

The man removed the bowler and inquired, "Herr Hitchcock?"

"I hope you're not an actor. I've already had one actor too many this morning."

"I'm Detective Inspector Wilhelm Farber." Hitchcock paled. Police. He was terrified of the police.

Hitchcock bravely struggled out of his chair and shook the man's proffered hand. "How do you do. I have no part for a policeman in this film, Herr Detective Inspector."

The man smiled. He liked Hitchcock on sight. He nodded at Alma while Rosie scurried away with Alma's order. "I am not looking for a part as an actor, although . . ." Hitchcock started to tremble. ". . . I was once told I might have a future in the theater. But no, I find police work much more challenging. Is there someplace we might talk in private?"

"I seem to recall being assigned a small office. Don't I

38

have an office somewhere in the vicinity, Alma?" Alma led them to the office. When the three were seated, Hitchcock behind a fragile desk with his hands folded over his stomach, wondering if Alma knew how to bake a cake with a file in it, asked Herr Farber, "Of what am I accused?"

"Oho, you are accused of nothing, Herr Hitchcock. Why are you so defensive?"

Why indeed? wondered Alma, who know Hitchcock's fear of the police and made a mental note to try to do something about that in the very near future.

"I am not being defensive," said Hitchcock. "I was just making a small joke. Terribly small, since you didn't find it funny."

"Anna Grieban was in your employ?" Alma didn't like the use of the word *was*.

Neither, apparently, did Hitchcock. "What do you mean, 'was'?"

"She is dead."

"Dear God," gasped Alma. Hitchcock feared the worst. Policemen don't arrive to announce death by heart attack or vehicular accident or infected hangnail.

"That is terrible news," intoned Hitchcock gravely, tempted to add, And where the hell do I get that competent a script girl on such short notice?

"She was murdered," said Farber.

"That's even worse news," commented Hitchcock.

"Quite brutally." Alma's hand covered her mouth, her face screwed up with horror.

Farber directed his attention to Alma. "You are connected with this film? With Herr Hitchcock?"

Hitchcock answered for her. "She is my assistant and my fiancée, in no particular order. And as of this moment, she is also my new script girl, with no increase in salary."

39

"Oh, Hitch, really," said Alma. He could see she was shaken by the terrible news.

"How did Miss Grieban die?" asked Hitchcock. Farber told them, sparing no gruesome detail.

"Twenty-nine stab wounds?" asked Hitchcock with a look of incredulity, while inwardly thinking, how delicious! "Twenty-nine! It was either the act of a maniac or a knifer badly in need of practice."

"She was not a pleasant sight. Her body was found by a tenant who is now in hospital in a state of shock." He looked from one to the other. "Tell me, please. What do you know of Miss Grieban?"

"I don't know too much at all," said Alma, "although I was the one who hired her. You see, coming from England to film here, we weren't too familiar with the film work force in Munich, so we asked around for suggestions. As a matter of fact, I think we got Anna with an introduction from Freddy Regner."

"Who is this Freddy Regner?" Farber had whipped a notebook and pencil from his inside jacket pocket and was taking notes, first, Hitchcock noticed, licking the lead end of the pencil. What a marvelous idea, thought Hitchcock, death from lead poisoning by someone who licks pencil ends. He heard Alma telling Farber that Freddy was a scriptwriter. Hitchcock added that Regner had a film shooting in the adjoining stage. "I would like to speak to this Regner."

"He's about," said Hitchcock. "In fact, he gave me a script to read this morning." He said to Alma, "I left it on my chair. I hope nobody pinches it." Alma couldn't care less about anybody's script; she was too preoccupied with the ugly thoughts of Anna Grieban's horrible murder. "Would you like Alma to fetch Freddy?"

"Soon. There's plenty of time."

Oh no, there isn't, thought Hitchcock, I've a day's shooting ahead of me, and every minute I spend with you is costing us money we can't well afford to spare. He heard Alma saying something about dining the previous evening with the Fritz Langs.

"Of course!" cried Hitchcock. "We saw her last night. Why, we're probably among the last to see her alive!" How, wondered Alma, can the man speak with such relish when a colleague has been so brutally dispatched? But then, she reminded herself, that's Hitch. His sense of humor would always transcend his sense of tragedy. "She was with this terribly fascinating man. Face very ghastly, very disfigured. Bad plastic surgery, or perhaps nothing much that plastic surgery could do to improve it. Undoubtedly a veteran of the late unpleasantness."

"You mean the war, of course." Farber's pencil flew across the page.

"Oh, indeed, I mean the war. My film is not yet completed."

"And did you speak to Miss Grieban and this man?"

"I was most anxious to," explained Hitchcock. "That face, I mean it is so distinctive, I want to capture it on film. But they had an argument."

"Ah! You overheard this argument?"

"Oh, no, they were on the opposite side of the room near the string orchestra." From the sound stage, they could hear Rudolf Wagner and the violinists tearing into a Lehár melody. "But we did see Anna slam her hand on the table, looking quite irate. . . ."

"A woman scorned, perhaps?" suggested Farber.

"A woman angry, that I can assure you," countered Hitchcock.

41

"And after she slammed her hand on the table?"

"She grabbed her handbag and fled."

"With her escort in pursuit?"

"No, he had to settle up the bill first. *Then* he pursued."

"You have no idea of this man's name?"

"None whatsoever."

"Perhaps Freddy Regner knows," suggested Alma. "We saw him speaking to the man here at the studio yesterday."

Farber lowered the pad and pencil, a look of fascination on his face. "You had seen him earlier in the day here?" Alma and Hitchcock nodded. "And you had no opportunity to speak to him *then*?"

"Sadly, no," said Hitchcock, looking like a dejected basset. "He was terribly quick on his feet. Now you see him, now you don't. Alma caught him right here on our sound stage peeping from behind a piece of scenery. At least Alma says she saw him. I didn't."

"I positively saw him," said Alma. "He seemed to be fascinated by an original melody composed by our pianist, Rudolf Wagner."

"Wagner seems determined to play it all this season," offered Hitchcock.

"It's very lovely." Alma began humming it and then blushed. The very idea of such frivolity appalled her, with Anna Grieban probably lying on a slab at the morgue.

"Charming," said Farber. "So, this is all you can tell me?"

Hitchcock's face was a blank. Alma shrugged helplessly. "Perhaps," began Hitchcock, "I should make a general announcement to the company of this awful tragedy, and then perhaps some others might come forward with some helpful bits of information about Anna. But, Mr. Detective, I must get on with my filming."

"By all means. Now I would like to meet this Fredrick Regner."

"I'll fetch him," volunteered Alma, and left.

As Hitchcock led the detective away from the office, Farber asked, "Your film, it deals with murder?"

"No, it deals with chorus girls, who, I might add, deserve to be murdered."

"You do not have much faith in this film you are making? Then why do you make it?"

"Because it was placed on a platter and handed to me. It is my first opportunity to direct."

"Congratulations! I hope you catch much success!"

"I hope you catch your murderer."

Hitchcock mounted the stairs to the stage of The Pleasure Garden and shouted for the company's attention. He told them the news of Anna Grieban's murder, which was met with a chorus of gasps and cries of "oh, no," and "*Gott im Himmel*." Hitchcock introduced Detective Inspector Farber and asked that he be given complete cooperation. Meanwhile, he added, Miss Reville would take over as script girl and work should commence immediately.

Alma had found Regner and turned him over to the detective, who led him to a secluded corner of the sound stage. Regner was of no help. Yes, he remembered the man with the disfigured face, but no, he had no idea who he was, a total stranger to him. The detective knew nothing of Regner's having said he directed the man to Stage Three when the man appeared on Stage One because Hitchcock and Alma had neglected to mention it. Yes, he had recommended Anna Grieban because she had been script girl on two of his earlier films and was quite competent. When the *Pleasure Garden* company set up shop at the studio, she hadn't worked for months and was destitute, and he was delighted to recommend her. "Surely," he reminded Farber, "you can see how squalid her quarters are."

"So you have seen them?" Farber was pleased to see the writer's face redden.

"Well, yes, once. She . . . er . . . one time invited me for a schnapps."

"I hope it was a good schnapps."

"Not bad," said Regner with an expansive smile.

Farber then spoke to Rosie Wagner, having been told by Alma that she was Anna Grieban's assistant. Rosie cowered as the detective began his questioning. "What's the matter with you?" he asked.

"I'm afraid!"

"Of what?"

"You!"

"Why, for pity's sake?"

"You won't arrest me?"

"What for?" He was tempted to say, Better such a plain frump should be kept under lock and key rather than be permitted to roam at large blemishing the landscape.

"When I was a little girl, my father always threatened to put me in jail!" Farber was interested in meeting a man of such admirable character and discrimination.

He said instead, "You must learn to forgive parents for the foolish threats they make to their small children. It is not easy being a parent. I have three of my own. Monsters, each and every one of them. Especially the two girls. Very devious and dangerous. They leave their roller skates on the staircase for me to trip over."

Rosie said something like "heh heh." Farber gave her the

benefit of the doubt and assumed that was what passed for laughter. She seemed less ill at ease now and picked at a pimple on her chin. "You will question my father?"

"Why?" Farber's hand holding the pencil was poised in midair.

"He also knows Anna Grieban. I mean knew. He is over there. At the piano."

"Ah! The one who composed the melody Miss Reville hums so charmingly. How nice, father and daughter working together." He wondered if what she had now said was "Ugh." "So what can you tell me about Anna Grieban?"

"She was very bossy. She didn't like me." Farber was beginning to adore the late script girl. "But I am a good worker." Farber asked Rosie about the man with the disfigured face, but Rosie could tell him nothing; in fact, Rosie added up to a wasted ten minutes. Farber dismissed her and went to her father.

"Poor Anna," said Wagner, having some free time while Hitchcock was busy solving the problem of a difficult trick shot. "She was a very intelligent person, but very unlucky."

"How so?"

"Well, you saw the sordid hovel she lived in."

Farber smiled. "She served you her schnapps there?"

"No schnapps. Tea and biscuits. Stale biscuits. She was poverty-stricken."

"But she made good money when she worked, didn't she?"

"Surely you jest, Herr Farber. In our miserable economy what is good money?"

"Yes, yes, I understand. Even millionaires are having difficult times."

Wagner wondered if the detective was a Communist.

45

There was a lot of that going around these days, but he didn't have the courage to inquire.

"There was also a tragedy with her husband."

"She has a husband?"

"Had."

"You knew him?"

"Oh, he was long gone before I knew Anna. I only met Anna on a movie about two years ago. The husband she married before the war. She was just a child then, she told me. But she loved him very much. From the way she described him, he must have had the looks of a Greek god."

"Not a German god?"

"I don't recall our gods being famous for their looks."

"So this husband was killed in the war, I presume?" asked Farber.

Wagner shrugged. "I don't know if he was killed or not, but he didn't come home to her."

"Now comes a very commonplace question in these investigations. Do you know if she had any enemies?"

Wagner told him with great satisfaction, "My daughter detested her."

"So I gather. But do you think your daughter capable of such a dreadful murder?"

"Rosie is a very dreadful daughter."

"So are mine. I have two."

"My sympathies."

"Did you know a friend of Anna Grieban's who has a tragically disfigured face?"

Wagner ran his fingers across the keys. "I never heard her speak of any such person." He softly began playing his own composition.

"You didn't notice him yesterday here in the studio?"

"At the studio, I notice only my piano and my employers. I provide mood music for the actors, the violinists, and myself, that is all we do here."

"That is a charming melody you are playing. It's your own, right?"

Wagner looked up from the keyboard. "How do you know this?"

"Miss Reville hummed it for me. She thinks you are very gifted."

"She is a lovely woman, Miss Reville. She told me she recommended me last night to Fritz Lang, the director."

"Oho, that's big time! Not like this fat man Hitchcock."

"Do not overestimate Mr. Lang, or underestimate Mr. Hitchcock. Is there anything else I can tell you?"

"I don't know," said Farber affably, "is there?"

Hitchcock had solved the problem of the trick shot. "All right, everyone," he shouted, "let's try to get this one in one take! Actors, please keep your positions until I call for action."

"Musicians!" cried Alma. The music began. The detective Farber now stood behind Hitchcock, watching the director's rear end quiver as he prepared the intricate scene. Alma stood next to him, and behind her was Fredrick Regner. Hans Meyer, the actor who professed to know about mountains, tiptoed about quietly in the background.

Hitchcock barked in succession. "Camera! Action!" The clapper boy held his board, on which was lettered the number of the scene and the day's date, in front of the camera, and the camera operator cranked away. Virginia Valli and Carmelita Geraghty came dancing out with the chorus, lavish smiles on their faces, doing their utmost to keep their high kicks in precision. Alma once again, as during the day before, was beginning to suffer from nausea induced by the cigar and cigarette smoke of the atmosphere players at the

Pleasure Garden tables. The orchestral trio was providing a bouncy melody that sounded something like a bastardization of "Alexander's Ragtime Band."

A chorus girl tripped.

"Bloody hell!" shouted Hitchcock as he began tearing at his thinning hair. "Cut! Cut! Goddamn it, cut!"

A deadly silence descended over the sound stage, a deadly silence broken by the crashing dissonance of the piano keys.

"I do not need any comments from you, Herr Wagner!" shouted Hitchcock, followed by some nervous tittering.

A woman's shriek scythed through the stage. Farber turned in the direction of the sound.

"My father! My father!" screamed Rosie Wagner. "Somebody has murdered my father!"

Rudolf Wagner had fallen across the keyboard, a knife in his back and a frown on his face.

Four

Detective Inspector Wilhelm Farber was seething with indignation. How dare a murder occur practically under his very distinguished nose while he was investigating an earlier one? And again, no witnesses. The two violinists, who gave their names as Martin and Johann, claimed to have been busy sorting and selecting sheet music in the respite provided by the clumsy chorus girl. When they heard the cacophony from the keyboard, they thought it was Wagner giving vent to frustration and impatience.

"He was frequently frustrated and always impatient," said Martin, wheezing, which he did when nervous.

Johann added, "I think he was also upset when he caught this person staring at him from behind that piece of scenery."

Farber asked Hitchcock, who was now convinced his movie was jinxed, "Do you suppose it's our friend with the shattered face?"

"I suppose it could be." He asked the musicians, "Did either of you see this man?"

Johann scratched his chin. Martin shifted from one foot to the other. Both were uncomfortable and wary. Army veterans who distrusted and despised authority, they were old friends and survived by remaining trapped within the limits of their meager ambitions.

Farber prodded them. "A man has been seen around here with a terribly disfigured face. Did either of you see him?"

After a moment, Johann spoke. "I caught a glimpse of him yesterday. But not today. I didn't see him today. Martin? Did you see this man?"

"I don't see anybody but my sheet music. You know how lost I get when I'm concentrating." He explained to Farber and Hitchcock. "I'm a very heavy concentrator. When I concentrate, I'm no use to anybody but myself."

"Thank you, gentlemen. You've been very helpful," said Farber. Hitchcock wondered if he was often given to such bizarre overstatement. When they were out of earshot of the musicians, Farber said, "You have just witnessed two superb examples of why Germany is so slow in recovering from the disaster of the war. Two idiots. Well, Hitchcock, I am stumped."

"We need a cup of strong tea." He led the way to the refreshment cart. It was now almost two hours since Wagner's murder, and Farber, with an efficiency that impressed the very fastidious director, had interrogated over two dozen people who had been stationed in the vicinity. The results were disheartening, but Farber never gave way to any emotional display of disappointment, even when Wagner's daughter Rosie carried on in anguish and hysteria and had to be sedated, a performance Hitchcock and Alma found suspect, knowing the animosity between the girl and her father. One of Farber's subordinates approached him as he stirred his tea and gave him some information. Farber listened gravely, thanked the man, and stared into his tea while Hitchcock wondered if the peasant type guarding the refreshment cart would challenge him to a hand wrestle if he reached for a pastry.

"Well, Herr Hitchcock." said Farber, "it seems the knife that killed Wagner is the same weapon that killed Anna Grieban."

Hitchcock's eyes widened with astonishment. "You mean the murderer carried that weapon onto the lot, as brazen as you please?"

"Why not? It can be brought in a briefcase, a handbag, a paper bag containing presumably a sandwich and a piece of fruit; it could be concealed in a newspaper. And now we know for sure there was a link between Grieban and Wagner."

"Perhaps they were lovers and a jealous lover decided to put paid to the situation."

"I can't much envision those two cooing at each other, could you?"

"I don't remember noticing any intimacy between them here on the set. But on the other hand, I haven't been noticing too much of anything except that I'm about to get behind in my shooting schedule and I can ill afford that. I know they've known each other for some time, but that's not unusual in film circles, especially in one so incestuous as this one in Munich. Film people are terribly clubby, even when they despise each other."

51

"How many more shooting days are left to your film?"

"I can afford another ten. Then I must start preparing the next one."

"Well, maybe the solution will materialize before you are finished here." Hitchcock doubted it, but did not voice the thought. He knew enough about murder to accept that, without witnesses or clues, the chances of apprehending the murderer would be slim.

"By the way," asked Hitchcock, wondering that if in fact there was a clue, information that Farber might have elected to withhold from him, "were there any fingerprints on the knife?"

"The hilt was wiped clean. And, what's worse, it's an ordinary kitchen knife, one that can be bought all over the country. A very cheap utensil."

"But effective."

They saw Alma walking briskly toward them. "Ah so, Miss Reville," said Farber with a smile, "and how is the daughter?"

"Well, you won't believe this, but Rosie's hysteria has developed into catatonia. She's been taken to a sanatorium." Alma took Hitchcock's cup and sipped his tea. "Awful."

"Yes, that's very sad," said Farber.

"I meant the tea."

Hitchcock reclaimed the cup and, his face screwed up with thought, stared into space. Alma busied herself ordering coffee and a sandwich while Farber made notes in his pad. "I wonder if catatonia can be faked."

"Not this case," said Alma. "I was there in the studio doctor's office. That nice young actor . . . what's his name again . . . Hans something . . ."

"Meyer . . . Hans Meyer . . . he climbs mountains . . ."

"Yes, Hans Meyer. He helped carry her to the office.

We saw her sink into this spell and for a moment there the doctor thought she'd had a stroke or some form of apoplexy. She went all gray. . . ."

"She was gray to begin with," said Hitchcock.

"This was a paler shade, dear, and then she broke out into this dreadfully cold, clammy sweat, and you can't fake *that*, my darling."

"No, I suppose you can't."

"Anyway, Herr Farber, I'm sure you'll want to discuss this yourself with the doctor."

"Oh, yes. I shall discuss it with the doctor. Then I shall write my report, and like the efficient detective that I am, I shall pursue all leads, especially when they are as nonexistent as in this case, and then go on to another case. And perhaps someday in the future, with any luck the near future, there will be a sudden stroke of luck and someone will remember something and bring it to me and I will have found my killer. And now, having shared one of my favorite fantasies with you, I shall go and speak with the doctor." He patted Hitchcock on the shoulder and then, to Alma's surprise, took Alma's hand, the one holding the sandwich, and kissed it. "Ah," he added, "knockwurst. How I adore knockwurst." And with that, he went in search of the doctor.

"Well, for heaven's sake! I've never had my hand kissed before."

"Don't become addicted. I'm not versed in continental manners. I suppose there's no point in resuming shooting until after the lunch break."

"The company's been at lunch for the past half hour. I told the third assistant to let them go when we took Rosie to the doctor's office. I might also add, our two American stars have gone back to their hotels . . ."

"No!"

". . . much too upset by Wagner's murder to be of any use to us in front of the camera. They promise to be on hand bright and early tomorrow morning."

"That blows it." He sought the comfort of the pastry tray.

"Not at all. I took the liberty of laying on a sequence of atmosphere shots you can take with the chorus, the dress extras, et cetera, et cetera, and that can give us a full afternoon's work. Besides, it'll give you more footage to work with when we get down to editing. It'll give the film a bit of an expensive look."

Hitchcock smiled warmly as he caressed Alma's cheek. "You are devilishly clever, Miss Reville. Promise to remain forever on my team."

She crossed her heart with an exaggerated gesture. "Now what do you think?"

"About what?"

"The murders, of course."

"Frankly, I'm not too sure what to think." He shared the information he'd received from the detective, and then they walked about the set for a while in silence. "It's patently obvious Anna and Wagner were mixed up in something together, or perhaps were privy to the same dangerous information."

"What kind of information, do you think?"

"I'm not quite sure. The disfigured face has something to do with it, I'll bet my last shilling on that. You know, there's Anna Grieban's husband."

"Presumed missing in action."

"Not at all. We don't know that for a fact at all. All we know is there's no sign or word of him *after* the war. He was supposed to be something special in the looks department."

"Hitch! Do you suppose the disfigured face is Grieban's husband?"

"That's what I've been thinking, strangely enough."

"And if he is, he came back and found her having an affair with Wagner and killed them."

"In 1925, seven years after the war ended? That's a terribly long period of procrastination, especially for a jealous husband."

"Supposing he was in hospital all these years, getting his face patched up."

"We've seen the results. He should sue."

"Skip the levity and concentrate on the facts." They were sitting on the stage of The Pleasure Garden, Alma having long since lost interest in her sandwich and now nursing her coffee. "He could have been sequestered in hospital for a good many years. We know of such cases in England. Let's say three or four years." She paused.

"I'm waiting." The company was beginning to straggle back to the stage, and Hitchcock was anxious to get on with his job.

"Then he's finally released. Looking the way he does and being the decent sort . . ."

"Decent sorts don't commit murders."

"They do in a fit of passion. Even decent sorts turn indecent when sex rears its inquisitive head."

"How would *you* know, Miss Susy Prude?"

"I've read Elinor Glyn. Anyway, upon leaving hospital and being decent about it, he remains in the background."

"Wouldn't Grieban know he was in hospital?"

"It's more than likely she didn't know. The way his face was shattered, dear God knows what happened to the rest of his body. How the poor soul must have suffered." She looked anguished for a moment and then continued her dis-

55

sertation. "Probably everything or just about everything of his was blown away . . . ."

"Oh, my dear, not *everything*!"

". . . his identification tags . . . all that sort of thing. . . ."

"But there's one flaw in your theory."

"And what's that?"

"His fingerprints. From the brief glimpses we've had of him, his fingers appeared to be quite intact."

"Hitch, must you be so tiresome?"

He got to his feet. "Time to get back to work." Then he went strangely silent.

"What's wrong?"

"You said this actor Hans Meyer helped carry Rosie Wagner to the doctor's office."

"Yes, he appeared quite concerned."

"What was he still doing hanging about? I saw him early this morning. I thought I'd gotten rid of him."

"Well, obviously you hadn't."

"I wonder if he's still around."

"No, he went with Rosie in the ambulance."

"A total stranger accompanies the afflicted mouse to the sanatorium? How odd."

"Perhaps he wasn't a total stranger. You said the film community here was wholly incestuous."

"I somehow got the impression that the unappetizing Rosie Wagner wasn't the sort to be offered up on anybody's plate. Farber shared that opinion too."

"Oh, come now, Hitch, We know loads of men and women who dote on ugliness. What's her name, that musical-comedy actress, the one who haunts the alleyways under the bridges in search of derelicts, and what's his name, that strange playwright who absolutely goes ga-ga over women with deformities? And what's his name, the author who left his wife to run off to Switzerland with a double amputee?"

"Why, my dear Miss Reville, I am thoroughly astonished at this revelation of the underbelly of your education."

"Don't play the innocent with me."

"Well, I suppose Herr Farber—I find him a charming man, by the way—will be on to Hans Meyer. It's not our problem. Our problem is right here . . ." which he emphasized with a wide gesture of his hands that seemed to encompass the entire stage, "so let's get to work."

La-la-la-la . . . la-la-la . . .

"Oh dear," said Alma, as her voice choked on the last *la*, "poor Rudolf Wagner will never ever be published." And to Hitchcock's perplexed astonishment, she burst into tears.

In London, long past business hours, a light still blazed in an office in Whitehall. Sir Arthur Willing was a tall, solidly built, distinguished-looking gentleman in his mid-forties. Now slouched in a chair at a conference table, he seemed to his colleagues to have shrunk. The two men with him watched as Sir Arthur carefully applied a lighted match to the bowl of his brier pipe. The other men were undoubtedly subordinates because they sat patiently like subordinates, waiting for their chief to light his pipe satisfactorily and address them. The thin young man with sparse red hair was named Nigel Pack. Nigel was now two hours late for a supper date with a secretary, but she was so besotted with him that she had told him he could arrive at her flat at any hour of the night and be warmly welcomed. It was a flat she shared with two other girls, but fortunately, they had separate bedrooms. Sitting across from Nigel was another young man, whose name was Basil Cole. Basil's sideburns and mustache met on his cheeks to give him the look of a perpetually inquisitive simian. Women sometimes weren't sure whether they were expected to kiss him or feed him peanuts.

"Well, now," said Sir Arthur, as he sat back with a discontented look on his face, "as my father would have said in a rare sober moment, we are in the shit."

"It's not all that bad, sir, is it?" asked Nigel.

"Oh, not all that bad," mocked Sir Arthur. "We lose two of our best informants in Munich, which means God knows if the others are in jeopardy too, and the man says, 'It's not all that bad, sir,' as though he were diagnosing a sprained ankle. And what do *you* think, Cole?"

Basil Cole folded his arms and spoke with authority. "I agree with your father. We're in the shit."

"And there's nothing we can do about it either," added Sir Arthur morosely. He turned to Nigel. "I suppose the others have been cautioned?"

"Duncan has gone to ground somewhere in upper Bavaria. The other one has chosen to brazen it out in Munich so he can keep an eye on Hitchcock and Miss Reville."

Sir Arthur leaned forward with his hands folded on the table, a pained expression on his face. "Exactly what is there about them that makes them so suspicious?"

"Miss Reville did seem to be playing up to Rudolf Wagner a bit." It was Nigel Pack who had spoken, and Basil Cole shifted in his chair.

Sir Arthur said, "Well, Wagner did have a bit of a reputation for womanizing, didn't he? He'd been having it off with Grieban, hadn't he?"

Basil Cole said, "Well, hadn't just about everyone? We know the woman for an easy mark. For a while there she was out on the streets. Her dossier tells us she sold her body to everyone but science."

"She was a good operator." And for Sir Arthur, that was the supreme accolade. "Aren't Miss Reville and Hitchcock engaged to be married?" Cole nodded. "Neither one of them has been previously involved?"

"That's right," said Cole.

"So I hardly think it likely Miss Reville was trying to arouse Wagner's sexual interest."

Nigel Pack picked up the thread of conversation. "But she did trouble to memorize the melody, and that's most bothersome."

"It's a charming melody," said Sir Arthur. "I'd hate to lose it."

"It's safe," said Cole.

"You mean so far it's safe," said Pack.

"At any rate, Reville did recommend Wagner's talent as a composer to the director Fritz Lang."

"Well, that's what's bothering me," said Sir Arthur, suddenly getting to his feet and pacing the room. "His wife's quietly active with this Hitler movement. She's a known anti-Semite."

"We're not without those in our own midst," said Cole.

"But not as virulently active as she is. That woman could be dangerous. Do you suppose she tried to recruit Hitchcock and Reville?"

"We don't know that for a fact," said Pack, "but they'll bear closer watching in the future. They're staying on in Munich for another film. And that's a rather sudden decision."

"Not all that sudden," said Basil Cole. "Balcon's operation . . ."

"Balcon?" snapped Sir Arthur.

"Michael Balcon. Hitchcock's producer and very good friend." Basil Cole was now referring to some papers on the

59

table in front of him. "Balcon's operation is a hand-to-mouth existence. He makes his deals where and when he can. Apparently the German side is quite pleased with Hitchcock's work and opted to continue with a second film. This one's to be called *The Mountain Eagle*."

"This could all be part of a clever plot to provide Hitchcock and Reville with a cover to keep them in Munich without arousing any suspicion, couldn't it?" Sir Arthur was having trouble with his pipe and seemed about to declare war on the bowl of tobacco, which refused to remain ignited.

"It could," said Cole, "but somehow, I seem to feel Hitchcock and Reville are actually innocent bystanders."

"Perhaps you're right, but I say we continue to keep them under close surveillance. That's a dangerous witch's caldron brewing over there in Germany. So we'll keep after Mr. Hitchcock and Miss Reville, if you don't mind."

"Oh, not at all, sir," said Cole and then, unable to resist, commented, "And thereby hangs a trail."

He understood the stony silence that followed.

Two weeks later in Munich, Hitchcock sat in his small office in the studio talking on the telephone to Michael Balcon in London. The connection as usual was terrible, and both were shouting.

"I said we did the last shot half an hour ago!" shouted Hitchcock. "The film is completed! Thank God it's completed!" He listened. "I didn't get that! What? What?"

"Congratulations! Is it any good?" shouted Balcon.

"I'll know better after the rough assemblage! Alma and I will get together with the editor first thing tomorrow morning and get cracking on it!"

"You'll have to work fast! *The Mountain Eagle* is scheduled to shoot in mid-July!"

"We'll make the date, not to worry. I say, Mickey, we're a bit short of cash here!"

"What did you say?"

"I said we're a bit short of cash!"

"Oh cash, cash, of course, that bothersome trifle. I expect to transfer a bank draft to you by next Monday."

"Sooner than that! We're existing on credit!"

"Don't worry about it, you'll be fine!"

Alma entered and took a seat. Hitchcock shot her a "heaven help us" look and shouted into the telephone, "It is unpleasant being short of funds!"

"What about the police?"

"I wouldn't dream of borrowing from them!"

"You nit, have they any fresh leads on the murders?"

"I don't know. Detective Farber hasn't been in touch in days."

"Oh, yes, he has," interjected Alma.

"What? What? Hold it, Mickey." He put his hand over the mouthpiece. "Is Farber here?"

"No, he got through to the stage. He wanted to speak to you, but I told him you were in a shouting match with Mickey Balcon in London, so he gave me the news."

Hitchcock looked apprehensive. "He knows who did the killings?"

"Oh, no. There have been no miracles. It's Rosie Wagner. She's been spirited away from the sanatorium. She's gone missing."

"Good lord, but how?"

Alma shrugged. Hitchcock shouted the news to Mickey Balcon. Then he had to remind Balcon who Rosie Wagner was.

"I say, Hitch!" Balcon shouted. "Do you suppose all this has the making of a good thriller?"

61

"Don't change the subject!" shouted Hitchcock. "Send the bloody cash or we hop the next train back to London!"

"Don't you dare! The money's on its way. Meantime, I'll advise our people at the studio to advance you enough to get by on until it arrives. How's Alma?"

"Hungry!" shouted Hitchcock, and slammed the receiver down on the hook. Bristling with anger, he leaned back in his chair. "What the hell do you suppose is going on?"

"Rosie's disappearance?"

"To hell with Rosie, she was a total crashing bore. With us. You and me."

"For heaven's sake, Hitch, I still love you."

"I know you do. That isn't what I'm referring to. Mickey's had a visitor from Whitehall. From British Intelligence. They cross-examined him about *us*."

Alma was delighted. "How marvelous! What have we done?"

"That's what they're trying to find out." He leaned forward. "My dear, it seems there's a suspicion that we're clandestinely up to no good. That we might be spies."

"Us, spies? You? Me? *Me*, who has been known to keep a secret for as long as three minutes?" She erupted with laughter. "Oh, that is wonderful! Oh, how delicious! And what did Mickey tell this gentleman from Whitehall?"

"He most politely told him to go to hell, but most politely. Alma? Remember a few weeks back when I said we're not in the midst of a spy thriller? Well, my dear, I rescind the statement. I have a suspicion we have become very innocently involved in a very troublesome situation." He arose from the chair and crossed around the desk to Alma and helped her to her feet. "We have another two months here in Germany, my darling. We must proceed with very great caution."

"Hitch," she said darkly.

"What is it, my love?"

"You've just sent a freezing chill up my spine."

"Oh, and mine too, mine too. Come, my love, let's repair to the canteen for some double whiskeys. We both deserve and need them."

La-la-la-la . . . la-la-la . . .

"And will you please scrub it with that bloody melody!"

"I can't seem to, Hitch. I just can't seem to."

BOOK TWO

London,
June 1936

Five

The years were kind to Alfred and Alma. They married December 2, 1926, after the shooting was completed on *The Mountain Eagle*, a film so incredibly bad, there are no longer existing prints ("Mercifully," commented Hitchcock). On Saturday, July 7, 1928, their daughter Patricia was born in their charming flat at 153 Cromwell Road in London. In 1929, Hitchcock directed his first all-talking film, *Blackmail*, and his leading lady was the luscious blonde Anny Ondra, whom Fritz Lang had pointed out to him in the restaurant in Munich, although her voice was dubbed by a British actress. In June of 1936, the Commonwealth emerged from mourning for the late King George V, who had died on January 17 of that year, and now speculated dolefully as to whether the somewhat inadequate King Edward VIII would fulfill his rumored threat to abdicate the throne unless he was permitted to marry the woman he loved, the ambitious American divorcée from Baltimore, Mrs. Wallis Simpson.

Eleven years after the unsolved Munich murders, Alfred and Alma were preparing their twentieth film. In the past two years, Hitchcock had begun to win an international reputation with such superb spy thrillers as *The Man Who Knew Too Much*, *The Thirty-Nine Steps*, *The Secret Agent*, and *Sabotage*. The script of his next feature, *The Lady Vanishes*, was giving him trouble. The writers, Sidney Gilliat and Frank Launder, were not extracting Hitchcock's vision from Ethel Lina White's *The Wheel Spins*; only Alma could do that, and in the back of his mind, Hitchcock knew Alma would have to take over the project. This would be his second film with producer Edward Black, the previous one, *Young and Innocent*, having fallen somewhat short of Hitchcock's usual mark, one of the rare occasions that found Hitchcock and the critics in agreement.

In addition to the Cromwell Road flat, the Hitchcocks had acquired a modest country home in the quiet, picturesque village of Shamley Green, near Guildford, less than an hour's drive from London. They called the cottage, which was their sanctuary, "Winter's Grace." They spent as much time in it as possible, and of late, Alma was there often alone. Hitchcock was usually at his office in the Gaumont-British Studios trying to get the script he wanted from his writers. This particular June day, Patricia had been taken away for a long weekend with her cousins, her Aunt Nellie's children. Hitchcock had phoned earlier to tell Alma he'd be home early, but he was bringing a surprise guest for dinner. Alma wasn't too fond of that kind of surprise, but at least on this occasion he had given her fair warning and she'd been able to prepare a passable dinner. She wasn't sure as to what to serve for the sweet—fruit and cream, which Hitchcock usually found boring, or a bang-up pudding calorically threatening. Hitchcock had gained so much weight over the past eleven years, Alma found herself smothered in guilt every time she tried to prepare a sensible meal for him. It was that look on his face when she gave him boiled fish and a vegetable, the look of a man betrayed, by a wife who deserved the firing squad, despite the fact that he loved her very much. Alma decided on sponge cake and jelly.

The phone rang.

Alma recognized the voice immediately. That damned woman reporter again, trying to get a story out of Hitch. "Miss Adair, I've told you three times today Mr. Hitchcock is at the studio. I haven't the vaguest idea when he'll be home," she lied gracefully. She didn't like Nancy Adair. She hadn't the vaguest idea what she looked like, because she was only a disembodied voice on the telephone, a voice in pursuit of her husband for the past three days. The determined voice of a free-lance journalist anxious to earn a few quid with some sort of story from Great Britain's most famous and most respected director. Why, even Hollywood was singing its siren song in his not unresponsive ear.

"I know he's at the studio because I'm parked outside the gate. They won't let me in without a pass."

"Well, then, hadn't you best go home?" Wherever *that* is, and let me get on with this bloody sponge cake recipe.

There were teardrops in Nancy Adair's voice. "Please help me, Mrs. Hitchcock. I only want a half hour of his time. This could mean so much to my career. It's so difficult for a woman to get a foot into Fleet Street. . . ." Well, then, thought Alma, try using some other part of your anatomy. And then Alma wondered if she had a good figure and worse, blond hair. Hitch was an easy target for a good figure

69

and a head of blond hair, peroxided or otherwise. She knew he privately swooned over such Hollywood blondes as Jean Harlow, Helen Twelvetrees, and Alice Faye. He was on the lookout for a blonde for *The Lady Vanishes*. The stunning Madeleine Carroll, who'd done two of his recent films, wasn't available, and his producer was loath to go to the expense of importing a blonde from Hollywood. "Miss Appleby . . ." that was Hitchcock's secretary, ". . . said if *you* asked Mr. Hitchcock to see me—"

Alma interrupted rudely, "I do not influence my husband in his profession, Miss Adair . . ." (And may God forgive me for that statement!) ". . . so I'm sorry, but I have to ring off. Good-bye." Alma hung up.

Nancy Adair, in a phone kiosk outside the entrance gate to the Gaumont-British Studios, slammed the receiver down and roughly shoved the door open. She crossed the street to her automobile while the guard at the gate admired her trim figure and her beautiful mane of blond hair. Dressed in a carefully tailored mannish suit in the style recently made popular by Marlene Dietrich, Nancy Adair appeared to be not yet thirty. Her face was a tribute to the art of her beautician, and her temper was a throwback to her late unlamented parents. She got behind the wheel of her car, slammed the door shut, lit a cigarette, and drummed her fingers on the steering wheel. She was a very determined young woman.

"But it is so dangerous for you to be carrying so much weight!" exclaimed Hans Meyer as he and Hitchcock emerged from the executive building and got into the back seat of the limousine that would drive them to the cottage. Hitchcock had gained weight while losing hair. Now in his late thirties, he considered himself still too young to contemplate mortality.

"You sound just like my doctor, who is a physical wreck." Hitchcock sat with his hands folded over his stomach. "I don't want to talk about myself, I want to talk about you and what's happening in Germany."

"What's happening in Germany is a *Schrecklichkeit*." It sounded ugly, and Hitchcock winced. "That means a fright, a dreadful horror, something terrifying."

"Like my first two films. Drive carefully, Edgar!" he admonished the chauffeur as they almost sideswiped a car driven by a blonde woman who pulled out of the opposite side of the street as they came out of the studio.

"Her fault, sir, the bloody bitch," said Edgar, who chauffeured only for Hitchcock, his regular job being that of studio carpenter.

"As you were saying, Hans."

"I don't know where to begin. I'm so lucky to have gotten out."

"You're not Jewish, are you?"

"No, but Nazi persecution isn't restricted to Jews. It includes Gypsies, homosexuals, intellectuals who refuse to bow before Hitler and his gang and are brave enough to speak out against him. . . ."

"There are some pretty awful films coming out of there," said Hitchcock, who'd recently had an offer to do a film in Berlin and firmly rejected it.

"How can they help but be awful, they're either Nazi propaganda or old-fashioned operettas."

"How did you learn you were on their blacklist?" Hitchcock wondered what had become of the man's pencil-thin mustache. Clean-shaven and tired, Hans Meyer had arrived

71

in England a fortnight earlier and couldn't believe his ears when Hitchcock's secretary said Mr. Hitchcock did remember the young actor who could climb mountains. What was more important, over the past decade, Meyer had made a good reputation for himself playing villains and oddball characters not only in German films, but in French and Italian ones as well. Hitchcock had seen a good deal of his work, and there was the possibility of a part for him in *The Lady Vanishes*.

"Well, when, after ten years of working steadily your phone stops ringing and your agent doesn't return your calls, you begin to suspect you have a problem."

"I should say so. Bloody agents. Now tell me the truth. What have you done to incur the Nazi's displeasure?"

"I had a falling out with Leni Riefenstahl. You know her work?"

"Oh, yes. I've run some of her things. She also climbs mountains."

"That was how we first met. It was in her film *The Blue Light*. Now she's a big favorite with the Nazis. There was a rumor she was for a while Hitler's girlfriend."

"I thought he preferred boyfriends."

"His tastes are eclectic. Actually, the suspicion is that he is asexual, but that is neither here nor there."

"It is for him."

Meyer sighed and rubbed his palms on his trousers. "Riefenstahl wanted me to join the Nazis, but I couldn't stomach that idea. You know, I always dreamed of going to Hollywood." Hitchcock smiled. "Well, a few actors have made it there, haven't they?"

"Well, Peter Lorre's gotten himself a contract despite his bad teeth and *his* obesity. He'll probably spend the rest of his career in thrillers."

Hans Meyer asked, "Do you think Mrs. Hitchcock will remember me?"

"Indeed, Hans Meyer, indeed. A week doesn't pass that we don't recall those awful murders. You see, Alma and I would love to do a film about that time, but we can't find the MacGuffin."

"The who?" Hitchcock explained the MacGuffin. "Ah so!"

"For a while there, we thought of using Rosie Wagner as our MacGuffin, but we could never figure out what might have happened to her. Have *you* any idea? You apparently were a friend of hers."

"No, I wasn't," said Meyers hastily.

"But you went along in the ambulance with her to the sanatorium."

"I felt sorry for her. I thought she was dying. She was so alone, that's what the studio doctor told me. Her mother dead. Her father murdered. So I volunteered to accompany her to the sanatorium."

"Do you know if she ever came out of that catatonic state?"

"She must have, to have run away from there the way she did."

"What way was that?" Hitchcock was wondering if at last he was on to something. Edgar the chauffeur was cursing the bad driving of the blonde woman in the car behind him. On two occasions she had seemed to be trying either to pass them or pull up alongside, and both times she'd almost crashed into cars coming from the opposite direction.

"Well, what I heard was that she disappeared quite mysteriously. Again it was the studio doctor who told me this when you so kindly gave me that bit in *The Mountain Eagle*."

73

"Don't *ever* mention that *awful* film again. Edgar! What the hell is going on? This is the road to Guildford, not Le Mans!"

"It's not me, Hitch, it's that bloody woman in the car behind us. She's a right proper menace, she is!"

"Well, try losing her!"

"What do you think I'm trying to do?" Edgar was perspiring, which was unusual for the always cool and collected young man.

Hitch turned to the actor. "What did the doctor tell you?"

"She seemed to have vanished in the night. No one saw her go. And if there were accomplices, no one saw anyone entering the hospital or leaving with her. Now isn't that some puzzle?"

"Indeed, it is quite some puzzle. Now let me think—that charming detective, Farber. I think it was Farber."

"Oh, yes. Wilhelm Farber."

"Did you ever have an occasion to cross his path again? On the last day of shooting of that *awwwful* film, he came by to say good-bye and thank Alma and myself for what little help we could give him, and he said he'd keep in touch and let us know if he ever solved the murders. But alas, we never heard from him again."

"As far as I know, they remain unsolved."

"And is Farber still in Munich?"

Meyer moistened his lips and then told Hitchcock, "Farber is dead."

Hitchcock's hand flew to his heart. "Oh, no!"

"Well, if you remember, he was rather a strange man. A sense of humor . . ."

"So unbecoming in a detective, unless it's in fiction," commented Hitchcock wryly.

74

". . . and a rigid sense of proportion. I heard he of-
fended the Nazis and . . . well, he was found dead in the
village of Dachau. . . ."

"Dachau. Oh, yes, that's not too far from Munich."

"About ten miles."

"Why would anyone want to be found dead in Dachau?"

Hans Meyer shrugged. "From what little there was in
the newspaper, he'd gone there unofficially, to investigate
something on his own, and he was found in a ditch outside
the village, his car wrecked, the body strafed with bullets."

"The poor soul. I wonder if he was on to something
involving the murders of Anna Grieban and Rudolf Wagner,
or if it was something else? We'll never know, will we?"

"Never, I suppose."

Hitchcock rolled down the window and shouted at
Nancy Adair as her car passed theirs. "You bloody stupid
incompetent bitch. Edgar! Pull into that driveway ahead and
let's be rid of that woman! Imagine! And she's a stunning
blonde, too!" Hitchcock rolled the window back up and then
sat back. They rode in silence for a while, Hitchcock waiting
for his rapid heart beat to return to normal and for his blood
pressure to settle down. *La-la-la-la . . . la-la-la . . .*

Hans Meyer smiled. "I remember that tune!"

"Alma doesn't let me forget it. It continues to haunt us
both after all these years. Alma's convinced it had some sig-
nificance. You know, when Alma said to Rosie Wagner before her father was murdered that she wished it had words,
Rosie said very mysteriously, 'Perhaps it does have words,'
or something like that. Now let's stop dwelling on the past
because you'll have to rehash all this for Alma and you can
do that while I try to solve my way out of the enigma of this
disappointing script my writers have handed me."

"This part you think might be right for me . . ."

"Doctor Hartz. A right proper villain. Trouble is, as he's written here, he has no charm. I like my villains to be charming. I like the audience to like them. So what do the writers tell me when I tell them Dr. Hartz has no charm? They tell me to hire a charming actor."

"I can be very charming, Hitch."

"I know, Hans. I know. I'm considering you very seriously. If this doesn't work, I'll see what I can do to help you here." He sighed a very deep and very heavy sigh. "There are so many refugees in London now looking for work in films. Half come from Germany and the other half are here because they're washed up in Hollywood. Conrad Veidt wants the part. Paul Lukas wants the part. And the actor's union is after me to hire a Briton for the part. Life can be so difficult."

Edgar the chauffeur crowed ecstatically. "She's blown a tire! The bloody menace has blown a tire!"

Ahead, they saw Nancy Adair struggling to change a tire. Hitchcock rolled down his window and shouted as they drove past her, "Hire a horse!"

Fifteen minutes later, they arrived at the cottage. The chauffeur, anxious to return to his wife in London, refused refreshment and left. Alma kissed Hitchcock as he led Hans Meyer into the pretty sitting room. Hitchcock asked her, "And do you remember this young man? He's eleven years older, minus his pencil-thin mustache, there are now some distinguishing shades of gray at the temples, and he's on the run from the Nazis!"

Alma threw up her hands and laughed. "The mountain climber! I can't for the life of me remember your name, but you're the mountain climber!"

"Hans Meyer," he told her and they embraced warmly.

"What a nice surprise! Hitch, fix the drinks. Dinner will be a while yet, I"m having a problem with the sweet."

"Oh, no sweet for me!" said Hitchcock, "I'm starting a diet."

"Catch me, Hans!" cried Alma. "I'm about to faint!"

Two hours later, after dinner, they sat in the sitting room with coffee and brandy. Over dinner, Meyer had re-hashed everything he had told Hitchcock in the car, holding Alma engrossed. Now she asked him, "But what about your family? It must be awful leaving them behind. My goodness, we don't even know if you're married. Are you?"

"I'm a free man," said Hans. "I was orphaned when I was a young boy and raised by my mother's family. They've left Germany for Austria, so they're quite safe."

"Well, then, we must try to do something for you here," said Alma, "mustn't we, Hitch?"

"We shall do our best. More brandy?" Meyer held out his snifter, and Hitchcock poured generously.

"By the way, Hitch. Some free-lance journalist named Nancy Adair has called here several times to try to set up an interview with you. I told her to call the studio. . . ."

"She has, and I have no time for her. Tell her to stop phoning here. Bloody nuisances, journalists—except, of course, when you need them."

The phone rang.

Alma's eyes narrowed. "If that's *her* again . . ."

"Well, *I'm* not answering the phone," said Hitchcock as he poured himself a refill.

"Perhaps it would help if I took the call?" volunteered Hans.

"Oh, by all means!" said Alma with a smile of delight. "Of course it might be Patricia, but you go right ahead."

Hans crossed to the phone. "Yes?"

"Could I please speak to Mr. Hitchcock? My name is Nancy Adair. . . ."

"Well, Miss Adair . . ." Hitchcock and his wife wearily exchanged a look. ". . . he is not available now."

While Hans Meyer handled Nancy Adair, Alma asked Hitchcock, "I think we should ask Hans to spend the night. Then he could go back into London with you in the morning."

"If it won't inconvenience you, darling."

"Oh, not at all, and I'd love to continue nattering. There's so much more I want to know about what's going on over there." She became suddenly grave. "Those lovely people we worked with in Munich. I wonder what's become of them."

Hans returned and overheard Alma. "A lot of them are now very loyal Nazis." Alma's shoulders sagged. "Miss Adair is in the village."

"Oh God!" cried Hitchcock.

"She wanted to come by, but I discouraged her."

"Bless you, dear Hans," said Alma. "And now, we think you should spend the night, unless you have pressing business back in London. Then we could arrange for a taxi from the village, but the expense is prohibitive. Otherwise, you can drive into town in the morning with Hitch. Edgar usually picks him up around nine. Do stay, I'd love so to hear more about what's—"

The phone rang.

"I don't believe it," said Hitchcock, "I simply don't believe it. If it's that woman again . . ." He waved the others back as Alma and Hans made a move to the phone. "*I'll* take it!" He struggled out of his comfortable chair and lumbered across the room to the phone. "Who is it?" he barked.

78

"Herr Hitchcock?" The voice at the other end was a man's and very faint.

"This is Hitchcock here. Who is this, please? I can barely understand you. Could you speak up, please?" He listened.

"Herr Hitchcock, this is Fredrick Regner." He seemed to be speaking with an effort. "Do you remember me? Munich? The Emelka Studios? I gave you a script to read . . ."

"Which I did not like! Freddy Regner, how the hell are you?"

"Freddy Regner!" cried Alma. "It's not really Freddy!" Hans Meyer stared at Hitchcock and sipped his brandy.

"It's really Freddy," Hitchcock said to Alma in a droll voice. Into the mouthpiece he said, "That was Alma to ask if it's really Freddy. How are you, Freddy? Where are you? Are you well?"

"I'm in London. I stay with a friend."

"We would like to see you as soon as possible. How can we arrange it?"

"Herr Hitchcock, I am not well. You see, I had a very bad time in Germany."

"How awful, Freddy."

"And getting out was not easy for me. But now I am here, and I hear you have this cottage in the country, and when there is no reply from your flat in London, I phone you here. Is this all right?"

"Of course it is. Where is this you're staying? If you're ill, I'll come to see you."

"I have a script for you, Herr Hitchcock."

"Not the same one you gave me eleven years ago," Hitchcock joked.

79

"I think you will find this one very interesting. I wish to send it to you now. Tonight."

"But if you're ill . . ."

"My friend, Martin Mueller, with whom I stay, he will bring it to you. If this is all right, please, I will put Martin on the phone and you will give him the directions."

"Yes, of course."

"And you will read the script right away?" There was no escaping the urgency in Regner's voice. "It is very important you read it right away. You see, it deals with Munich. When we were in Munich. The murders."

"How marvelous! Alma and I have been trying to do one of our own, but we've had no luck. Alma, darling! Freddy's done a script about the murders in Munich!"

"How marvelous!"

Hans Meyer smiled at Alma, and they listened as Hitchcock gave simple instructions to Martin Mueller. Then Regner came back on the phone for some final word.

"Herr Hitchcock. You must be very careful. The script must not fall into the wrong hands. There are many dangerous people here in London who are friendly to the Nazis, and the script is a danger to them. Do you understand me, Herr Hitchcock. Do you? Do you understand?"

"I do. I most certainly do. Do you have a doctor looking after you?" But the line had gone dead. Hitchcock stared at the phone, and then hung up the receiver. "Most mysterious. Most mysterious indeed. Imagine Freddy Regner after all these years. You knew Freddy, didn't you, Hans?"

"Oh, many years ago at the studio. But we were merely acquainted. He sends you this script with his friend?"

"Yes. Someone named Martin Mueller. Does that ring a bell, Hans?"

"Mueller is a very common name in Germany. Like Jones or Smith here."

"Here, Hans, Smith is Smythe." said Alma, "and Jones never stands alone. It is usually combined with a hyphen and a pretentious other surname, like Jones hyphen Hepplewhite. Something like that."

Back in his chair and warming his snifter of brandy between the palms of his hand, Hitchcock was preoccupied.

"Is something wrong, darling?"

"I'm not sure. That's what I'm puzzling." He repeated Regner's words of warning.

"How melodramatic, Hitch," said Alma. "It's like a scene out of one of our movies."

"Yes, as a matter of fact, it reminded me of Lucie Mannheim's warning to Robert Donat in *The Thirty-Nine Steps* when she staggers into his bedroom with the knife in her back."

Hans Meyer spoke. "If I'm to spend the night, I must tell my friend in London so he won't worry when I don't return. May I, please?"

"You have to jiggle the hook for the village operator," said Alma, "and then she'll put you through." Hans went to the phone, and Alma said to Hitchcock, "Imagine that. He's written a script about the Munich murders. Poor Detective Farber. How he would have loved to have read it."

Hitchcock said nothing.

La-la-la-la . . . la-la-la . . .

"I wonder if there's something about *that* in the script?" Hitchcock said.

Six

Martin Mueller was a small man with big problems. The antiquated British Ford he was driving was no match for the rutted road leading to the Hitchcock cottage. He'd had little previous experience driving in the British countryside; in fact, he had little previous experience driving in Britain. Twice he almost collided with cars coming at him from the opposite direction because he kept forgetting the British drove on the left-hand side of the road. The British—oh, these British, hospitable, yes, but friendly, no. Would he ever come to accept tepid beer and sausages that were composed largely of oatmeal? And the wireless. The BBC. All that delicate music suitable for tea dancing. And the language, the peculiar language. Boiled sweets meant hard candy. A kip was a bed for the night and not an abbreviation for a herring. And a butcher's wasn't a place to buy meat, it was cockney slang for having a look at something. ("Butcher's hook, have a look, get it, Martin?" "*Nein*, I don't.")

There was a fine drizzle, and the metronomic beat of the windshield wiper was making him sleepy. He saw a cottage ahead and referred to the directions Hitchcock had dictated. That had to be the place. It was ablaze with light, and it was after midnight; that must be Hitchcock waiting up for him. He accelerated and pressed on. As he reached the driveway to the cottage, he passed a parked car that seemed to be unoccupied. He drove a few feet into the driveway and parked. He switched off his headlights and then picked up Regner's manuscript, which was in a sealed envelope on the adjoining seat. To protect it from the rain, he put it inside his jacket and held his hand tightly around the manuscript. He got out of the car, shut the door, and hurried up the driveway, which was lined with beautifully trimmed hedges. He heard nothing but the falling of the rain.

If this wasn't the Hitchcock's cottage, he had no idea what to do next except phone Regner in London for new instructions. This would make Freddy angry. It would mean Freddy would have to phone Hitchcock again, feigning illness and asking for fresh instructions. He'd have to phone Mueller back at whatever kiosk Mueller would be fortunate in locating in this desolate area. He heard the piano. The melody. Rudolf Wagner's melody. This is it. I'm here. His face brightened.

Then the knife was plunged into his back.

Mueller gasped as he stumbled forward. The blade was so sharp, he almost didn't feel it. But he felt the hands tearing at his arms, tearing at the jacket. This made him angry.

It was a new jacket. He had saved to buy it for months. Now there would be a rent in the back where the blade penetrated, and not even a master tailor would be able to disguise the tear. Martin scrabbled together a fistful of dirt and pebbles and rolled over on his side, now beginning to feel the pain, and threw the dirt and pebbles into his assailant's face. Whoever it was, he wore a balaclava on his head protecting everything but the eyes, the vulnerable eyes. The assassin cried out in pain and stumbled backward. With a Herculean effort, Martin Mueller struggled to his feet and, weakly crying Hitchcock's name, reached the front door and rang the bell. He heard his assassin curse and run in the opposite direction.

At the sound of the doorbell, Alma's hands froze above the keyboard. Hitchcock said, "I'll answer the door," and waddled past Hans Meyer, who stifled a yawn. The Hitchcocks had urged him to go to bed over an hour ago, but he insisted on staying up and sharing their vigil. Hitchcock opened the door, and Martin Mueller fell into his arms. Hitchcock shouted for help. Alma and Hans came running and helped carry Mueller into the house.

"Inside my jacket," gasped the dying man, "in my jacket." Hans Meyer moved toward the jacket, but Hitchcock was already fumbling with the zipper.

"Oh, my God," said Alma, her face pale and drained of blood, "that knife! It's been plunged in to the hilt! Hans! Get the operator! Tell her to send a doctor and the police! Hurry!" Meyer hurried to the telephone.

Hitchcock removed the envelope from inside the jacket and flung it onto the couch. He didn't know what to do with Mueller and decided it was best to leave him lying prone on the carpet near the fireplace. He knew it was dangerous to try to remove the knife without medical knowledge and tried his best to comfort the man. Mueller's lips were moving, but no sound emerged. Meyer was shouting into the telephone, and Alma had poured a brandy and was holding the glass to Mueller's lips. He shook his head with an effort, too weak to accept the liquor. Alma placed the glass on the coffee table and fought back tears. He was such a young man, so small and so vulnerable, and the jacket seemed to be new; it had that wonderful leathery smell of a newly bought windbreaker. He's probably not yet thirty, thought Alma, and saw a look of fear in Mueller's eyes as he stared at something happening behind her. She turned and saw Hans Meyer lifting the envelope from the couch. Instinctively, Alma crossed to Meyer and said, "Thank you, Hans. I'll take that."

Hans Meyer handed her the envelope and, clutching it to her bosom, Alma returned to Hitchcock's side. Hitchcock was gently pressing the man for Freddy Regner's phone number and address, but Mueller's eyes were closed and his ears unheeding. Hitchcock felt with his fingers gently at the base of the man's neck. There was no pulse beat. Hitchcock sat back on the carpet. "I think he's dead."

"Your poor carpet," said Hans Meyer, "it's soaked with blood. I'm afraid it's ruined."

Alma looked up at him and thought, what a strange observation at this tragic moment. "The carpet is replaceable," said Alma in a shaking voice, "the man isn't." From somewhere out in the road she heard a motor revving and then the sound of a car driving off with a screeching of tires. She went to the window and drew the curtain aside, and although she could hear the car driving off, she could see nothing.

"Thank God Patricia isn't here," said Hitchcock. He had risen and gone to Alma at the window and put his arm around her shoulder.

"I just heard a car drive off. Do you suppose . . ."

Hitchcock read her mind. "You'll tell the police." As if on cue, in the distance they could here the shrieking of the on-off, on-off of the police siren.

"I suppose that'll be the sheriff," said Alma.

Hitchcock groaned. "I hope he's brought a translator. I can never understand a word he says. Come on, we need brandy. It isn't every night we have a murdered man falling into our arms. Here. I'll take that." He took the envelope from Alma, went to his desk, opened the center drawer, and, after placing the envelope inside, locked the drawer and pocketed the key. "Brandy, Hans? You might as well. I'm afraid we're in for a long session with the local police. Everything they know they've gleaned from watching Hollywood movies; we must be very patient with them."

Five minutes later, Peregrine Hunt, the village sheriff, arrived with his two constables, who were callow youths with a shared IQ, in Hitchcock's opinion, of less than thirty. Peregrine's wife was the local postmistress and telephone operator. Between them, they ruled and terrorized their small world. The Hitchcocks called them the Lunts. Peregrine's false teeth were ill-fitting, and he was frequently inarticulate. The Hitchcocks, however, had more or less learned to unscramble him on the frequent occasions when they came across him shopping in the village. As the local celebrity, Hitchcock suspected Peregrine lay in ambush waiting to attack the director and engage him in conversation. Peregrine's wife, who had the strange name of Effinasia (which Alma pronounced "Euthanasia" and when with the woman sometimes wished to commit), was a movie buff and could recite great gobs of dialogue from almost all of Hitchcock's talkies, a reputation recently overshadowed by her devastating impersonation of Mae West at a local charity ball. In the policemen's wake arrived the local doctor, Oliver Grundle, whom Alma had described, when he was first introduced to her several years earlier, as belonging in a production of *A Midsummer Night's Dream*. He was a spare, angular man, certainly past fifty, and given to saying "oh my" and "tsk tsk" and prescribing aspirin and strong tea for everything from influenza to tuberculosis. When he saw the body he tsk tsk'd, said, "Oh my," and then knelt at Mueller's side.

"He's dead," said the doctor, and Hitchcock restrained from congratulating him. "Stabbed in the back," the doctor continued, and Hitchcock refilled his brandy snifter. "Murdered," the doctor said. "Nothing much I can do here except have him removed to the morgue." He thought for a moment. "We don't have a morgue." Hitchcock briefly played with suggesting the body be placed on display in the window of the general store but then decided frivolity would only add to the doctor's confusion.

"We'll have to take him into Guildford," said Peregrine Hunt with almost admirable authority. He turned to one of his underlings and said, "Ring Effinasia and tell her to send the coal wagon." That wasn't exactly what it sounded like, but the young man was studying decoding in his spare time and was able to convey the order over the phone to Mrs. Hunt, who usually closed the switchboard down at one A.M. but in a police emergency gallantly stood by her post like the captain of a sinking ship.

"Coal wagon's coming," said the young man with a big smile for everyone that largely went unnoticed.

"Now then, Mr. Hitchcock, what can you tell me about the deceased and how he came to be lying on your carpet with a knife in his back?" Peregrine produced a pencil and notebook, and for a brief instant, Alma hungered for the presence of the late, urbane German detective, Wilhelm Farber.

The testimonies of the Hitchcocks and their guest were brief and to the point. They told the sheriff the whole story from Regner's phone call to the delivery of the envelope by the murdered man. Hitchcock could see Peregrine Hunt knew he was in over his head and tactfully suggested Scotland Yard be notified and asked to participate. While the sheriff procrastinated before coming to a decision, Dr. Grundle helped himself to a shot of gin and wandered around the room admiring the prints with which Alma had decorated the walls. By the time the coal wagon arrived, Peregrine Hunt had asked his wife to connect him with Scotland Yard, and Hitchcock, foreseeing a long night ahead of them, suggested to Alma a large pot of coffee and some sandwiches would be in order. Hans Meyer accompanied Alma to the kitchen, and she was grateful for the assistance he had volunteered.

Hitchcock took a seat at his desk, aching to unlock the top drawer and have a look at the manuscript. Peregrine Hunt had suggested they cover the corpse with a sheet, and Hitchcock directed one of Hunt's young men to the hall cupboard at the head of the stairs. He was too weary to undertake the assignment himself. While waiting for the men from Scotland Yard to arrive, Hitchcock reran in his mind as many of the incidents that he could recall of the murders in

Munich. Then he replayed his mysterious conversation of a few hours ago with Fredrick Regner. Alma and Hans Meyer entered with trays of coffee and sandwiches, and Hitchcock said, "Now where in the hell do we find Fredrick Regner?"

"Regner. Fredrick Regner." Detective Superintendent Michael Jennings of New Scotland Yard was a twelve-year veteran of the force and a man begrudgingly admired and respected by his peers. He was a no-nonsense police officer who had divorced his wife two years after joining the force when he found her constant complaints about his line of work prevented him from concentrating fully on his job. He later heard she'd left England and worked as a nurse in a leper colony in Hawaii. In a crowd, Jennings became every-man, unrecognizable. This helped make him a superior asset in an investigation. Hitchcock admired his brisk efficiency as he took statements from the Hitchcocks and Hans Meyer and then turned his attention to locating Fredrick Regner. "I'll contact Immigration first thing in the morning. They'll have to have a record of him. Can't enter the country without registering, you know." He once again returned to the place on the carpet where Martin Mueller's body had lain, the corpse long since having been removed by coal wagon to the morgue in Guildford. He stared down with such intensity, Hitchcock wondered if he expected to find some answers written there. Another Scotland Yard officer entered the house and gently closed the door behind him, grateful that the rain had stopped and hungry for the warmth of the bed he shared with his recently acquired wife.

"There's nothing much of use in the victim's car, sir." His name was Peter Dowerty, and he had just recently been assigned to Detective Superintendent Jennings' team. Jennings liked him, but would never tell him that.

"Well, tell me what you found, then we'll see if there's nothing much of use."

Alma and Hans had moved through the room with their trays of refreshment, and sandwiches and mugs of coffee disappeared so rapidly that Alma was reminded of the plague of locusts sent to devastate the persecutors of the Israelites.

Peter Dowerty cleared his throat and told his superior officer he'd found a page of directions on the seat next to the driver's, or at least he assumed that's what it was, as he recognized English place names, but everything else was printed in a foreign language he deduced was probably German. There was a map of London and vicinities in the driver's compartment, along with a bar of chocolate and a half-eaten cheese sandwich. "Cheddar," said Dowerty and Alma fell in love with him.

"No registration?" asked Jennings gently.

"Here, sir." Dowerty handed Jennings the registration. Jennings read aloud in a soft, almost cultured voice, "Martin Mueller, age twenty-eight, single, Caucasian male, et cetera, et cetera, et cetera, residing at eight-oh-oh-three Liverpool Road, London. Well, we'll have a look into that right now. Dowerty, get on to Phone Directory in London and see if there's a listing for Mueller." Dowerty obeyed instructions efficiently. There was no listing for Martin Mueller at eight-oh-oh-three Liverpool Road. "I thought not," said Jennings almost smugly, "house numbers on Liverpool Road don't run into four digits."

Hans Meyer yawned and then apologized for yawning, and Jennings told him he could go to bed if he liked, inasmuch as Jennings had his statement and could see little else that he might add to the investigation. "Now, Mr. Hitchcock . . ."

"Yes?" Hitchcock drew out the word as though he were pulling on a string of chewing gum. Actually, he was chewing on a ham sandwich and wondered why Alma had forgotten to provide mustard.

"This manuscript the man brought you, do you suppose it might have some bearing on the murder? I mean, let's look upon this carefully. An old acquaintance phones and asks you to read a scenario. It can't wait until tomorrow or be sent through the post, but it must be brought to you tonight. And"—he referred to his notes—"he warns you there would be danger if it falls into the wrong hands. Now who could the wrong hands belong to?"

"Probably some other director," replied Hitchcock with equanimity.

"Could I have a look at this manuscript?"

"Why, certainly." He caught Alma's eye in her reflection in the mirror that hung over the desk. He also saw past her to Hans Meyer at the foot of the staircase, who was about to ascend, and then, deciding not to, turned to observe the scene between Hitchcock and Jennings. Hitchcock unlocked the drawer, removed the envelope, and then slit the envelope flap with the desk knife. He removed the manuscript, which was bound in a purple cover. Hitchcock made a face.

"Is anything wrong?" asked Jennings.

"I loathe the color purple. I find it vulgar. It puts me in mind of purple pasts and purple rages and a dreadful movie I once saw called *Riders of the Purple Sage*, but we mustn't let me digress. This manuscript is terribly thin for a film

91

script. Do you mind if I have a look first? After all," he said with his trademark enigmatic smile, "it was meant for me."

"By all means," said Jennings with admirable patience. It was obvious, at least to Alma, that the man wanted to complete his investigation and get back to headquarters and instigate a wider operation.

Hitchcock announced, "It has no title." He turned a page. "And it is not a scenario at all. It is a treatment for a proposed scenario. I assume you've had some experience with movie jargon, Mr. Jennings?"

"Some."

Hitchcock handed him the script. "You have a look. It means nothing to me. Don't let us keep you up, Hans. I think there's very little of interest here."

Hans took the hint and went upstairs. Jennings was flipping pages and then said, "There's a musical notation here."

"Oh, really?" said Hitchcock blithely. "I once directed a musical, *Waltzes from Vienna*. It was a disaster. It was neither Viennese nor did it waltz very well."

Jennings returned the script to Hitchcock. "I'm afraid what little I've scanned means nothing to me. Murders in Munich, a disappearing girl . . ." Alma thought her breath would stop. "And this melody composed by the . . . am I correct? Is there such a thing as an atmosphere musician?"

"There was, back in the days of silent movies. It was supposed to help put the actors into the mood to emote. On occasion it was effective."

"I see. One last question, and then I'll let you get to bed. I suppose we could all use some sleep." Peregrine Hunt was already asleep sitting upright on the couch. The doctor had long since departed, and Hunt's callow assistants sat near the door to the kitchen with expressions of total disinterest. Jennings was addressing Alma. "You're positive you didn't see the car you heard driving away shortly after the murder?"

"Heavens, no. I heard it from a distance, obviously out on the road somewhere, and besides, the hedges lining our driveway are quite tall. It's impossible to see over them."

"Only if you stand on the top rung of a ladder," advised Hitchcock. Jennings could tell it was time to end his investigation for the moment. There was no escaping the underlined irritation in Hitchcock's voice, and it was now almost four in the morning. There'd be little sleep for any of them.

A few minutes later, as Jennings and his two assistants got into their official car, with Dowerty taking the wheel, Jennings asked, "Could you find a decent tire print of the car Mrs. Hitchcock heard?" The third man, Angus McKellin, a dour Scotsman who had made his way to London from Glasgow as a teenager, spoke up:

"It was all scuffled and useless, sir. The car had been parked on a stretch of grass. I could try again if you like."

"No point in bothering," said Jennings, as Dowerty drove out of the driveway, "it was probably a hire car. Even if we trace it, we'll find a false name and driver's license."

McKellin said cheerfully, "Mrs. Hitchcock is a bonny woman, don't you think, Chief?"

Chief was thinking, but not about Alma Hitchcock. His mind was on Fredrick Regner's manuscript. He had seen enough to convince him a more thorough investigation of the material was called for, but he did not wish to arouse the Hitchcocks' suspicion. He took out his pocket watch and glanced at it. A call to Sir Arthur Willing would have to wait for a few more hours. The irascible old gent would never tolerate the interruption of his beauty sleep.

Hitchcock and Alma were in the kitchen, seated next to each other at the table, hungrily reading the manuscript. "The typewriting is a disaster," commented Hitchcock. Alma was too absorbed to comment. She read faster than Hitchcock and prodded him to hurry it up a bit. "Stop rushing me," said Hitchcock testily. "This has to be read with great care."

Half an hour later he sat back and rubbed his eyes. Alma's head rested in the palm of her hand, her elbow propped up on the table. "Well, my beloved, what do we make of it?"

"It's quite obvious, Hitch. We're in the midst of an espionage intrigue. We've been smack in the middle of it beginning with the murders in Munich. And it's quite obvious the protagonists in the London section, the film director and his wife, are you and I."

"How terribly unpleasant. In this story"—he tapped an index finger on the manuscript—"I murder someone, you're kidnapped, and I flee in fear of the police and go on this long dangerous search throughout the countryside for the head of the spy ring. We already did that one in *The Thirty-Nine Steps!*"

"And the melody's there. *La-la-la-la . . . la-la-la . . .*" She clapped her hands together. "I'll bet it *does* have words. You remember, Rosie Wagner said perhaps it does have words; well, I'll bet you a shilling will get you a pound it's in the notations. Let's go to the piano." With alacrity, Hitchcock picked up the manuscript and followed Alma to the piano, where she seated herself. She took the manuscript and flipped the pages until she found the musical notations. She sent Hitchcock to the desk to find a pencil, and he grimaced at the bloodstained carpet. Once Alma was in possession of the pencil, she softly played the notes so as not to awaken Hans Meyer, whose room was above them. She studied what she had written and then shrugged with frustration. "Just notes. *Do mi fa sol, sol fa sol* . . . it means nothing to me."

"We need some sleep. We're all fuzzy now. There's too much to think about and we must think about this clearly."

"Do you think we'll find Freddy Regner?"

"What makes you think we won't?"

"I suppose Mr. Jennings will call all the German refugee organizations in search of a lead, but still, but still . . ."

"But still *what*?"

"I think Freddy Regner will be found when he bloody well wishes to be found." She thought for a moment and then said, darkly, "Hitch? Do you suppose we've been set up?"

"Set up as what?"

"I was just remembering. When we were in Munich after we completed shooting on *The Pleasure Garden*."

"Well, what about it?"

"You were shouting over the phone to Mickey Balcon in London how desperate we were for fresh funds. And he told you then someone'd been around from Whitehall asking questions about us." Hitch was no longer sleepy.

"Yes, I remember. I've never forgotten." Alma followed him back to the kitchen. Hitchcock almost forgot the manuscript, but Alma reminded him and he reclaimed it from the piano. In the kitchen, Alma plugged in the teakettle and set out two mugs. Through the window, the first rays of dawn were appearing, but neither Hitchcock nor Alma entertained thoughts of getting some rest. Their adrenaline was hyperactive.

"Hitch. In *The Lady Vanishes* . . ."

His eyes widened. "The little old lady who disappears! She teaches the two young people a melody she's learned in the mountain inn where they were all staying. And at the end of the story, the melody turns out to be a secret code. Now how the hell do you suppose eleven years ago in Munich some spy foresaw that I'd be using a coded melody in a film I hope to be shooting a few months from now?"

"The answer is terribly obvious. Nobody foresaw any such thing. It's a coincidence. Coded melodies have appeared in several spy films made by the Americans. There was that awful one with Constance Bennett . . ."

"I wonder if she'd be right for *The Lady Vanishes*. She's shooting here at Gaumont-British some thriller with Oscar Homolka and . . ."

"Hitch! We've got to get that melody decoded."

"Not so fast, my girl. Not so fast." The kettle whistled and Hitch watched distractedly as Alma prepared their tea. "Tomorrow morning, I suggest we move back to the flat in London."

"Why, for heaven's sake? It's so beautiful here."

"Beautiful? There's a miserably bloodstained carpet in the next room. I had a murdered man fall into my arms. We're delivered a mysterious manuscript that predicts me as a murderer and you as a kidnap victim, and you want to sit in the country and admire the beauties of nature. Why, my dear Alma, whatever became of your terribly British sporting instinct? My dear, if we are being set up, I say we must cooperate." He held up the manuscript. "You know what a bloody awful time we have finding some good filmable material. Well, here's a potential right here in my hand. But we must go about this carefully, very carefully. We have the welfare of our daughter to consider."

"Oh God!" cried Alma.

"What? What is it?"

"I've just thought of that dreadfully persistent Nancy Adair person! If that poor creature only knew what went on here and she missed it all, I think she'd slit her wrists!"

"And not a moment too soon," said Hitchcock, as he lifted his mug of tea and sipped.

The door opened and Hans Meyer poked his head in. "Good morning!" Startled by his sudden appearance, Alma cried out.

"I'm so sorry if I startled you!"

"Oh, my God, Hans," cried Alma, "I'd forgotten completely about you."

"I didn't," said Hitchcock softly, and took another sip of tea.

Seven

It pleased Sir Arthur enormously when running into old friends he hadn't seen for years to hear them exclaim, "Why, Arthur, you haven't changed one bit." But he had; they knew it, and he knew it, change being inevitable. Early the morning after the Hitchcocks' unpleasant adventure at the cottage, Sir Arthur sat in the conference room at Intelligence headquarters reaming the bowl of his pipe with a matchstick. With him were his longtime aides, Nigel Pack and Basil Cole, and Detective Superintendent Michael Jennings. Nigel Pack's thinning red hair had gone the way of all thinning hair. He was bald, fifteen pounds heavier, and unhappily married to the woman he'd begun dating eleven years earlier when she was a secretary. Basil Cole had remained a bachelor, and all traces of facial hair had long ago disappeared when he overheard a woman in a restaurant commenting on his thick mustache and sideburns. "The last time I saw a face like his, Tarzan was feeding it a banana."

Jennings was staring out the window at the thickening fog, an odd occurrence for a day in June, waiting for Sir Arthur to comment on the previous night's event at the Hitchcock cottage. Sir Arthur was now tamping down tobacco into the pipe bowl and wondering aloud why a fresh pot of tea hadn't been ordered. Nigel Pack buzzed a receptionist and ordered the tea, "What about this actor person, Hans Meyer?" asked Sir Arthur. "What do we know about him?"

Jennings referred to his notebook. "Recently arrived seeking refuge from the Nazis. Apparently blacklisted in their film industry for some months. Has had a pretty fair career acting in Germany, France, and Italy, fluent in several languages. Has applied for a visa to the United States. Worked in a Hitchcock film in Munich back in '25."

"Anything political?" asked Basil Cole.

"We've still to complete our research on him."

"No family ties? No wife?"

"No wife. Family left Germany several years ago."

"Jewish? Homosexual?"

"No, and probably no. But then, one is never too sure about that these days, is one?" He heard a chair squeak, and Jennings looked at Basil Cole, who seemed uncomfortable.

"Well, you're doing a good job, Mr. Jennings. I assume you've got some of your best people on the Hitchcocks?"

"Around-the-clock surveillance. I've put several men on the actor." Jennings stifled a yawn and rubbed his eyes as a secretary entered with the fresh pot of tea.

"Ah! Here's the tea! That'll perk you up, Mr. Jennings. Give me your cup." Sir Arthur sounded like a pantomime dame. Jennings was thinking what Jennings needed was a day's sleep, but oh, what the hell, for king and country (not that he thought this bloody king was a symbol to respect).

In their cozy flat at 153 Cromwell Road, Alma was slicing bread for toasting. The fog was seeping through the windows, and Hitchcock had tried caulking the window seams with towels, but it never worked. He had been on the phone all morning with refugee organizations, trying to locate Fredrick Regner, but with a frustrating lack of success.

"Stop scowling, darling," advised Alma, "it makes you look a villain."

"It's absolutely maddening. I wish that detective would get back to me."

"If you stay off the phone, he might be able to get through." The phone rang. "See what I mean?"

Hitchcock cradled the phone between his chin and shoulder as he studied a section of the Regner manuscript. Into the phone he said somnolently, "Yeeeessss?"

"Mr. Hitchcock? At last!" chirped Nancy Adair. "I'm Nancy Adair!"

Hitchcock, his hand over the mouthpiece, said to Alma, "Gangrene's set in." Into the phone he said with mock affability, "Ah, Miss Adair, we seem to be missing each other, like an army of nearsighted soldiers." Alma was tuning in the radio, listening to the news. Hitchcock was listening to Nancy Adair pleading for an interview. "One moment please, Miss Adair." Hitchcock's hand was back over the mouthpiece as he addressed Alma, "There'll be no getting rid of the nuisance until I agree to see her. Can you stand it if I ask her up?"

"Get it over with, as Mother used to say when spooning castor oil into my mouth."

100

Nancy Adair's voice caressed Hitchcock's ear with gratitude while Alma wondered aloud why there was no news about the murder of Martin Mueller. Hitchcock looked at his pocket watch and said, "Perhaps there'll be something in the afternoon papers. After all"—he puffed himself up like a pouter pigeon—"I *am* Alfred Hitchcock."

Alma was buttering the toast as Hitchcock returned to the manuscript. "What are you doing?" she asked.

"I'm doing a breakdown of all the steps Regner's outlined for us in his treatment."

"Stop saying *us*, as though we're his protagonists."

"Well, he has written about a film director and his wife, hasn't he?"

"Just a device to pique your interest and your ego. There are a hell of a lot of holes in that story. There are at least three big enough to drive a hearse through."

"What an unfortunate analogy. But you're right. There are more loose ends here than I left dangling in *Sabotage*. For example, his denouement doesn't identify the culprit behind it all. That's very sloppy of him; his plots were always so meticulously worked out. And that melody, which I am growing to loathe and detest with the passion I usually reserve for any Ivor Novello creation, continues to make no sense. *Do mi fa sol, sol fa sol.*" He took a bite of buttered toast and stared out the window. "Damned fog. Damned Freddy Regner." The phone rang. "Damn Nancy Adair." Into the phone he said, "Yeeeessss?"

"Mr. Hitchcock? Detective Superintendent Jennings here." Hitchcock pantomimed Jennings' identity to Alma, who smiled as she poured their tea. "Sorry to be so late getting back to you, but I've been tied up in a meeting all morning."

"I was wondering if you've been able to locate Fredrick Regner, Mr. Jennings."

"I'm afraid not, Mr. Hitchcock. It appears he has probably entered the country illegally."

"Is that possible?" Hitchcock knew it was possible, but often found a pose of naïvete got better results when he was nosing about for information.

Jennings was a jump ahead of him. "We both know it's very possible. He's not registered with Immigration, which means he probably came by private boat and was landed somewhere along the coast that's known to be unpatrolled."

"That's probably why he took ill," commented Hitchcock between sips of tea.

"Oh, of course. You said Regner told you he was ill. That's what he told you; it doesn't mean he is."

"That's a thought, isn't it? Feigning illness so as not to blow his own cover. By the way, Mr. Jennings, there's been nothing about the murder on the wireless. Is this a deliberate omission?"

"I should think you'd be grateful. You don't want to be besieged by hordes of reporters, do you?"

"I don't mind," replied Hitchcock with a trace of annoyance.

Jennings laughed. "You film people! Always hungry for publicity."

"Mr. Jennings," said Hitchcock solemnly, "publicity helps sell film tickets."

"Have you a film to sell right now?"

"Where have you been of late, Mr. Jennings? Tibet? My film *Sabotage* is showing in the West End at the moment, and it can use all the help it can get."

"Well, Mr. Hitchcock, for the time being, we've decided to keep a lid on the case, until we can get more information on Regner and the victim. But I'll continue to keep in touch."

"I am most grateful for small favors. Good-bye, Mr. Jennings." Hitchcock said as he replaced the phone in its cradle, "wherever you are." He repeated Jennings' end of the conversation almost verbatim, and Alma put her hands on her hips, very irritated.

"Bloody cheek of the police. Why don't we give the story ourselves?" Hitchcock found her sly look endearing.

"Do you think we dare?"

The doorbell rang.

Alma's hands were now folded as she leaned against a kitchen counter. "You can't be faulted for letting it slip to our beloved Miss Adair."

The doorbell rang again. "Patience," commented Hitchcock as he waddled to the wall intercom, "is obviously not one of her virtues." Into the intercom he asked, "Yeeessss?" and Nancy Adair's voice squawked back her identity. Hitchcock buzzed her in and then crossed to the door and held it open. Alma examined herself in the sitting-room mirror and decided there was no room for improvement. They could hear their visitor nimbly racing up the stairs, and Alma commented she sounded like an ibex leaping from alp to alp. Nancy Adair arrived on the landing, and Hitchcock's heart skipped a beat. When she appeared in the doorway, face glowing like a klieg lamp, Alma's mouth set into a grim, tight line. A blonde. A slim, beautiful blonde.

"So you're Nancy Adair," said Hitchcock as she came into the room and shook his hand. "This is Mrs. Hitchcock." Nancy Adair shook Alma's hand with a firm grip.

With a synthetic party smile, Alma asked the reporter, "Tea? Whiskey? Port? Wine?" Tea for all was decided on,

103

and Hitchcock and the blonde sat across from each other while Alma repaired to the kitchen.

"Well, Nancy Adair. You certainly don't look like a Nancy Adair."

Nancy was rummaging in her oversized handbag for a notebook and pen as she inquired a bit flirtatiously, "And what did you expect me to look like?"

"Like one of the usual undersexed Fleet Street gorgons, especially the overambitious ones. Exactly whom do you write for?"

"I'm a free lance. I thought you understood that. This interview is geared toward a newspaper syndicate in the States. I understand your film *Sabotage* is opening there soon."

"Yeeesss. Sylvia Sidney, who plays the spy's wife, is quite a favorite there. You know the old saying. 'Laugh and the world laughs with you, cry and you're Sylvia Sidney.'"

"May I quote you?" she asked eagerly.

"That's what you're here for." He had settled back in his chair with his hands folded across his stomach, wondering whether to warn her that inanities could drive him to violence. But, surprisingly enough, she had come prepared with a list of intelligent questions, most of which he replied to with cheerful good humor. Alma served biscuits with the tea and hoped they weren't stale; the tin had been in the larder for weeks.

Twenty minutes later, Hitchcock referred to the clock on the mantel and began fidgeting. Nancy Adair asked, "And your next film?"

"It's to be called *The Lady Vanishes*. It is adapted from a novel by Ethel Lina White, *The Wheel Spins*. It's a spy story."

"Your last five films have been spy stories, haven't they?"

"Yes, I seem to be in a bit of a rut. But spies are such interesting people, don't you think?" Actually he knew they weren't. He knew they were usually dull, unhappy, frightened, and had bad teeth.

"I don't know. I don't think I've ever met any spies." She gave a small laugh, and Alma crossed and then recrossed her legs. "Have you?"

"I sometimes think I have." Hitchcock was scratching his chin. "I think I met some eleven years ago in Munich. Anyway, Alma agrees with me they might have been spies, don't you, dear?"

"Yes," said Alma, wishing to be rid of Nancy Adair, but Hitchcock was regaling her with the story of the Munich murders.

"That's a *mar*velous story!" exclaimed the blonde. "Why's it been kept under wraps all these years?"

"I really don't know," said Hitchcock, "I suppose if the victims had been internationally famous, they might have merited a headline in this country. But unfortunately, they were as obscure in life as they were in death."

"Like the man who was murdered last night?"

Alma almost dropped her teacup as Hitchcock asked, "How do you know about that?"

"Have you forgotten I was in your village at the time?"

Alma asked, "You mean you stayed on after I discouraged you?"

"Well, frankly, I was going to call back later to try to persuade you to change your mind, so I had dinner at the inn and spent the night. The woman on the switchboard apparently phoned the innkeeper's wife and told her about the

105

murder. While serving my breakfast she told me. I suppose by now the entire village knows the story."

Hitchcock said to Alma, "So much for Mr. Jennings' lid." Nancy Adair had gotten to her feet.

"This is such a charming flat, Mrs. Hitchcock. I'd like to put a little something about it into my story. Do you mind if I look around?"

Alma gathered up the tea-things on a tray and led the way to the kitchen. "There's not terribly much to see. It's quite an ordinary little flat. We don't spend as much time here as we used to. We love the cottage so." Hitchcock followed them into the kitchen, reminding himself to reprove Alma for serving stale biscuits.

"And are these your notes for your new film?" Miss Adair was at the table unceremoniously flipping through the manuscript pages. What cheek, thought Alma. Hitchcock took the manuscript and placed it face downward over his own sheet of notes.

"I don't like my notes to be read by others, Miss Adair," scolded Hitchcock.

"I'm so sorry. Once a reporter, always a reporter."

Alma interrupted. "Hitch, I think we're going to be late for the meeting. You'll have to forgive us, Miss Adair, but we've a production meeting at the studio."

Hitchcock was staring at the blonde intensely. Then he exploded. "You tried to run us off the road yesterday!"

"Oh, dear, I was afraid you'd recognize me."

"Recognize you! I should throttle you!"

"I wasn't trying to run you off the road, really I wasn't. I was trying to get your attention. . . ."

"You most certainly got *that!*"

Alma said to Hitchcock, "You didn't tell me anything about it."

"I didn't want to worry you."

"I know it's a bit late after the fact," said Alma, "but I'm worried now."

"I won't keep you any longer," said Nancy Adair as she hurried back to the sitting room and set about gathering up her things. "I'm so grateful for the time you've given me, Mr. Hitchcock."

Hitchcock was holding the door open for her. "Be sure to send me a copy of your story when you've written it."

"Absolutely. Good-bye, Mrs. Hitchcock, the tea was lovely."

"The biscuits were stale."

Alma glared at Hitchcock, and after the reporter was gone and the door was shut she said, "I didn't like that woman."

"You're missing the important point," said Hitchcock as Alma followed him back to the kitchen.

"And what's that?"

"She apparently didn't try to peddle Martin Mueller's murder to a newspaper."

"Oh!"

"Exactly. Oh."

"Maybe she did, but the police got on to all the papers and asked them to hold the story."

"Maybe. But I don't like it one bit. I think I should advise Detective Jennings about this." Hitchcock phoned New Scotland Yard but was told Jennings was away from his office. Hitchcock left his name and phone number. He returned to making notes while Alma phoned her sister-in-law and chatted with Patricia.

"Patricia's having a lovely time," Alma told Hitchcock as she placed the tea-things in the sink. "The fog's ruined their plans for a picnic, so they're going to a flick instead. Fred

107

Astaire and Ginger Rogers. Hitch, you're not listening to me."

"It's this bloody manuscript. Something's not right with it, and I can't put my finger on it. It's quite obvious Regner expects me to fill in the blank spaces in the story, but I can't see how." He sat back in the chair, which groaned. "I just don't know how to penetrate this."

"Perhaps you should have given Miss Adair a crack at it," said Alma wryly.

"Perhaps I should give you a crack and be done with it." The phone rang. "That may be Jennings." He crossed to the phone. "Yeeeessss?" He listened and then hissed to Alma for quiet at the sink. She shut the taps and turned to Hitchcock with interest. "Where are you? You sound very strange. And your manuscript . . ." Alma crossed to her husband. ". . . is most peculiar. I don't think there's anything much I can do with it until I discuss it with you. And what's more, the police are looking for you. Mueller's been murdered. That's right, murdered, right on my bloody doorstep, and no pun intended." He said in an aside to Alma, "The poor bastard's terrified, and we have a dreadful connection. Doesn't sound the way he sounded last night. Hello, hello, hello. This is a terrible connection." He listened, his face screwed up as he strained to unscramble the other end of the conversation. "Of course I know where it is. I'll be there as soon as possible. Taxis are hell in a pea souper like this, but we'll be there." He slammed the phone down. "Regner's at the tea cottage by the Serpentine in Hyde Park."

"Of all the silly places to park oneself in a fog." Hitchcock grabbed the sheet of paper on which he'd been making notes, folded it and slipped it into his inside jacket pocket. Alma was in the sitting room at the mirror putting on her hat.

"Come on," urged Hitchcock, "we've no time for fussing." They hurried out of the flat, Hitchcock closing the door behind them. As they hurried down the stairs, they could hear the phone ringing, but there was no time for turning back.

In his office, Michael Jennings decided to let the Hitchcocks' number ring a few more times and then gave up. Then he returned his attention to Peter Dowerty, who was seated across the desk from him. "Strange. He phoned only half an hour ago."

"Hitchcock?"

"Yes. I suppose they've gone out, but in this weather, one need but question why?"

"Angus will be on their tail." He referred to his notebook. "Shall I get on with this?" Jennings nodded and leaned back in his chair, hands folded behind the back of his head, staring at the ceiling and absorbing the information he was hearing. "The blonde was quite a looker and spent at least a half hour with the Hitchcocks. She fits the description of the woman the sheriff reported was at the inn last night in Shamley Green."

"He didn't report any other strangers in the village?"

"Just some lorry drivers who had coffee and sandwiches at the local coffee shop. It stays open late for the lorry drivers."

"You got a good look at this woman?"

"Yes, sir."

"Despite the fog?"

"I was under the lamppost which was where she parked her car."

"And so?"

Dowerty smiled broadly and winked. "I wouldn't mind finding her head on my pillow the next morning."

"The license number, you nit. Did you get the license number and did you check it out?"

"Yes, sir, yes, sir," said Dowerty hastily. "I've got a tracer on it. I recognized the code number on the license plate. It's from a car-hire firm."

"And when she left the Hitchcocks?"

"I was on the other side of the street then. She might remember if she'd seen my face under the streetlight, and I didn't want to arouse her suspicion."

"All you aroused was yourself."

"Sorry, sir."

"Anything else?"

"Angus arrived to replace me."

"And you distinctly heard her say into the intercom, 'It's me, Nancy Adair.'"

"Yes, sir."

Jennings yawned and stretched. "You know something, Dowerty, I sometimes think police work could be very injurious to one's health." The phone rang. "Get that, will you, Dowerty? I'm feeling a bit wilted."

Dowerty said into the phone, "Detective Superintendent Jennings' office."

In the sitting room of their flat, Hitchcock, looking harassed, asked to speak to Jennings. When Jennings came on the phone, he told him about being called away to meet Regner in Hyde Park. "He wasn't there," said Hitchcock, "and of course it was most annoying, especially in this dreadful weather. But I'm afraid we fell into some sort of trap."

"Trap? What do you mean? You weren't attacked by someone, were you?" Jennings was clutching the phone tightly, his concern infecting Dowerty, who leaned forward, to be able to catch snatches of Hitchcock's conversation.

"Oh, nothing so melodramatic. It seems we were

tricked out of the flat so someone could break in and steal Regner's manuscript." He could hear Jennings relaying the information to Dowerty. "It's not a terribly good manuscript, but then, it's the only clue we've got, isn't it?" Then he remembered. "Hold on! I made a sheet of notes of my own and that's safely in my jacket pocket. Now why would anyone want to steal a manuscript? That's a bit hairy, don't you think?" Then he thought again. "I wonder if it could be that blasted Adair woman."

Jennings played his role suavely and asked, "What Adair woman?"

Hitchcock told him about her persistence in seeking an interview, which he'd finally granted, and then remembered to tell Jennings of his experience with her on the road to the cottage the previous day. Jennings carefully made notes and then asked Hitchcock, "Is there anything else missing from the flat?" Hitchcock told him Alma had made a hasty inventory and certainly no jewelry was missing, although there was nothing else of much value in the place.

On another phone in Jennings' office, Dowerty was listening to Angus McKellin's report on the wild-goose chase trailing the Hitchcocks to Hyde Park, McKellin phoning from the kiosk across the street from the Hitchcocks' building, a vantage point from which he could still keep an eye on the place. Dowerty told him Jennings was getting the details from Hitchcock himself on the other phone, and McKellin rang off, wishing the bloody fog would lift.

Hitchcock was saying to Jennings, "My conversation with Regner last night was quite brief and certainly fraught with emotion on his part, but I should have guessed I was being fooled by an imitator."

"Perhaps it wasn't an impersonation," suggested Jennings. "Perhaps it really was Regner."

111

"Why would he wish to steal his own manuscript?"

Jennings smiled and said, "Quite right, Mr. Hitchcock. Quite right. Is the lock on the door badly damaged?"

"Not badly damaged at all. It was picked by an expert. We shall have it replaced immediately." He listened. "No. I haven't heard from Hans Meyer at all. I seem to recall his mentioning several interviews he had scheduled for today. What? Let me think . . . yes . . . that's it. He said he was staying at the Royal Court." He listened again. "Oh, of course, Mr. Jennings. If anything freshly sinister erupts, I shall be on the line immediately. Good afternoon." He rang off and then said to Alma, "I'm very hungry."

"I'll fix something." As she went to the kitchen, Hitchcock took the sheet of notes from his pocket and reread them. He reread them again and then again until he heard Alma call him to the kitchen. As he entered the kitchen, the phone rang.

"Yeeessss?" Hitchcock inquired, as Alma dished eggs and bacon onto two plates. "How very peculiar. Thank you very much, Mr. Jennings. If I hear from him, I'll let you know."

"What's very peculiar?" asked Alma.

"Hans Meyer has checked out of his hotel and left no forwarding address."

Eight

At five that afternoon, Angus McKellin was in the kiosk across the street from the Hitchcocks' house reporting to Detective Superintendent Jennings. "Mrs. Hitchcock went out to do some shopping at about three P.M. but wasn't gone long. She went to the butcher's and the greengrocer's around the corner, and when she returned I could see she was carrying what looked like the afternoon newspapers."

"Cinema people do a bit of reading," commented Jennings glumly. "I suppose there should be two of you doing the surveillance, one to cover her and one to cover him, but we're too damned shorthanded here."

"Actually, sir," said McKellin, "ever since we come back from Hyde Park, I've had this feeling that *I'm* being watched."

"Don't be neurotic."

"I try not to be, sir," he said, wondering what it was to be neurotic.

"When's your replacement due?"

"In three hours' time, sir. The fog seems to be worsening. Bleeding awful for June."

"Be grateful you're not a bride. We'll speak again later." He hung up. There was another call waiting for him. "Jennings here. Yes, Mr. Hitchcock?"

"Something slipped my mind when I reported the robbery. It's about Nancy Adair." He repeated the curious fact that she apparently hadn't reported the murder of Martin Mueller to one of her newspaper contacts.

"Yes, that is curious," agreed Jennings, cursing himself for not having thought of that himself, but then he was swamped with so much, the occasional lapse in the detecting process was forgivable. He tried never to be too hard on himself. "Good thinking, Mr. Hitchcock."

"And there's something else," Hitchcock said matter-of-factly.

"There's nothing in the newspapers about Mueller's murder."

"Oh, that too, of course. How clever of you to guess we've bought the afternoon dailies. But actually, Mr. Jennings, I thought you'd like to know we're expecting a visit momentarily from Hans Meyer."

Jennings leaned forward with his elbows on the desk. "Did you ask him where he was staying?"

Hitchcock replied, "He said he'd moved in with a friend to save on expenses. Do you want him to contact you?" And for what reason, wondered Hitchcock.

"Yes, I'd appreciate that. By the way, for your informa-

114

tion, I've had a tracer on Miss Adair. She seems to be operating out of her hired car."

"How very odd," commented Hitchcock.

"She doesn't seem to have a fixed address. No telephone, not even ex-directory."

"Neither listed nor unlisted," Hitchcock was telling Alma who was studying the sheet of notes Hitchcock had drawn up from Regner's manuscript.

"Probably camping out in some bed-sitter in Earl's Court," suggested Alma. "That type is prone to live that way." Hitchcock repeated her suggestion to Jennings.

"Yes, that *is* a thought," said Jennings blandly. "By-the-by, have you had that lock on your door replaced?"

"Can't be done until morning. But no matter, we're in for the night. I'll have Hans phone you when he gets here. How much longer will you be in your office?"

"Oh, indefinitely, I should think. Good-bye, Mr. Hitchcock."

Hitchcock joined Alma at the table, drew up a chair, and reclaimed his sheet of notes. "Now let me see. The director, thinking he has murdered his assailant and fearing the police, goes to the church where Orwell sought food and refuge. Now, who the hell is Orwell?"

"George Orwell," Alma informed him. "The writer. In his memoir, *Down and Out in Paris and London,* he's terribly poor and sleeping in doss houses and begging meals from charity. He frequented a church near King's Cross Station where the kindly vicar fed vagrants bread and tea."

"Do you suppose there's still a kindly vicar dispensing tea and kindness and possibly information at this church?"

"Probably. England's up to its hips in kindly vicars. The way they seem to proliferate, I should think we should consider a plan to enter the business of exporting them." She thought for a moment. "What possible information would one get from a vicar other than the quickest directions to heaven?"

"If I knew, my dear, I wouldn't be questioning." He tapped his finger on the sheet of notes. "But here it is." He read aloud. "'Seeks refuge at church Orwell knew and information from vicar.'" Hitchcock was humming under his breath. "Damn! Now *I'm* humming that bloody melody. I say, do you suppose the vicar at that church might have connections with Germany? You know what I mean, someone in Germany who is passing information to him which he passes on to Whitehall. Do you suppose that could be it?"

"Oh, I do hope so!" said Alma with unrestrained enthusiasm. "It's such a delicious idea. Why haven't we thought of using something like that?"

"We can't think of everything, although God knows we try. Now let me see . . . after the church, the man goes out into the countryside, his destination somewhere in the Midlands, the village of Medwin and a woman named Madeleine Lockwood. Where's that map of Great Britain gone to?" Alma went to the sitting room to search for the map. She found it in the desk and brought it to Hitchcock. He opened the map, muttering under his breath, "Medwin, Medwin, Medwin . . . probably one of those places even missionaries haven't heard of. Well, I'll be damned. Here it is. Medwin! Ha! Why the peculiar look on your face?"

"I was just thinking. The climax of the story has everyone converging on this one man who has information both sides are after, but Regner never tells us who he's actually spying for, us or them."

"Perhaps both. He's probably a double agent."

"Well, if both sides know his identity, why don't they go directly to him?"

"Because they don't know who he is. Why don't you read this thing carefully!"

"I have, and don't shout at me."

"I'm sorry, but this damned insistence of yours on logic. Everything can't be logical! Look around us. Hitler, is he logical? He's absolute nonsense, but there he is with his Chaplin mustache and his master race, ha! And what about our pale excuse for a king and his mordant passion for an American divorcée? I thought that situation died with silent pictures! The man I'm searching for is someone who filters the information to others; that's who we're looking for. And now I'm beginning to see where Regner has been so deucedly clever."

"Kindly share that with me."

"Be patient and bear with me. Eleven years ago in Munich, Anna Grieban and Rudolf Wagner are murdered. In the script, Regner gives them other identifications, but what the hell, it's patently them. They were spies working for the British government."

"You're not sure about that."

"I have to be sure about that, or there's none of your bloody logic to Regner's plot line. Now be quiet and listen." Alma's face was a model of stoicism. "That bloody melody of Wagner's was a code, one that possibly still exists. If codes aren't broken by the opposition, they age beautifully, like a decent wine. Now the person who murdered them is possibly the man with the disfigured face, remember him?"

"Oh, of course! The MacGuffin."

"Perhaps he is, we can't tell yet. Then there's Hans

Meyer and that dreadful daughter of Wagner's; what was her name again, Rosie?"

"Rosie. Whatever became of Rosie?"

"God knows. She's probably a member of the Nazi party and fingering all her neighbors. I wouldn't put it past her. And, of course, my dear, there's Regner himself."

"Ahhh! I've had him in the back of my mind."

"You can move him up forward now. Then, my dear, there's us."

"We didn't murder them."

"True. But remember what Mickey Balcon told me on the phone at the time? There'd been inquiries about us from Whitehall."

"Oh, my dear, you mean they thought we were spies too?"

"Yes, but it's more sinister than you think. They suspected us of possibly spying for the *Germans*."

"What cheek!"

"Why not? We were there when the murders were committed. You adored Wagner's melody and recommended him to Fritz Lang as a composer. And we stayed on in Munich to do a second film. Why couldn't we have been spies? It ties up very nicely, as a matter of fact. I wish we'd used that kind of logic in *Secret Agent*. Anyway, we come to the present. Hans Meyer is in London. And Regner. And he phones us. He's sending this manuscript with Mueller. The whole damned procession is listed right here in my notes, taken directly from Regner's manuscript. Except he didn't predict Mueller's murder."

"Well, he's not exactly Nostradamus."

"But he's been pretty damned shrewd. The more I talk this thing, the smarter it gets. Have you noticed there's a bit of *The Thirty-Nine Steps* in this story? The director thinks he's a murderer and goes to ground, especially since he's terrified of the police. Now that's a bit close to the bone."

"Oh, you probably told that psychosis of yours to Regner back there in Munich."

"Of course I did. I've told it to just about everybody else."

"I didn't notice you trembling when the police came to the cottage last night."

"I did perspire a bit, but not that anyone'd notice. Now stop digressing! Why would you be kidnapped, or whatever name he's given to the woman in his scenario?"

"To make you talk, if they think you're a spy and have information they want."

"But which 'they'? As the Americans would say, the good guys or the bad guys?"

"That, my darling, belongs under the heading of 'suspense.'"

"Yes. Quite right. I wonder what's keeping Hans Meyer? You don't suppose he thinks he's going to be asked to share dinner with us."

"He'd better not. There's just enough for the two of us."

"What's on the menu?"

"Chops, a vedge, and salad. You said you were dieting."

"Must you believe everything I say?"

"You wish I would, but I don't. And now who's digressing?"

"Sorry." He referred to his notes and mumbled, "Vicar . . . Medwin . . . Madeleine Lockwood . . ."

"Madeleine Lockwood. Nice name for an actress."

"Regner has her as a onetime music-hall singer. Not a bad touch. Now let me see . . . itinerant circus . . . I suppose we could get a list of any of those out touring the hinterlands. According to Lockwood, there's danger in the

119

circus but Regner doesn't specify what. And then the script reaches its climax in a Channel village . . . nice touch . . . village from which the villain can make a hasty exit abroad in case of emergency." He referred to the notes again and mumbled.

"What did you say?" Alma had been making notes of her own, attempting a more orderly rundown of the bare bones of Regner's story.

The doorbell rang.

Sir Arthur Willing wasn't happy. The cause of his unhappiness was the purloined scenario. He said to Nigel Pack and Basil Cole, both of whom impatiently wished he'd call it a day but suspected they'd be trapped with him for hours, "The scenario is in dangerous hands. That poses a serious threat to Mr. and Mrs. Hitchcock."

"What do you suggest we do?" asked Basil Cole, stroking his nonexistent mustache and then with embarrassment removing his hand from his face.

"I suggest we do nothing and await further developments. Jennings has them under surveillance, three men sharing a twenty-four-hour watch. It should be six men, one for each of the Hitchcocks, but Jennings is shorthanded; so much for Scotland Yard's annual budget."

"But if the Hitchcocks are in danger?" questioned Nigel Pack.

Sir Arthur waved his hands with irritation. "We're surrounded by danger! Everyone's surrounded by danger! We could be struck by a bus or a taxi or a lorry! We could be hit by a stray bullet!"

"Where from?" asked Basil Cole.

"Basil," said Sir Arthur wearily, "I'm beginning to suspect you could use a vacation."

* *. *

From the landing outside their apartment, Hitchcock shouted down the stairwell, "Hans, is that you?" There was no reply. Alma stood in the doorway.

"Hitch, I don't like this one bit. Come back into the flat at once."

"Well, you heard him plainly on the blower. He said he was Hans, it sounded like Hans!"

Alma screamed.

They hadn't heard the men who had come soundlessly up the stairs. Professionals. Experts. They knew their job well. Hitchcock was pushed from behind and fell face forward into the sitting room. Alma ran to the window to cry for help, but one of the assailants was too quick for her. He grabbed her and pinned her arms behind her. Hitchcock got to his knees and shouted at the man. The man said to the men behind Hitchcock, "Shut him up." Hitchcock looked behind him and saw a man coming at him, right hand upraised, wielding a cosh, ready to bring it down on Hitchcock's skull. Hitchcock, with amazing grace born of desperation, scrabbled to his feet and raced into the kitchen. He found a meat knife, but the other two men were prepared for him when he came running back into the sitting room to defend his beloved Alma. Each man stood against the wall at opposite ends of the doorway, and as Hitchcock came dashing in, one tripped him, sending him back to the floor again, the other coshed him, and Hitchcock, still clutching the knife, passed out. Alma struggled with her captor, who snarled at the man with the cosh. "Let's get her the bloody hell out of here, before the other one comes to." The man with the cosh, Alma noticed, had a facial tic just under his left eye. Hitch, she was thinking, my darling Hitch, don't be dead. My dear, dear darling, don't be dead. As they

121

dragged her from the flat, she thought she saw the shadow of a fourth person from the stairwell leading to the roof. Whoever you are, you bloody fool, she thought, help me. Help me.

In the phone kiosk across the street from the Hitchcocks' house, Angus McKellin, huddled on the floor with an ugly bruise on his right temple, began to stir. He began to rouse himself, but not in time to see Alma being dragged from the house by the three men and spirited away in a hearse. He struggled to his feet and fought to orient himself. It was an automatic reaction to dial headquarters, but the phone's wires had been clipped. He fought to focus his eyes and could see the door to the Hitchcock house was ajar. He staggered across the street and up the stairs, and when he came to their landing, through the open door he could see Hitchcock lying on the floor. He did not see the knife in Hitchcock's hand because it was no longer there. It was in the hand of the fourth person, who had been waiting to search the flat after the three men went off with Alma. "Mr. Hitchcock!" shouted McKellin, "Mr. Hitchcock!" He ran to the fat man and knelt at his side. The knife was cruelly and brutally plunged into McKellin's back. He died instantly, his mother would later be glad to know. The bloodied knife was withdrawn from the body and replaced in Hitchcock's right hand. Then the phone wires were cut, and from the kitchen, Hitchcock's sheet of notes was taken.

The man with the tic was at the wheel of the hearse. In the back, Alma had been bound and gagged. The windows of the hearse had been blacked out from within. The two men with Alma were smoking and joking, and the man with the tic was confident they had little idea where he was taking the hearse.

*   *   *

Hitchcock's eyes opened slowly. The pain at the back of his head was excruciating. He was clutching something in his right hand. It felt like a knife hilt. Slowly and with great care, he turned his head to look at his right hand. "Oh, my God," he whispered. The blade was covered with blood. Hitchcock released the hilt and struggled to his knees. Alma! Where in God's name was Alma! He got to his feet, and it was then that he saw Angus McKellin's body. Hitchcock's body began to tremble. "Alma!" he cried, "Alma!" but there was no response from Alma. He kneeled beside the body and stared at the face. Although the incident with the three assailants had been nightmarish, Hitchcock registered their faces in his memory. The man with the tic under his left eye who had attacked Alma, the other two who were perfectly cast as thugs, but the dead man on the floor was neither of them. Hitchcock went from room to room crying Alma's name, but she wasn't there. Then he stared at the knife. My God, he realized, my God! The knife killed the man lying there, that ugly red stain on his back. I was holding the knife when I came to.

My God! I've killed a man!

The police! I'll be taken into custody! He was perspiring, and yet his blood had gone cold. Not the police. Not for him, not the police. Alma. He must find Alma. Hitchcock sat on a chair staring at McKellin's body. He had to think, and think hard. It was uncanny. This was in Regner's scenario. Hitchcock a murderer, Alma abducted. The son of a bitch! Had he set them up? Had Regner set them up? Hitchcock was angry. That was a good sign. Anger filled him with determination, and in that state, Hitchcock could become a tiger in action. He hurried to the kitchen to retrieve his notes and saw they were gone. "Bastards," he muttered, "bastards." But having worked on those notes for so many hours and gone over them repeatedly with Alma, he had committed them to memory. Then Hitchcock dwelt for a moment on Detective Superintendent Jennings. Should he take a chance? Would the man believe his story? He was a policeman. Hitchcock didn't trust policemen. In the bedroom, Hitchcock found his old plaid jacket and put it on. From the top shelf of the closet he took a dark hat and pulled it over his head. He felt around for the tin box and found it, his and Alma's hidden store of cash kept there for emergencies. He emptied the box of its contents, well over a hundred pounds, and knew Alma would forgive him. Alma! He must at least alert the police about Alma.

John Bellowes, their solicitor. He would call John and tell him what had happened. John would know what to do. Hitchcock went back to the sitting room to the telephone and groaned with dismay. The wire had been cut. The bastards thought of everything; why couldn't his scriptwriters? He rushed from the flat, down the steps, and hurried across the street to the phone kiosk. Damn, damn, damn! The wires were clipped there, too! Such efficiency had to be admired. In the dense fog, Hitchcock pulled up his jacket collar and went hurrying in search of another kiosk. They couldn't have vandalized all of them along Cromwell Road.

John Bellowes was a rare species of solicitor. People liked him. He was sympathetic. He didn't drone on and on in the lawyerese that most normal people found boring. He was a sensible man married to a sensible woman he'd met while a student at Oxford. Bettina, his wife, had a wealthy father, which again made a great deal of sense. The Bellowes, with their two young sons, ages nine and six, lived quite sensibly in a sensibly detached house in Hampstead.

This night John and Bettina had planned a quiet evening together. After supper, with the boys sensibly tucked in bed, they planned to play backgammon, after which Bettina would sensibly read a chapter or two of the latest Evelyn Waugh and John would sensibly study his briefs for the next day. Then Alfred Hitchcock phoned and nearly drove John Bellowes out of his senses.

"What do you mean, you *think* you've killed a man and Alma has been abducted? Hitch, are you drunk?" Bellowes barked into the phone while Bettina stood behind him wringing her hands like a silent screen heroine about to be tied to the rails. She liked the Hitchcocks, although she thought the director was too fat and his wife a bit aloof, but then, they were cinema people and John warned her all cinema people were a little strange, especially directors and their wives.

Hitchcock shouted into the phone. "I am not drunk, and this is a nightmare. Now listen carefully. Oh, God, how my head aches!" He carefully told him the story of the attack by the thugs, Alma's abduction, his awakening with a bloodied knife in his hand, and a fourth man lying dead from a stab wound in his back. "No, I haven't the vaguest idea who the dead man was. No, I did not look for any identification. My mind was not on identifying him. My only thought was to run and somehow find Alma. I didn't even stop to wipe my fingerprints from the knife hilt."

"Well, that wasn't very clever," editorialized John Bellowes.

"In times of stress, I'm hard put to be clever. Now listen carefully. . . ." He instructed his solicitor to phone Jennings at Scotland Yard and relay the information to him. "And when you're finished, put in a good word for me. I have to go now."

"Hitch! Hitch!" Bellowes shouted into the phone, "Where are you going?"

"I'm going to church!"

"Hitch! Hitch!" Bellowes shouted, then said to his wife, "He's rung off."

"Darling, I've never heard you shouting so forcefully before," said his wife, "Is something wrong? What's Alfred done?"

"His worst, my dear, he's done his worst. And Alma's gone missing."

"What? Alma's missing? Alma isn't the type."

He ignored her as he phoned Scotland Yard and asked to be put through to Jennings, who listened carefully to Bellowes' opening line and then asked him to hold on a moment. He shouted for a stenographer into his intercom, and when one came on, told him to get on to an extension phone and take down every word of the conversation. Then he returned to Bellowes, who thoroughly and succinctly relayed the information he'd received from Hitchcock.

"The murdered man. He didn't know the identity of the murdered man?" Jennings had paled. It could be Angus McKellin. He looked at his wristwatch. It was not yet eight o'clock, when McKellin's replacement was due to come on duty.

"He didn't." Then Bellowes added, as the convincer to illustrate Hitchcock's befuddled state of mind, "He didn't even wipe his fingerprints from the knife hilt!"

Jennings glared at the mouthpiece while thinking, thank God for small favors. He asked Bellowes to repeat his name, phone number, and address for the benefit of the stenographer and advised him he'd be in touch with him. "And be sure to let me know if you hear from Hitchcock again!" Jennings rang off and ordered a squad car with three detec-

126

tives in it to meet him in the driveway in five minutes. Then he got through to Sir Arthur Willing on Willing's private line, who after he had digested Jennings' information, said softly, "Tally ho, we're off to the races." Then Sir Arthur instructed his secretary to round up Nigel Pack and Basil Cole; there was a long night's work in store for them.

Hitchcock took the tube to King's Cross Station. He decided it was safer and more anonymous than taking a taxi. The train was crowded, and Hitchcock huddled against the door, his hat pulled down in an attempt to shield his face, his hands plunged into his jacket pockets. The turning wheels seemed to be saying "Alma-Alma-Alma-Alma," and Hitchcock's mind was a jumble. He could hear Rudolf Wagner's melody counterpointing the roll call of names racing through his mind: Wagner, Grieban, Rosie, Regner, Hans Meyer, and the man with the disfigured face. Jennings. John Bellowes. Dear, dear, lovable, dull John Bellowes. Hitchcock hoped he'd found Jennings.

While Hitchcock was undergoing the long tube journey to King's Cross Station, Jennings, Peter Dowerty, and two other detectives were hurrying up the stairs to Hitchcock's flat. There had been no sign of Angus McKellin on the street, and it was still not yet time for his replacement to appear. Jennings feared the worst, and found it in Hitchcock's flat.

"It's Angus," said Peter Dowerty, who knelt by the body for a clearer look at the face. "Somebody'll hang for this."

Nine

Emerging at King's Cross tube station, Hitchcock quixotically wished he'd retained the murder weapon to cut his way through the pea souper. It had grown thicker and heavier, and he was breathing with an effort. Ahead of him was a newspaper kiosk lit by a kerosene lamp. The owner was a shabby little man missing his upper front teeth and sporting what appeared to be a week's growth of beard. He hawked his newspapers spiritedly while wishing the fat man now confronting him would decide which paper to buy and go on about his business.

"Is there a church nearby?" asked Hitchcock, hardly a picture of piety.

"Which denomination, guv?" The little man's head was cocked to one side; he resembled a scruffy starling.

"I believe the vicar serves tea and bread to the homeless."

"You don't look particularly hungry, guv."

"As a matter of fact," said Hitchcock, on the verge of bristling with indignation, "it's long past my dinner and my lunch was nothing remarkable."

"You sound like a toff down on his luck, guv."

"My luck of late hasn't been terribly remarkable either." He wondered if Bellowes had reached Jennings and the wheels had been set in motion to rescue Alma.

"Well, now," said the man, scratching his beard, "you mean Mr. Peach, Mr. Lemuel Peach. If you turn the corner there past the pub, across the street is Mr. Peach's church. He's usually in the basement."

"Thank you. You're most kind." While getting his directions, Hitchcock had managed to scan several newspaper headlines. There was nothing about him and the murder at the cottage. He was beginning to feel unnecessary. At the corner outside the pub, he was accosted by a prostitute with Joan Crawford shoulders, broad and padded. A cigarette hung precariously from her lips, and her string purse dangled from a wrist. "'ello, dearie," she said, and Hitchcock imagined he could do a two-step across her breath, "love for sale."

"Loathe that song," snapped Hitchcock and continued on his way to the church. What the prostitute shouted after him to do was a physical impossibility. The church was located in a cul-de-sac, and as Hitchcock approached it, he could see it was in a sorry state of disrepair, perhaps a metaphor for his own life at the moment. There was a tiny blue light over the basement door, and with great care, Hitchcock made his way down the stone steps, eroded by centuries of footsteps. At the heavy wooden door, he thought he could hear some shuffling about from within. He tried the knob, but the door was locked. He found a bellpull and tugged it. After a few moments, a little wooden door in the larger door opened and Hitchcock saw a pair of steely blue eyes staring out at him. A stentorian voice inquired:

"Are you a good Christian?"

Hitchcock swallowed and responded gravely, "One of the best."

"I don't know you, you haven't been here before, have you?" There was a hint of an accent—not North Country, not Welsh, either.

"You come highly recommended. I've been told you serve bread and tea."

"You don't look hungry."

"Looks can be deceiving." He almost added, And so can vicars—that is, if it was the vicar guarding his gates like Cerberus in the Underworld.

"There's no bed for you tonight. I'm all full up."

"I don't need a bed. I . . . I'm used to sleeping rough."

"I should well imagine that, with all that flesh on you. Come in." The door was unbolted and opened, and Hitchcock entered the basement. There was nobody there except the man he assumed to be Lemuel Peach. There was a long wooden table on which rested loaves of bread and urns that Hitchcock imagined contained the tea, but no downtrodden other than himself. There were a number of cots in evidence against two walls, but none of them was occupied. A most peculiar charitable hostel, Hitchcock decided. When the door shut behind him with what sounded like an ominous clang, Hitchcock examined his host as he shot the bolt back into place. He was wearing a business suit, a polka-dot bow tie, and, for reasons known only to the man himself, a green eyeshade, the kind usually sported by croupiers in third-rate gambling casinos in Hollywood Westerns. "This way," said the man as he led Hitchcock to the table, sliced some bread, drew a mug of black tea, and served the mean repast to his guest, who was lacing and unlacing his chubby fingers nervously. "Why are you uncomfortable?"

"Are you the vicar? Are you Mr. Peach?"

"I am Lemuel Peach."

"You don't look like a vicar."

"Most nights I dress in mufti. One gets so bored with clerical drag." His face hardened. "What do you want? You're not really hungry. If you were, you'd be wolfing the tea. Were you expecting drippings with the bread? I don't serve drippings here. This isn't your mum's kitchen, you know, this is a house of God, and my God is a bit skint."

Hitchcock leaned across the table, his attitude 'Let the devil take the hindmost.' "Mr. Peach, I have come for information."

"What information I can impart you can find in the Bible."

"Where's Fredrick Regner?"

Too quickly, the man said, "I don't know what you're talking about."

Hitchcock was getting impatient and angry. "Mr. Peach, in the past twenty-four hours, there have been two murders and a kidnapping, events that give every dangerous sign of reaching epidemic proportions, thanks to a scenario conceived by Fredrick Regner." He recited for the vicar the contents of Regner's manuscript.

When Hitchcock was finished, Peach asked, "But how does it end?"

"That's what I'm trying to find out."

Very softly, Mr. Peach said, "You are a very foolish man. You are treading where angels fear."

"I'm very determined, and I'm very angry. My wife has been stolen, and I find corpses cluttering up my landscape most dismaying and most depressing. You and this church are in the scenario, which means you're part of this tapestry of espionage!"

"Tapestry of espionage? How fruity. You must have been bitten by the Baroness Orczy. Your language belongs to *The Scarlet Pimpernel*."

"You yourself come from Germany, don't you?" It was a stab in the dark, but Hitchcock was rewarded when Mr. Peach's eyes narrowed threateningly.

"If you have come here to make trouble for me, there are those who can make trouble for you."

"You're hardly offering me pious words of comfort. How unlike a vicar you speak. If you're really a man of the cloth, you're cut from a very peculiar bolt." And then it exploded in Hitchcock's brain. "My God! I'll bet you're not Lemuel Peach at all." He moved backward as the man's hand slowly reached for the bread knife. "You don't frighten me, whoever you are. You're not Peach, are you?"

"I said I am Lemuel Peach."

"That's what you say, but I suspect you aren't. I don't care for any more bread, thank you. You can put the knife down."

"I think perhaps you should stay the night after all. It would be unchristian to deny you a bed on a night like this. You haven't told me your name."

"My name is Nemesis," said Hitchcock archly.

"I don't much care for Greeks," said the possible vicar, "and I don't much care for threats."

"You work for the Germans."

"I work for God."

"You are part of a network that stretches from here to a village on the Channel coast."

"Your scenario is poppycock."

"My instincts aren't. Why threaten me with the knife?"

"Because you're talking like a madman. I get a lot of loonies here, but they're rarely given to violence."

Hitchcock had backed away to the door. With one hand, he was fumbling behind his back to open the bolt. "I think I understand why you're in Regner's scenario."

"Did it mention me by name?" shouted the vicar, if he was the vicar.

"No, not by name. It just said 'the vicar.' I'll bet there have been a lot of vicars here named Lemuel Peach. A real vicar doesn't sport frivolous bow ties. Real vicars are dedicated men."

"I, too, am a dedicated man!" stormed the improbable vicar as he sent the knife expertly flying at Hitchcock. Hitchcock yelled and stepped nimbly aside. The knife imbedded itself in the wooden door just a few inches from Hitchcock's head. Hitchcock was now positive this man was not a vicar as he went rushing out the door, eager to be swallowed up by the fog. He ran up the stone stairs and across the street without thinking of the possible danger of moving vehicles. When he reached the pub, he stopped to catch his breath.

"Changed your mind, dearie?" asked the prostitute, who had crept up behind him on little tart's feet.

Hitchcock continued his flight, and as he ran, he was suddenly reminded of the recurring nightmares he had suffered in Munich eleven years ago, and wondered if those pursuers were once again hot on his heels. He saw a fish-and-chips shop and went in. Later, holding a newspaper cone filled with fish and chips, a hot mug of tea and milk at his elbow, he tried to make sense of his encounter with the obviously ersatz Lemuel Peach. That's what Regner had insinuated in his manuscript. Peach's church had been taken over by spies. He had to be right, or why would the bogus vicar hurl a knife at him? It couldn't have been his comment about frivolous bow ties. He filed a mental note to get this information to Jennings through John Bellowes as soon as he'd finished his supper. He couldn't remember fish and chips ever having tasted this good before.

Nigel Pack's wife was called Violet, at the moment a name appropriate to the color her face had turned at Pack's announcement he was returning to Whitehall, where he would probably be working for the rest of the night. "I should never have married you!" she stormed.

"Quite right," agreed Nigel as he changed his shirt, damning Sir Arthur Willing and Basil Cole and Alfred Hitchcock and all disciples of espionage and wishing he'd chosen to become a plumber's assistant. "Ours is a marriage shipwrecked on the shoals of deceit. You thought our life would be a glamorous one with a possible accrual of wealth. Well, now is the moment of truth. Working in British Intelligence is tiresome and tedious, but it is all I'm equipped to do. We can't accrue wealth because you spend my money as fast as I acquire it."

"*Our* money." She practically spat the words at him.

"And we can't divorce because we don't dare. We can't afford it."

She sat at her dressing table, absentmindedly picked up a hairbrush, and began stroking her hair. "I think I'll go spend some time with Mummy and Daddy. The sea air, I think, would do me a world of good."

"I'd prefer you didn't."

She slammed the brush down. "I'm bloody bored with what you do and don't prefer I do."

"You will remain right here in London until this matter of the Hitchcocks is resolved. Then we'll see what we can do to improve our sorry situation. I can assure you, having lost my friends, my hair, and my self-respect, it would be no great ordeal losing you."

Violet was now morose. She said sadly, "Sunday is Daddy's birthday. I don't think he'll be celebrating too many birthdays in the future."

"Wire him flowers."

"Go to hell."

"If you lead the way."

Basil Cole had returned to the offices of British Intelligence almost an hour before Nigel Pack and in high good spirits. He'd been tracked down at his club, where he was losing heavily in a friendly poker game and was grateful for the rescue. Sir Arthur Willing was unhappily completing a lonesome dinner at his desk. "You're dining rather late, sir."

"This is Whitehall, Mr. Cole, not the French Riviera." Sir Arthur was grumpy, which meant he'd had neither gin nor wine, and there was a strong possibility events were not turning to either his direction or satisfaction. "Where's Pack?"

"I don't know, sir," said Basil Cole as he sat opposite Sir Arthur and read some memos his superior pushed across the desk to him. "Wasn't he contacted?"

"Over an hour ago, for God's sake. They found him at some dinner party at the Italian Embassy. He spends an awful lot of time partying with those people, seems to me."

"I think it's his wife, sir. Violet is partial to exotics."

"Violet is a frump."

Cole finished reading the brief memos and blew a low, mournful whistle. "Bad stuff, this, murdering a detective. They really think Hitchcock did it?"

"His fingerprints are on the knife hilt."

"Well, if he did, it couldn't have been deliberate. I mean if his flat was raided, his wife abducted, he must have panicked—"

"Oh, bother your suppositions. Jennings is on to it, and he's a very capable man. We've a long night ahead of us."

"I gather Hitchcock is still at large."

"Very much so. But we'll catch up with him."

"We usually do." Basil Cole smiled brightly.

"Here's Pack at last," grumbled Sir Arthur. "What kept you?"

"Sorry, sir. The fog. My taxi crawled here."

"What are those scratches on your face?"

"I cut myself shaving."

The knowledgeable Basil Cole refrained from commenting, 'Next time use a razor blade instead of Violet's fingernails,' but instead handed Nigel the memos and watched him sink onto the sofa and read them.

At the same time as Hitchcock was eating his lonely dinner and Sir Arthur's aides were converging in his office, Alma Hitchcock was sitting on a settee in a beautiful drawing room of a mansion she suspected was located somewhere in Mayfair. She was sipping from a glass of what tasted like a superior Madeira while waiting to be served a promised dinner, and wondered if the man with the tic under his left eye would continue to provide companionship through the meal. He had come into the room only a few minutes earlier, and

136

she hadn't seen him since being transferred from the hearse into a delivery van somewhere in Regent's Park, under the cover of fog and darkness and the animal cries from the zoo. She remembered that. It could be a clue of the sort Hitch adored using. Of course his animal cries at the end of the film would turn out to have come from a nearby secreted gramophone and the transfer would not have occurred in Regent's Park but at some other venue. The man with the tic was pouring himself a Scotch and soda. He was in his early forties, and his clothing was nondescript, appropriate to anonymity. His hair was very black and parted in the middle, and his face would be an attractive one were it not for the overactive tic. He continued to say nothing, and Alma found him and his attitude annoying.

"I assume you have a name," she said, surprised at the unnaturally high pitch of her voice.

"Oh, yes. My family could afford one." He sat on a piano bench and sipped his Scotch and soda.

Suave, thought Alma, he's been studying Ronald Colman. "You're not going to tell me your name?"

"What's in a name?"

"Identification," riposted Alma. "If you won't tell me your name, will you kindly tell me what the hell's been going on? Where is my husband?" The man said nothing. "What do you expect to gain by abducting me?"

"You'll recognize that in due time."

"I see. Can you at least explain this business in Regent's Park? We might have all been killed when that delivery van sideswiped us."

"I'm a very good driver."

And indeed he was. Somewhere in Regent's Park, a delivery van had appeared from out of nowhere, Alma of course not knowing what it was from the interior of the blacked-out hearse, but later recognizing what kind of vehicle it was when she was transferred into it from the hearse. When the hearse skidded to a stop, the delivery van alongside it, the rear hearse doors were suddenly flung open, and the thugs who had helped kidnap Alma drew guns but were quickly overpowered by four men who beat up the thugs mercilessly.

"Your goons were very brutally beaten by those four . . . men . . . I suppose, for want of a better description. Why were they tied up and left in the hearse?"

"To be found and put into jail, of course. Why else?"

He didn't have to sound so condescending, thought Alma; he was treating her like an idiot child. "What about the men who brought us here? Shouldn't *they* be put into jail?"

"It would hardly be cricket jailing your saviors."

"Saviors? This is most confusing." She felt like Alice on the second leg of her journey through Wonderland. "Why weren't *you* trussed up and left to be jailed?"

"I was not one of *them.*"

"Then what were you doing with *them?* You let *them* strike my husband!"

"Mrs. Hitchcock, all in good time."

"All right. All in good time. And how long am I to be held prisoner here?"

"Don't you like this room? I'm told it was decorated by Syrie Maugham." He pronounced the name as though he thought it should be written with lightning.

"I see." Alma managed a small smile. "Then we're somewhere in Mayfair. That's Syrie Maugham territory."

"We could be in Hampstead or Hammersmith." She

knew he was playing with her. "Mrs. Maugham has on occasion condescended to work those lesser territories."

She was beginning to suspect that the man with the tic was possibly to the manor born, not just in a manner born. Or else he subscribed to some very posh magazines. Now she remembered Patricia. "My daughter!"

"She's with her Aunt Nellie. Quite safe and by now comfortably tucked into bed and asleep."

"You know so much about us. Who are you? What's going on? Where's my husband?"

"Ah! Here's dinner." A butler entered, followed by a woman pushing a serving cart. The butler looked as though he might have had some experience in the prizefighting ring, and the woman looked as though she might be more comfortable as a matron in a women's jail. "Mrs. Hitchcock, you must be famished!"

In the fish-and-chips shop, Hitchcock was demolishing his third serving and feeling once again on top of the world. The next step was to get to the village of Medwin and locate Madeleine Lockwood. He remembered on the map the village was somewhere to the west of Brighton, which meant trains for Medwin or connecting to Medwin would leave from Victoria Station. He looked at his pocket watch. He might still make it to Victoria before the last trains left, which was usually around midnight. But first he would phone John Bellowes and have him relate the adventure at the church to Jennings. Probably by the time Jennings got around to raiding the church, the bogus Lemuel Peach would have decamped. On the other hand, probably not. Spies, as Hitchcock had come to know them, especially

139

when portrayed by Peter Lorre, could be a thoroughly brazen lot.

The shopkeeper's harsh voice jolted Hitchcock. "I'm closin' up."

"Oh. Yes. Sorry if I've kept you."

"Want another portion first?" He'd been silently admiring Hitchcock's appetite. He himself was a spare eater, finding the rancid odor of fish and chips reprehensible, although the business was profitable.

"Thank you, no. I think I've had enough."

"You're not from around these parts, are y'?"

"Well, actually, I'm not. How could you tell?"

"From your speech and the way when you eat, you don't slop all over yourself."

"I had very strict parents. Good night." He reluctantly returned to the chilling fog while anxiously seeking a phone kiosk. When he found one, it was on a street that seemed dark and sinister, foreboding of danger, and Hitchcock found himself looking over his shoulder. He couldn't see too far under the circumstances and he entered the kiosk while fishing in his pocket for some pennies. Bellowes' line was engaged, and Hitchcock cursed the solicitor under his breath. He dialed again after a brief wait, and it still was engaged and Hitchcock hoped it was because one of the children had been taken suddenly ill. He didn't like the Bellowes children; they had expressed a desire to grow up to become policemen, which immediately placed them in the enemy camp. The hell with it, thought Hitchcock; I'll throw caution to the winds. He dialed Scotland Yard and asked for Detective Superintendent Jennings. It was a long shot. He assumed the man had gone home to his comfortable bed by now. He wondered if he had a comfortable wife or an uncomfortable mistress or both. Jennings was there. "This is Hitchcock speaking."

"Where are you?"

"In a kiosk."

"Where?"

"In greater London."

"We've a warrant out for your arrest."

"I did not kill that man. Didn't my solicitor get through to you?"

"He did."

"Didn't he explain the facts to you?"

"He did. At the moment I find them prejudicial."

"It's the truth."

"Mr. Hitchcock, that was one of my best men who was murdered."

"Oh, dear. That is unfortunate."

"It's more than unfortunate, Mr. Hitchcock; it's damned tragic. The murder of a police officer calls for death by hanging."

"And well it should. I'm sure you'll find the killer." Hitchcock reminded himself this phone call could be traced and began to hurry the conversation. "Now listen to this. I've just had a very strange experience that warrants your immediate investigation."

Jennings listened attentively to Hitchcock's adventure in the church at King's Cross Station. So did Peter Dowerty, who listened on the extension, and so did an engineer who was trying to pinpoint the location of the kiosk from which Hitchcock was speaking.

"And then," concluded Hitchcock, "he threw the bread knife at me, and as I look back at it, it was quite a professional effort. Fortunately, it missed me by a hair. Mr. Jennings? What news of my wife? Is there any word of Alma?"

"Not yet. Now listen, Hitchcock—"

Hitchcock interrupted, "Th-th-th-that's all, folks," and abruptly hung up. He left the kiosk, his mind on Victoria Station, but he found he was disoriented. He couldn't remember the direction of the tube station. When he fled from the church, he had run blindly until coming across the fish-and-chips shop. He hastened back to the shop to ask directions of the owner, but when he got there, the place was dark and the door was locked. There wasn't a soul on the street. Hitchcock decided to stumble along in the fog until he came upon someone who would direct him to the tube.

And then, from somewhere ahead of him, he heard the buskers.

It unmistakably had to be buskers. He could hear the plunk-plunk of a banjo and the rattling of finger sticks and the tap dancing of feet on the pavements and high whining voices singing of Burlington Bertie, and with renewed hope, Hitchcock hurried in the direction of the sound.

What a strange place for buskers, thought Hitchcock. They're a long way from their usual turf. They belong in the West End under the bright lights of the theaters and in the shadows of the expensive restaurants, not in King's Cross. Perhaps they're a local group.

And how come they were about at this hour of the night? He began to feel apprehensive, with second thoughts of the advisability of approaching them for direction to the tube. He had stopped under a street lamp and decided to reverse his direction.

From out of nowhere they appeared, heading in his direction. He could count five of them, all men, dressed in their busker suits, on which were sewn thousands of colorful buttons; more colorful buttons were sewn on the caps they wore jauntily. The banjo plucked and the sticks clacked and three men danced, albeit clumsily, and Hitchcock was very frightened. The buskers looked like sinister phantoms conjured up by some unseen demon, conjured up to find Hitchcock and terrorize him. He began to back away, but the buskers were fanning out, surrounding him.

"Money for the buskers," demanded one of the dancers, with a weasel's face and a rat's nose.

"Money for the buskers," said the one clacking the sticks; ugly warts were covering his face, and scraggly yellow straws were hanging down from under his cap.

"Give us your money, guv," said the third busker, and a thin stilettolike weapon appeared from under his jacket.

Hitchcock wanted to shout, but his vocal cords were paralyzed with fear. His money, he mustn't part with his money, he would need it for the odyssey ahead of him. On the other hand, he mustn't part with his life, as then both odyssey and money would be pointless. If he tried to escape, he knew he could never outrun them. They were not only younger, though he was still what he considered to be a youthful thirty-six, but they were each of them a good four stone lighter than he was. Still, he continued to back away.

"The lolly, guv, the lolly." This busker had a running nose that he wiped on the back of his hands.

Where are the police, wondered Hitchcock, at this hour of the night? Why aren't they abroad to protect innocent subjects of the king? But then, on the other hand, a constable was the last person Hitchcock wanted to deal with this night.

Then he heard the agonizing screeching of tires as an automobile drew to a stop beside him.

"Get in quickly!" shouted a woman's voice.

The door to the passenger's side was pushed open, and Hitchcock jumped into the car, pulling the door shut as, with a further agonizing screeching of tires, the car drove away at top speed, rescuing Hitchcock from the menace of the thieving buskers.

"Thank you, thank you very much," gasped Hitchcock, as he reached for a handkerchief with which to mop his sweaty brow.

"How lucky I came along, Mr. Hitchcock."

Hitchcock turned for a better look at the woman. He recognized Nancy Adair.

"As is frequently said," murmured Hitchcock, a very wary expression on his face, "'out of the frying pan . . .'"

Ten

"**A**nd exactly where are you driving?" Hitchcock asked Nancy Adair, who was hunched over the steering wheel, straining to see ahead through the fog.

"Wherever you tell me. But we're not going to get too far in this dreadful fog."

"Miss Adair. Among the many things I learned from my father, I learned the following: 'He travels farthest who travels alone.' Did you learn anything comparable from your father?" She said nothing. "You did have a father? They're quite inexpensive."

"Oh, yes. I had a father. And we're wasting petrol tooling around like this. Where do you wish to go?"

He squinted through the windshield and could see they were somewhere near Kensington Gardens. "Pull over."

"Why?"

Hitchcock was wondering if she thought he was her captive. "I want to talk to you."

"It would save time if we talked while driving to your destination."

"My destination is the nearest curb. Now pull over."

She parked the car and turned to him. "Well?"

"How did you know where to find me?"

"Sheer luck."

"I don't believe you. You've been trailing me."

"I want a story."

"I gave you the interview."

"It was charming. I know there's a better story. Ever since the murder at your cottage, I knew something hot was coming to a boil."

"Why didn't you sell that information to the newspapers?"

"Because I thought they'd already gotten it from their informants at Scotland Yard." Hitchcock look quizzical. "Don't be naive, Mr. Hitchcock. The newspapers have spies, well-paid informants, all over the place. Everyone's for sale. Everyone has a price."

"How cynical."

"It's a dog-eat-dog world, right?"

"I'm not a fool, Miss Adair. I may be slightly bewildered at the moment, and at a disadvantage, but I realize you've been trailing me for several days, ever since you started badgering my secretary and my wife to set up the interview. You were outside the studio yesterday waiting for me to come out, and when I did, you followed me to the cottage. You almost ran us off the road."

"In truth, that was quite foolish of me. I thought by forcing your car to stop, I could get my interview then."

146

"That was rather a desperate and dangerous measure. You might have killed all of us." Hans Meyer. My God, Hitchcock thought suddenly, Hans Meyer. He never came to the flat. Instead, those brutes appeared.

"I could see your chauffeur was quite expert at the wheel. I wasn't worried."

"How did you know where to find me tonight?"

She was lighting a cigarette. It was French, and the odor was unpleasant. Hitchcock rolled down his window and then couldn't decide which was worse, the smoke or the fog.

"It began after the interview. When I left your house, there was a man at the opposite side of the street standing near the phone kiosk. I'd seen him there when I arrived for the interview. It was quite obvious you were under police surveillance."

"Yes. I recently gathered that."

"So my instincts told me there was a better story to be had. Tonight, I drove by your house to see if the surveillance was a twenty-four-hour vigil. I saw you come chasing out of your building and rush to the kiosk. But you didn't use the phone—"

"The wires were cut."

"Ah! Then you went tearing down the street and I lost you in the fog for a while. You're terribly quick on your feet, Mr. Hitchcock," she said, gracefully not adding, for a man his size.

"I'm always quick when prodded. Then you found me again."

"That's right. You were coming out of another kiosk and disappeared into the tube."

Hitchcock wished she'd be done with the damned cigarette. He also wished he were carrying a portable lie detec-

147

tor. "You must be prescient to have located me several hours later in King's Cross."

She smiled. "Not at all. When I was looking at that manuscript on your kitchen table, I did manage to scan most of the first page before you took it away from me. It said Orwell's church in King's Cross. I knew that particular line traveled to King's Cross, so I drove to King's Cross. I knew I'd be there ahead of you, so I stopped for a sandwich. When I got to the church, I saw you being admitted to the basement. Then, when you came tearing out of there, I rolled down my window and shouted at you, but you didn't hear me. You seemed to be in a panic."

"I'd had a bread knife thrown at me."

"In church?"

"Oh, yes, stands to reason. There's so much blood and gore in the Bible, right?"

"I don't know. I've never read it."

"Oh, you should. Some of it's quite racy."

"Well, anyway. I kept after you. I saw you accosted by that woman."

"She was a whore. I disapprove of whores."

"And then I thought you'd go back into the tube, which I must say made my heart sink. I hadn't the vaguest idea where I could pick up your trail again." She stubbed out her cigarette in the dashboard ashtray. "But my luck held. You went past the tube, and I followed you to the fish-and-chips shop."

"Why didn't you join me there?"

"Frankly, I wasn't quite sure how to explain my presence."

"But you are now."

"Rescuing you from the buskers made it easy."

Hitchcock looked perplexed and then said, "Well, I

suppose your being there was quite fortuitous, and I thank you. But here is where we part company."

She grabbed his wrist as he started to open the door at his side. She had a very strong grip. "Mr. Hitchcock, you need me."

Hitchcock bristled with indignation. "I need you to let go of my wrist, young woman."

"Mr. Hitchcock. I know why you're running. I, too, know someone at Scotland Yard. I know your wife has been abducted. I know a policeman was murdered in your flat, and I know you are the Yard's number-one suspect."

"With your sublime talents, Miss Adair, you should soon be ruling the world."

She smiled. "Just a small portion. I'm not greedy." She removed her hand from his wrist. "I phoned my friend while I was having my sandwich. He pleaded with me if I knew where you were to tell him so he could capture you and win a citation. But I protected you."

"What a good story. All that's missing is some heavy breathing."

"You need me, Mr. Hitchcock. You're a celebrity on the run. A very fat celebrity. Alone, you are easily identified. With me, you are a heavy-set man traveling with a younger blonde companion. Think it over, Mr. Hitchcock. By tomorrow morning, there'll be a hue and cry. You are now involved in two murders and your wife's abduction. This fog won't cover the city forever. Once it lifts, it narrows your chances of escaping detection. You'll soon be recognized. You need me."

Hitchcock did some heavy thinking. She was lighting another cigarette, and he resisted the urge to tear it from her mouth and fling it out the window. Miss Adair, he now realized, was most certainly a formidable woman. As an opponent, she was a serious threat. As an ally, she might indeed be quite useful. "In my films," said Hitchcock, "the young woman accompanying the man on the run is usually an unwilling accomplice, marking time until a chance to escape and grass to the police. You're not unwilling, but I'm sure if I say no, you'd tell the police about me, wouldn't you?"

"Maybe yes. Maybe no." There was something continental now to the lilt in her voice, and for the first time since meeting her, Hitchcock studied her face. Even in the darkness of the car, because she had prudently not turned on the inside light when they parked, he could see a hardness in her face. She wore too much makeup, especially the mascara on her eyelashes and the heavy application of rouge and lipstick. She was probably at least five years younger then he we was and about ten years shrewder. "Well, Mr. Hitchcock?"

"Miss Adair, I realize I am in what is best described as a tight spot. And for a man my size, as you have eloquently emphasized, it's an uncomfortable squeeze. Yes, I can use an ally, and I shall confer that dubious honor on you." His voice deepened. "But I warn you, should you at any time betray me, I will involve you as my accomplice. I will show you no mercy."

"Mr. Hitchcock, the fact that I'm here, and not turning you in to the police, already brands me a criminal." She gunned the motor. "Where to, Mr. Hitchcock?"

"A village called Medwin. It's somewhere beyond Brighton, but farther inland. I assume you have a map of England?"

"There's one in the dashboard compartment." She pulled away from the curb. "It's late. We should think of somewhere to spend the night."

Hitchcock blushed, but in the darkness, she couldn't see this. "I'm not in the least bit tired."

"You will be." She laughed. "Don't worry. I know you won't make any improper advances."

"But what about you?"

"Mr. Hitchcock, I assure you, you're not my type. Now then"—she was peering ahead through the windshield—"somewhere along here there's a ring road that gets us on the road to Brighton. Ah, there it is." They drove in silence for a while. "A penny for them, Mr. Hitchcock."

"Oh, to you they'd be worth a great deal more."

"You are thinking about your wife?"

"I always think about Alma. Now more than ever, but somehow, I think the police will find her and find her unharmed. I think she's been taken in case a trade is necessary."

"A trade? What do you mean?"

"Mrs. Hitchcock for Mr. Hitchcock. Don't be so obtuse, Miss Adair. I know you're a very clever schemer. You know from the opening paragraphs of the scenario that I'm on a trail that's to lead me to a master spy, a spy ring, blood and thunder and all that."

"Then this will be even more exciting than I expected."

"And it will also be terribly dangerous, I should think. My life in jeopardy, and all that."

"And now mine too!" chimed in Nancy Adair lustily, adding a hearty "Ha-ha!"

"What an odd target for levity." said Hitchcock, "the prospect of a violent death. I should like to examine that further when I get the opportunity. You know this isn't a lard devised by some of my writers, though God knows those ninnies would be hard put to come up with an adventure like this one. We're in John Buchan territory now, and that's

151

a very tricky terrain. There have been two men murdered, and there's definitely a link to the two murders in Munich back in '25."

"Ah? There were earlier murders?" Hitchcock told her. "Well, that's another kettle of fish, isn't it?"

"Not too late to back out, Miss Adair."

"Are you mad?"

"No, but I think you are."

Her grip tightened on the steering wheel and they drove in silence for a while. Then she said cheerfully, "I offered you a penny."

"Well, since we're attached to each other now and it will be necessary from time to time to share my thoughts with you, I've been thinking about the man who was with me yesterday on the drive from the studio to my cottage."

"Oh, him. Who was he? From the brief glimpses I got of him, he seemed very attractive."

"He's an actor named Hans Meyer. A refugee from the Nazis. It was he I was expecting earlier this evening, and instead those thugs appeared, knocking me out and taking Alma. I was wondering what had become of him."

"Perhaps he arrived when you were knocked out, panicked, and fled."

"No, he rang our bell just a few minutes before we were attacked. We spoke on the intercom. I buzzed him in."

"Then that is how the attackers got into your building. As he entered, they overpowered him, knocked him out, and then went about their business. They obviously knew what they were doing."

"The Scotland Yard man on watch had to have seen them."

"Weeelll," she said, drawing out the word as an intimation of Hitchcock's apparent naïveté, "if I spotted him so easily this afternoon, then they certainly must have known he was there and knocked him out. An easy matter creeping up on him in this fog and coshing him."

"Of course." He smiled. "I said you were very clever. Well, then, after that he must have regained consciousness and come up to the flat to see what had happened . . ."

"And in a panic, you thinking he was one of the attackers returning to finish you off, you stabbed him in the back with the bread knife."

"Oh, not at all." Hitchcock was obviously annoyed. "Just because I complimented your prescience and your cleverness is no reason to jump to conclusions. I was knocked out by those men, and it still hurts, damn the eyes of whoever hit me. Yes, I had the knife, I'd run into the kitchen for it and I was still clutching it when I was hit, but I assure you, young woman, as I have assured my solicitor and Detective Superintendent Jennings of Scotland Yard, when I awakened with the blade of the knife all bloodied, it was quite obvious someone else had stabbed the detective and then placed the knife back in my hand. It's a very old ploy; Edgar Wallace used to do it to death in his overheated thrillers."

"You've spoken to your solicitor *and* to Jennings at Scotland Yard?"

"You saw me using the kiosk the first time. Did you think I was dialing for the correct time?"

"Your solicitor is quite understandable, but Scotland Yard? They could have traced the call and caught you."

"But they didn't, did they?" Hitchcock felt delightfully smug. "I know how the coppers operate; I direct thrillers. I knew they'd try to trace me. I just spoke at greater acceleration than usual, and bob's your uncle, here I am, and where are we?"

153

"Hopefully on the road to Brighton. Keep your eyes peeled for a bed and breakfast. There are dozens along the route to Brighton."

"They'll be terribly suspicious our checking in at this hour of the night and without luggage."

"No, they won't. They'll think we're wise getting out of this fog and away from the lorries on the road. And anyway, I'm getting drowsy. There! Up ahead on the right! What does that sign say?"

Hitchcock strained to read it and finally managed. "It's a funeral home. Perhaps we should stop and put them in touch with Scotland Yard."

"That's funny." She didn't laugh. "You're not so tense anymore. You're beginning to trust me."

"You're right. I'm not so tense anymore." He settled into silence and dwelt on Hans Meyer. After a while, he began to link the actor to a line from *Hamlet*, about there being something rotten in Denmark.

After his frustrating chat with Hitchcock, Jennings cursed himself, Scotland Yard, and the damn fool of an engineer who finally located the kiosk from which Hitchcock had called but had long since abandoned. Jennings immediately set about orchestrating an invasion of the basement at the church in King's Cross. He assigned Dowerty and three other men to masquerade as bums seeking food and shelter. He gave them Hitchcock's description of Lemuel Peach, complete with polka-dot bow tie, and shortly before midnight, the four men arrived at the solid wooden door to the basement of the church. Dowerty tugged at the bellpull and waited impatiently.

"Try the doorknob," one of his men whispered from behind him. Dowerty tried the doorknob and they went in.

154

"There's nobody here," whispered one of the men.

"Then why are you whispering?" snapped Dowerty. "Have a look through there." He directed one man to a door beyond the table on which rested the tea urns and the loaves of bread. Dowerty felt an urn, and it was cold. "Strange," he said, "nobody here at this hour. No poor unfortunates turning up to doss down?" He looked at the cots. "Hello? Who's that then on the cot under the window?"

The detective who had gone through the door beyond the table reported there were stairs leading upstairs to the church. But Dowerty was transfixed by the man lying face down on the cot with a bread knife protruding from his back. He lifted the head gently. "Mr. Lemuel Peach, I presume," he said, after recognizing the polka-dot bow tie. "Mr. Jennings isn't going to like this one bit."

The house offering bed and breakfast which Hitchcock and Nancy Adair selected was on the road just outside Brighton. Hitchcock fretted like a peevish rooster about rousing the innkeeper at his hour, but Nancy overrode his fears. "Do you have a handkerchief?" she asked as they pulled into the driveway and parked.

"Of course I do. What do you need it for?"

"Keep it over your face and pretend difficulty breathing. I'll do the talking." He followed her up the wooden stairs of the porch, and she twisted the bell on the door. The porch boards creaked under their weight, and Hitchcock had the feeling the building was so fragile, one wrong move and it would come tumbling down around their heads. "Come on, come on," urged Nancy impatiently as she twisted the bell on the door again.

"Coming! Coming!" They heard the voice coming faintly from inside the house, a voice, Hitchcock imagined, as fragile as the structure they were trying to enter. The door opened and a woman's head came poking out, wearing a nightcap. "Oh," said the fragile voice breathlessly, "people!"

Nancy Adair smothered the woman with charm. "I'm so sorry to disturb you at this hour, but we've gotten lost in the fog and it seemed too dangerous to continue, and my husband suffers so from asthma and this fog is wreaking hell with him." Hitchcock expected the little lady to burst into tears, but all she did was dart her eyes back and forth from the blonde to Hitchcock and back again. "I do hope you have a room for us."

"Oh, I do indeed, ecksherly." Hitchcock decided she meant "actually," and with that pronunciation sized her up as belonging to that race of British gentlewomen who, having fallen upon hard times, swallow their pride and go into business as hoteliers on a small scale. "Come in! Come in! It's truly awful out." Hitchcock prayed it wouldn't be truly awful in. "I have a very nice room on this floor behind the staircase. It's a guinea including breakfast, which is served promptly at eight A.M. Um . . . if you would just register here." She indicated a ledger on the front desk. Nancy found a pen alongside the ledger and signed in. Hitchcock, handkerchief over his face, making ugly noises as he gasped for breath, looked over Nancy's shoulder. She had signed them in as Mr. and Mrs. Jennings. Cheeky little devil, he thought, and not without humor. "I'm Miss Farquhar." She turned a sympathetic face to Hitchcock. "You poor soul. How you're suffering. I could prepare a steam inhalator for you. It would be no trouble at all. I've got one in the kitchen. My father suffered from asthma, so I know the agony you're going through. It killed him, asthma did, and it was a terrible death. He was a long time dying." She was a long time leading them to their room.

She unlocked the door, pushed it open, and clicked the switch. The room, Hitchcock could see with an inner sigh of relief, contained two single beds. "How nice," said Nancy Adair. "Isn't it nice, darling? And there are two beds, too." She said to Miss Farquhar, "When he has one of these attacks, it's best he sleep alone. Isn't it, darling?" Hitchcock sat on a chair and wheezed painfully.

"Oh, dear, I could do that inhalator for you in no time." Miss Farquhar seemed overdetermined to be a ministering angel.

From behind the handkerchief, Hitchcock said, "I'm feeling much better now that we're indoors." He had found a pound note and a shilling in his pocket and offered it to their hostess. "You said a guinea?"

"Oh, you can pay in the morning after breakfast," said Miss Farquhar, but Hitchcock pressed the money on her. He had every intention of being out of the place before breakfast. "The bathroom's just across the hall, and I can assure you you won't disturb anyone when you use it. There aren't any other guests in residence at the moment. I guess the fog's discouraged that. I'm usually quite full at this time of the year. You'll find plenty of towels, and there are extra blankets in the cupboard. Would you care for a cup of Bovril before turning in?" Poor lonely thing, thought Hitchcock; she's so loath to leave us.

"I don't think so. We'd as soon turn in. It's so late and we're so terribly tired, but you're most kind." Miss Farquhar bid them good night and went slowly upstairs to her bedroom.

Hitchcock shoved his handkerchief into his jacket pocket and asked Nancy, "Did you bring the map in with you?"

She waved it at him. He got up, crossed to her, and

unfolded the map. "Medwin, Medwin, Medwin," he muttered as he looked for the village. "Here it is. Medwin. Just north of Ridgewood. I suppose we can breakfast in Ridgewood."

"What's wrong with breakfasting here? It's paid for."

"I can't quite hold a handkerchief in front of my face while dining. I plan for us to be out of here long before breakfast." Without undressing, he stretched out on one of the beds.

"Don't you want to wash up, or anything?"

"I'll wash in the morning, and I have no pressing urge to do anything."

She sat on the other bed after removing her jacket. Hitchcock could now see she was sensibly dressed in a skirt, blouse, and the jacket. The beret she'd been wearing she now flung across the room, where it landed atop a dresser. She kicked off her shoes, and as she unrolled her stockings, she asked him, "What are we looking for in Medwin?"

"It isn't a what. It's a who. A woman named Madeleine Lockwood."

"And who is she?"

"All I know is that she was once in the music halls and was at one time the mistress of a highly placed person."

"You read this in the scenario?"

"Yes."

"You didn't bring the scenario with you?"

"It was stolen from the flat yesterday."

"You didn't tell me that!"

"I didn't tell you a lot of things." If Alma were in the room, she'd recognize he was on the verge of dropping off. His responses were getting slower and softer.

"But you memorized it?"

"I made my own notes. I always do a breakdown of scenarios for myself. Not much of a scenario. Very sloppy on Regner's part. I more or less memorized my notes. Went over them so often, and then . . ." He was snoring softly.

Nancy Adair took her purse and went to the bathroom. In the bathroom, she stared at her face in the mirror and then smiled a wry, crooked little smile. She whispered, "So far, so good," and then ran the bath.

At three o'clock in the morning, there was a heated argument going on in Sir Arthur Willing's office between him and Detective Superintendent Jennings. Also present were Nigel Pack, Basil Cole, and Peter Dowerty, the latter still disguised as a bum.

"I insist not a word of this be leaked to the press," said Sir Arthur, "at least not for another twenty-four hours. You have got to go along with me in this. Hitchcock is in enough jeopardy as it is. I mean, having a bread knife hurled at him . . ."

"And it miraculously reversing itself and landing in his assailant's back."

"You can't think Hitchcock killed the man!"

"The man isn't who he was claiming to be. He told Hitchcock he was the vicar, Lemuel Peach, but Lemuel Peach is away on holiday. He's at a retreat somewhere north. I got this from the church caretaker, whom we roused in the building next door."

"Then who's the dead man?"

"We don't know. I should know by morning."

"Didn't he have *any* identification?" asked a mystified Sir Arthur.

"He'd been stripped clean. There was nothing in his pockets."

"And no prints on the knife hilt."

Jennings was wishing the man would disappear in a puff of smoke. He was tired. Dowerty looked as if he needed toothpicks to prop us his eyelids. Sir Arthur's aides were staring ahead like zombies. They all needed some rest. "Sir Arthur, we've been through all this. We need some rest. You want this kept out of the papers, I'll defer to your demand. But it's not helping us trace Hitchcock or locate his wife."

"She's quite safe," snapped Sir Arthur.

The look on Jennings' face was one of incredulity. "You know this for a fact?"

"Mr. Jennings," said Sir Arthur as he ignited the tobacco in his pipe bowl, "I wouldn't lead you up the garden path." A well-beaten trail, he silently surmised. "There are times when one should have faith in British Intelligence."

"It doesn't help when you keep things from me."

"Sometimes that's necessary. Please trust me, Mr. Jennings. I'm one of the oldest whores in this game, and I'm usually respected for giving full value."

Nigel Pack interjected with what he thought was great charm, "He doesn't always confide in us completely either, Mr. Jennings, if that's any comfort to you."

"I'm not looking to be comforted," said Jennings coldly, "I'm looking to solve three murders, locate a missing woman, and prevent further bloodshed."

"Well, I've told you the missing woman is safe," said Sir Arthur, "and I certainly wish to see justice done. And as to the avoidance of further bloodshed, I've never been very good at prognostication. But let us hope there won't be any."

"I think we should call it a night," suggested Jennings. Dowerty seconded the motion.

Basil Cole said to Sir Arthur, "You must be dead-tired, too, sir."

"I'm not dead yet," said Sir Arthur as he continued to puff on his pipe, "or hadn't you noticed?"

Alma couldn't sleep. She'd been provided with night-gown and robe and other necessities, and the man with the tic had been terribly charming when he bid her good night and locked her into the room. There were bars on the window, too, and her view was of a small garden guarded by a wall that seemed at least five storeys high and obscured any further view beyond. What was being done to find her? she wondered. And Hitch. What of her poor darling Hitch? She'd seen him coshed and fall forward to the floor still clutching the kitchen knife he'd so bravely tried to use to rescue Alma. She prayed he wasn't seriously injured.

She paced the floor, her head aching with thoughts that were mostly confusing and puzzling. Her lavish surroundings (and this bedroom was an absolute stunner), the kind deference with which she was being treated, the thoughtfulness in telling her Patricia was quite safe. Sleep, sleep, she thought with a sigh, perchance to dream. Where are you, Hitch? Where are you now? Are you at home asleep?

Hitchcock was not at home, but he was asleep, and he was snoring. Nancy Adair lay on her bed staring at the ceiling, damning herself for not owning a pair of earplugs.

BOOK THREE

The MacGuffin

Eleven

Basil Cole was a tidy man. His obsession with fastidiousness had resulted in the defection of friends, lovers, and relatives, all expendable as far as Basil was concerned. His devotion to British Intelligence bordered on the fanatical, which made him a valuable asset to Sir Arthur Willing. Where the firm, as it was known in Intelligence headquarters, demanded utmost loyalty, Basil demanded from the firm utmost neatness. Lying in bed at 4 A.M. in the morning after the marathon session with Sir Arthur, Jennings, and Nigel Pack, Basil was too troubled to sleep. Leaving the Intelligence offices and not able to find a taxi, he had walked home, a distance of less than a mile. The fog was beginning to ease and drift out to the Thames, and from there presumably out to the sea where, as far as Basil was concerned, fogs belonged. The walk had refreshed Basil, and by the time he arrived at his very tidy flat just off upper St. Martin's Lane, he was wide awake and annoyed. While walking, he had thought back on the meeting and had come to the conclusion it was most untidy. There were too many loose ends dangling, and Basil wanted them neatly threaded into place. To Basil, every assignment should be like a well-planned sampler, such as the perennial 'God Bless Our Happy Home' neatly stitched by himself (a hidden vice), which hung in his foyer.

As far as he was concerned, the sampler that represented Hitchcock, his wife, and the murders was too hastily designed. The colors of the threads were all wrong and were clashing. Over his head there hung a cloud that Basil labeled 'The Sin of Omission.' Information was either being withheld, or misfiled in several minds, or just untidily ignored. For example, Sir Arthur was an incredibly intelligent man, yet he never dwelt on those two unsolved murders in Munich eleven years ago. Every attempt Basil made to allude to them was waved away, yet most of the principals involved in that case were once again headliners. The Hitchcocks, Hans Meyer, Fredrick Regner. The only missing character was Rosie Wagner, who, when last heard of prior to her disappearance, had been judged to be battier than a failed movie starlet. Neatly, tidily, Basil lined up the facts as he got out of bed, put on his Sulka bathrobe, went to the kitchen, and prepared his morning tea. In Munich in 1925, Anna Grieban, script girl–informant for British Intelligence, brutally stabbed to death in the shower. Rudolf Wagner, pianist and composer, another informant for the firm, stabbed in the back at the studio, where the murderer might easily have been apprehended but nevertheless escaped detection. Eleven years later, there is Regner with his strange scenario deliberately directed at the Hitchcocks, and his emissary, Martin Mueller, is stabbed to death on Hitchcock's doorstep. The next day, the manuscript is stolen, the Hitchcocks are attacked, Mrs. Hitchcock is spirited away, and Hitchcock, while unconscious from a blow to the head, is set up to appear as the murderer of the detective, Angus McKellin.

And just a few hours ago, Sir Arthur told Jennings Alma Hitchcock was perfectly safe. How did he know? If the firm had her, why hadn't he told either Nigel or Basil? They had been working together for over twelve years now, and to Basil's knowledge, he had always shared all information with them, even the most highly classified, give or take an occasional omission. But now, he was in default. And that was terribly untidy.

The kettle whistled, and Basil poured the hot water into the teapot, part of a set willed him by a maiden aunt who had perished in an avalanche in Switzerland. Only her skis were recovered, and they'd been willed to his cousin Ben in Norfolk. While the tea steeped, Basil went to the window and looked out. There were the signs of a gray, somewhat reluctant dawn, which just about summed up Sir Arthur's sudden withholding of information—gray and reluctant. Doling out that tidbit about Mrs. Hitchcock's safety was obviously done to bring Jennings back from the explosion he appeared to be on the verge of detonating. Jennings had been very square with them. He shared everything. He withheld nothing. He was a good man to have on your team. Basil, while barely knowing him, admired him. He recognized a brother. Jennings was also fastidious, very neat, very

167

tidy. The way he'd gone about investigating the false Lemuel Peach.

Basil poured a cup of tea and waited for the wilted leaves to settle to the bottom of the cup. And, while waiting, he became determinedly resolute. He would confront Sir Arthur and demand to know the whereabouts of Mrs. Hitchcock. After all, it was always up to him to tidy things up.

Alma was awakened from a fuzzy sleep by the sound of a cart being wheeled into the bedroom. She hadn't heard the door unlock and propped herself up on her elbow. There they were, the unholy team, the butler who looked like a prizefighter and the maid who looked like a jail matron. For her own amusement, Alma named them Dempsey and Brunhilde. Brunhilde wheeled the cart to the center of the room while Alma wondered if she would be joined by the man with the tic. As she got out of bed and put on the negligee provided her the night before, she saw there was enough food on the cart to feed a needy family.

"I don't eat much breakfast," said Alma. "Is what's-his-name joining me?"

"What's-his-name?" asked Brunhilde as Dempsey poured tea. Her voice was a bassoon's.

"The man who I assume is my host."

"Oh, *him*. Blinky." Blinky! Now why haven't I thought of that? thought Alma. "He's gone."

"Gone? Where to?" Alma wondered if it was anything she'd said last night that had caused Blinky to defect. How dare he go when she was just getting used to him! She had even been looking forward to the possibility of breakfasting with him. He was her only familiar in this maddening situation into which she'd been caged, and as far as she was concerned, she was his responsibility. How dare he depart without so much as a "by your leave" or a "so long, honey, it's been nice knowing you but I have to push on"?

"He's been called away," said Dempsey, who was surprisingly soft-spoken and cultured. "He's got an engagement elsewhere." The look he exchanged with Brunhilde didn't escape Alma. "He's a musician by profession, you know."

"I didn't know. I know nothing about him except that he's kidnapped me." Alma sat in the chair held out for her by Dempsey and eyed the stewed prunes in the bowl in front of her with suspicion. "I don't fancy stewed prunes."

"There's rhubarb and apricot, if you prefer," offered Brunhilde as she whisked the prunes away to oblivion and lifted the cover of a small salver in which the rhubarb and apricots, also stewed, looked to Alma as though they'd been laid to rest without the benefit of a clerical oratory.

"I'll just have some tea and toast."

Brunhilde shrugged.

Dempsey said, "He plays the saxophone."

"What? Who does?" This is unreal, Alma was thinking, terribly unreal. Hitch will adore it. We must try and find a place for it.

"Blinky does. He's quite good," said Dempsey.

"Saxophone players are so rare in my life," said Alma. "Where's he gone to fulfill this engagement?"

"Now, mum," chided Dempsey, "that would be telling."

A sudden anger enveloped Alma. "So what's to become of me?"

"I don't rightly know, mum," said Dempsey as he poured Alma's tea. "I don't read leaves."

For the first time in hours, Alma burst out laughing.

                            *   *   *

"Why, Miss Farquhar," asked Hitchcock, "have you been lying in ambush all night?"

He and Nancy Adair had been tiptoeing out of the bedroom at 6 A.M. and found the little lady ensconced behind the front desk, adjusting a lovely watch she had pinned to her dress.

"I see you're over your asthma attack. I'm so glad." It hadn't occurred to Hitchcock to camouflage his face with his handkerchief, as he hadn't expected to find the landlady awake at this hour.

"Thank you so much," said Hitchcock with an affable smile. "The room was most comfortable, and now we must be on our way, mustn't we"—he turned to Nancy Adair, who stood behind him—". . . dear."

"But I've breakfast for you!" Miss Farquhar looked as though she'd just been told war was declared. "Kippers and bangers and bacon and stewed tomatoes and eggs and hot muffins and butter and jelly and tea and sweet rolls . . ."

". . . alive, alive, oh . . ." murmured Hitchcock.

"We really can't," interrupted Nancy, "we're overdue in Medwin." Hitchcock wanted to kick her for mentioning Medwin.

"Medwin? What a strange destination."

"Why?" asked Hitchcock, "is something wrong with it?"

"On, no, no. It's just that it's such a tiny little village, nobody ever seems to go there intentionally."

"Well, obviously you've been there," said Hitchcock.

"Oh, yes, I have a cousin there. Cousin Phoebe. Phoebe Allerton. Actually she's a cousin twice removed. We were girls together. She lived with us when she was a child. Oh, you must have some breakfast."

                            170

Actually, Hitchcock was quite famished and admitted it. He chose to be oblivious to Nancy's look of annoyance and her tut of impatience and followed Miss Farquhar into the small dining room, where the breakfast was charmingly laid out on a sideboard. "Oh, doesn't this all look delicious, dear?" asked Hitchcock as he helped himself. Nancy Adair settled for tea and a sweet roll. As Hitchcock piled food on his warmed plate, he asked his hostess, "When visiting Medwin, have you ever chanced to come across a Miss Madeleine Lockwood?"

"Oh, yes," chirruped Miss Farquhar, "she's a spy."

Hitchcock almost dropped his plate. Nancy Adair's chin dropped, but she hastily raised it again. "A spy?" Hitchcock moved to the table while Miss Farquhar indicated where he should sit.

"Well, I don't know if she's still involved in espionage these days, but during the Great War, she was a very well-known spy. She wrote a book about it. I have a copy. Would you like to have a look at it?"

"Indeed I would, if it isn't too much trouble." He and Nancy exchanged a look. Nancy was lighting one of her French cigarettes, and Hitchcock demanded she wait until after breakfast. Miss Farquhar went into the next room, which was labeled The Library, while with annoyance Nancy stubbed out the unsmoked cigarette.

"Imagine that, dear," said Hitchcock as he piled egg and bacon on his fork and then consigned it to his gaping mouth, "our Madeleine a spy. I wonder how Freddy Regner knew all this?"

"Maybe he read the book."

"Oh, do you suppose there was a German edition?"

"I doubt that," said Miss Farquhar, as she returned and

handed Hitchcock the slim volume. "The book was privately printed."

"I see." There was a picture of a young Madeleine Lockwood on the back of the dust jacket. Hitchcock studied the portrait. "She was quite a beauty. Look, dear"—he showed the picture to Nancy—"wasn't she quite a beauty?"

"Yes, quite a beauty." She might have been commenting on a side of gammon.

"She isn't any longer," said Miss Farquhar, as Hitchcock thumbed through the slender book.

"Lost her looks, has she?" asked Hitchcock.

"She did after the scandal."

"Won't you sit down, Miss Farquhar?" Hitchcock's charm was ingratiating, and the landlady sat. "Now what was that about a scandal?"

"She had a lover in the military. Very highly placed. Quite a rich man, too. She brought him down."

"How do you mean?"

Miss Farquhar leaned forward and whispered conspiratorially, "He told her *secrets*."

"How unwise of him."

"Indeed. He was disgraced. Cashiered out of the army. Strings were pulled to keep him from a more serious penalty. It was all very hush-hush. Powerful family. Links to the royals, you know."

"Oh, them." Nancy Adair was examining a fingernail. Strange woman, thought Hitchcock. Terribly strange. With this kind of information Miss Farquhar was providing, if Hitchcock were a reporter, even a free-lance one, or especially a free-lance one, he'd be taking notes. Madeleine Lockwood was becoming a more fascinating link in their chain of progression, and now more than ever he was looking forward to meeting her.

"Them indeed. He was known to be quite matey with the late King George. Taught young Edward how to play polo."

"Is all that in this book?"

"Oh, no. The book's contrived from whole cloth. All very glamorous, you know, the gaiety and joie de vivre of spying."

"Of course," said Hitchcock, *"pour le sport."*

"So Madeleine Lockwood is to receive you! Well, what do you know! She's such a recluse!"

"Is she? Then she's not friendly with your cousin Phoebe?"

Miss Farquhar leaned forward again. "Actually, Phoebe is one of the few villagers she permits to cross her threshold. Well, she does need someone to shop and run errands. And Phoebe's not much trouble, as she's a bit light in the head."

"And quick on her feet."

"She gets around quite nimbly for a woman her age. She's almost seventy. So's Madeleine, as a matter of fact."

Hitchcock's eyebrows were raised a scintilla. "That would place Miss Lockwood in her fifties when she was spying for us during the war."

"She wasn't spying for us. She was spying for *them*."

"The Germans? Well, I'll be blowed! How'd she keep from being condemned to the firing squad?"

"Him and his connections!"

"Theirs must have been a rather late-in-life love affair."

"Does love respect timetables?" asked Miss Farquhar quaintly.

"I suppose it doesn't." Hitchcock resisted the urge to pinch her cheek.

Hitchcock looked again at the photograph of Madeleine Lockwood. "She doesn't look fifty in this photo."

"Why should she? That photo was taken forty years ago, when she was cavorting in the halls."

"Hmmm. I wonder." Hitchcock had lost all interest in breakfast. Nancy Adair was tapping a finger impatiently on the tabletop, while trying to summon up the courage to light a cigarette.

"Yes?" said Miss Farquhar.

"I was wondering if you could help us."

"More tea?"

"No, thank you. Miss Adair and I . . ." He heard an intake of breath. It came from Nancy Adair.

"Who's Miss Adair?" asked Miss Farquhar.

"That's my professional name," said Nancy swiftly. "In private life I'm Mrs. Jennings, but I write under the name Nancy Adair."

"Oh, of course! So many writers use pseudonyms." She turned to Hitchcock. "You were wondering if I could help you? Do you need directions to Medwin?"

"We need an introduction to Miss Lockwood."

"I thought she was expecting you!"

"She isn't. She doesn't even know we exist." Hitchcock spoke rapidly, hoping to assuage the little lady's sudden look of dismay. "It's like this. Nancy and I are collaborating on a book about espionage, and we're especially researching little-known spies. You know, those who didn't make headlines or met tragic demises, such as our Miss Lockwood." He hoped she'd be softened by his proprietorial attitude toward Madeleine Lockwood. "You probably don't know, but there are people who have heard of her and consider her a minor legend, such as my German acquaintance whose name you heard me mention a few minutes ago. Isn't that so, dear?" Nancy managed a smile as she thought the hell with it and lit a cigarette. "So, my dear, generous Miss Farquhar, that is what finds us on the road to Medwin and here enjoying your generous hospitality."

"You'd like me to phone Phoebe and ask her to intercede with Miss Lockwood?"

"Is it too much to ask?"

"Not at all. From what I've heard from Phoebe about Madeleine's monstrous ego, she might be more than delighted to be tempted back into the limelight."

"Mind you, Miss Farquhar, we're not offering her a tour. We'd just like to spend some time with her and interview her. I suppose it's too early to phone cousin Phoebe?"

"Not at all. She's up with the birds. I'll be right back."

When Miss Farquhar left the room, Hitchcock said to Nancy Adair, "Wasn't this a most fortunate stroke of luck?"

"Most fortuitous."

"You don't sound terribly enthusiastic."

"I'm just anxious to get on with the program."

"May I remind you, young lady, that this is *my* show. You foisted yourself upon me in a supporting role. To take it a bit further, I'm the director here and I call the shots."

"Of course, *Mr*. Director."

"And sarcasm is uncalled for."

"I'm sorry. Forgive me. I slept very badly."

"So did I."

"Like hell you did."

Miss Farquhar returned. "Phoebe will try to arrange it!"

"That was quick!" exclaimed Hitchcock.

"Why waste time when it is so cruelly evanescent?" She gave them directions to Cousin Phoebe's house in Allerton, and Hitchcock was effusive in his gratitude for Miss Farquhar's help. She saw them out to their car and as they drove off waved them good-bye with a lace-trimmed blue handkerchief she had stashed in her meager bosom. Then she went back into the house, marched directly to the library where there was an extension of the front-desk telephone, and put through a call to a number in London.

Hitchcock was reciting aloud, "Phoebe Allerton, 22 Hollyhock Lane, turn right at the petrol station as one enters Medwin. How long do you think it will take us to get to Medwin?"

"I should think within a hour, if we're lucky. But lorries are beginning to appear on the road, and we just might get stuck in traffic outside Brighton."

"Nancy?"

"Yes?"

"Have you met Miss Farquhar before?"

Nancy started to stammer and then corrected herself. "What made you think that?"

"They way you suddenly went silent at breakfast. Up till then, there'd been no shutting you up."

"I told you. I was tired. It takes me a long time to get going in the morning."

"It took you a long time to settle on a place for bed and breakfast last night."

"Mr. Hitchcock," said Nancy evenly, "you've been involved in too many spy stories. Now settle back and relax."

He settled back, but he didn't relax. His mind was racing and probing and examining and sifting fact after fact after fact. Supposition and possibility ran hand in hand, and suspicion had triggered a red light of caution in his mind. Somehow, there had to be a way of losing Miss Nancy Adair.

*　　*　　*

"I don't like that. I don't like that one bit." Sir Arthur Willing was wearing a suit of Irish tweed that bagged at the knees and the elbows. He thought the circles under Basil Cole's eyes were unbecoming, and he wished Nigel Pack would stop jiggling with his left leg the right leg he'd crossed over it. Detective Superintendent Jennings was about to take the floor but decided politically to wait until Sir Arthur was finished expressing his displeasure at the news he'd recently received and shared with them. "What do we know about this woman called Nancy Adair? Very little, I gather."

"Very little indeed," said Nigel Pack. "We've had a tracer on her after finding out she'd been in the village the night Mueller was murdered at Hitchcock's cottage. She has no telephone, no address, and of course no background."

"Meaning, in other words, she wasn't born, she was created." Sir Arthur exhaled. "I don't like this one bit. Anyway, very astute of dear Miss Farquhar to have phoned us once she recognized Hitchcock from photos she's seen of him and wondered why he was traveling incognito to a visit a former spy." He took a breath and then continued, "And with a blonde chit who looked nothing like pictures she'd seen of Mrs. Hitchcock. Deucedly clever of the old darling. Arrange to send her something, will you, Basil? Chocolates or some books. I'd suggest cash, but I remember her pride, though it did goeth before her fall. Too bad we had to drop her." He addressed Jennings. "By the way, the woman signed them in as Mr. and Mrs. Jennings."

Jennings chuckled and scratched an ear. "That's nice to know. At least we know she's aware of my identity. Now how would she know I was the detective assigned to the case? I suppose we have an informant at the Yard. . . ."

177

"Or here," added Sir Arthur. "Anyway, let's hope Miss Farquhar doesn't suffer a similar fate as our bogus Lemuel Peach. Hitchcock has been leaving only corpses in his wake. Sad that we couldn't have foreseen that possibility. What's troubling you Basil?"

"Miss Farquhar."

"Why she was dropped? She couldn't keep a secret."

"How Hitchcock and this blonde woman just happened to choose her place to spend the night."

"I should suggest, dear Basil, that the answer would lie somewhere with this pseudonymous Miss Nancy Adair, inasmuch as I doubt Hitchcock's ever heard of our Miss Farquhar before last night. Now then, Mr. Jennings. You're looking anxious to get on with it."

"I am. There's a lot on my plate and I'd like to get to it." He shifted in his seat as he referred to his notebook. "We've identified the impostor of Lemuel Peach."

"Ah! What a nice way to start the day," said Sir Arthur.

"His real name is Nicholas Haver, and he was born in Munich. He has visited this country before on two occasions, and on both occasions was apprehended and deported for suspicions of espionage. I emphasize suspicions, as nothing could be proved, but the authorities deemed it expedient to kick him the hell out."

"And unfortunately for him, he bounced back a third time." Sir Arthur clucked his tongue. "How do these people keep slipping back in after they've been booted out? They're so awfully good at that sort of thing. Every time one of ours gets caught, we have to work out elaborate exchanges to gain their freedom or else arrange to fix pensions for their widows."

"May I continue, Sir Arthur?" Jennings was beyond disguising his impatience. Sir Arthur nodded his head, wondering why Basil Cole was still looking distrait. "Haver was a musician by profession. In fact, he was a violinist in a trio at the Emelka Studios in Munich when the pianist of that trio was Rudolf Wagner."

"How marvelous!" exclaimed Nigel Pack. "Well, that should tidy that up." At the mention of "tidy," Basil shot Nigel a look.

"It doesn't tidy anything up," said Jennings, "because if he had murdered Wagner, the other violinist would have seen him. As it was proved, both musicians' hands were busy with violin and bow. Also, there's no record of Haver's espionage activities until two years ago, which means he's fairly new at it."

"How'd he get to the King's Cross Church?"

"Through the caretaker, who's done a flit."

"You think he's one of them, too?" asked Sir Arthur.

"I don't think so. He's had the job for years and probably found Haver's offer of a sop irresistible."

"Anything about when Haver joined the Nazis?"

"Some two or three years ago. Recruited by some woman. I've little more there. At any rate, Haver was part of the chain set up here to transfer information."

"Now how do you suppose Fredrick Regner knew all that? It's there in his manuscript, so he had to know."

"We know Regner's had access to many secret documents, which is why he had to flee Germany. They'll kill him if they catch him."

"What else have you got?"

"Hans Meyer continues at large. We can't get a thing on him."

"Well, he's bound to surface sooner or later," said Sir

179

Arthur grouchily. "They always surface sooner or later. Is that all, Mr. Jennings?"

"That's all this morning. sir. And if there's nothing else from you, I'd like to return to the Yard."

"No, and thank you very much. I think we're progressing nicely. Basil, what the hell is bothering you *now*?"

"If I could have a private word with you, Sir Arthur," said Basil as the other two rose to leave.

"About what?" snapped Sir Arthur.

Basil Cole drew himself up bravely. "It's about tidiness, sir."

"Tidiness?"

"Tidiness."

Twelve

Phoebe Allerton was aptly named. She twittered like a bird. Her hands fluttered when she spoke, and her eyes were as big as an owl's, if not especially reflecting wisdom. Her charming cottage at 22 Hollyhock Lane in the very modest little village of Medwin dated back to the early sixteen hundreds and, during the nineteenth century, Miss Allerton told them, had been the scene of a series of brutal murders.

"They found six bodies under these very floorboards," said Phoebe Allerton. Hitchcock didn't believe one word. They were seated in the sitting room, where the tables were stacked with piles of murder mysteries. Miss Allerton was probably a feminist, as she seemed to favor women authors. Hitchcock saw books by Agatha Christie and Dorothy Sayers and Ngaio Marsh and Mary Roberts Rinehart and Mignon Eberhart but not the work of a single man.

"And what were the murders known as?" Hitchcock decided to jolly her along until she made up her mind to take them to meet Madeleine Lockwood. They'd been with her for almost half an hour, having located the cottage without a problem and succumbing to her offer of lemonade and her own special chocolate biscuits because Hitchcock recognized the elderly woman's hunger for companionship, however brief.

"Why, they were known as the Hollyhock Cottage Murders! Haven't you heard of them?" She was refilling their glasses with lukewarm lemonade and Nancy Adair was trying to catch Hitchcock's eye to have him make the old lady get on with it.

"I'm afraid I haven't. Has anyone written about them?"

"*I* am." Despite her years she leapt from her chair with the grace of a prima ballerina escaping the lecherous advances of a Fokine faun and scurried to a desk at the opposite end of the long, narrow room. She grasped a thick loose-leaf book and brought it to Hitchcock. Then she stood back with hands clasped in front of her, her face warm with anticipation and possibly expecting applause as Hitchcock opened the book to the first page.

He read the title aloud for Nancy Adair's benefit: "*Blood and Gore*" She'd caught his eye and he got her message, but there was little way of relaying to her that Miss Allerton would have to be humored until she was ready to move on their behalf. He said to the old lady, "The title's a winner."

"You *do* like it!" Her voice was piccolo-tweety.

"Adore it. How long have you been writing this?"

"Almost forty years."

"I shall look forward to reading it."

"Couldn't you read some of it now? I'd value your opinion." The hands were fluttering and her feet were shuffling and Hitchcock feared she might be about to take off in flight.

"I'm afraid there isn't time, Miss Allerton. You see, it's terribly important we meet with Madeleine Lockwood."

Miss Allerton retrieved her book and held it tightly to her almost nonexistent bosom. "*Her* book's lousy. Had to publish it herself. Limited edition. Got *him* to pay for it." *Him,* thought Hitchcock, the lover cashiered out of the army? "It's all fantasy." She took her book back to the desk.

Nancy Adair decided to take matters into her own hands. "Does Miss Lockwood live nearby?"

Miss Allerton sat and arranged her skirt, then she spoke. "She lives just across the road. The big house with the thatched roof. You may have noticed it when you parked your car. It's very imposing from the outside. *He* bought it for her fifteen years ago or so. Inside it's a mess. You'll see for yourself. She's a mess too. Sometimes it seems as though her mind is wandering, but I know it's mostly playacting. She's an incredibly shrewd person. But when it seems her mind is wandering, well, you'll just have to be patient and steer her back to whatever track you want her on. She used to be in the theater." She spoke directly to Hitchcock. "She takes direction well."

She knows who I am! Hitchcock thought. Aloud, he said, "We're here to interview her for our book on espionage."

Miss Allerton's voice went limp. "You're writing a book too? Is there anyone who *isn't* writing a book?" She did little to masquerade her exasperation. "A book on espionage? Are you spies *too?*"

"Good heavens, no," said Hitchcock, "we're just researching a book about them."

"Filthy profession, that. It's what brought Jane down."

"Jane who?" asked Hitchcock.

"She sent you here! Jane Farquhar!"

Hitchcock's mouth was suddenly dry. He had a quick look at Nancy Adair, who had suddenly busied herself with nibbling at a biscuit and avoided his eyes. Hitchcock had a sip of his awful lemonade and then asked, "Jane Farquhar was a spy?"

"She wasn't a terribly good one. She blabbed all over the place. Began when she was a nurse abroad during the war. Prisoner-of-war camp. She was the head sister there. Well, some of those prisoners had been pretty highly placed in the German hierarchy and they just talked and talked to our Jane. Jane, of course, took her information to the authorities and the next thing you know, she's got two professions. Nursing and spying. She didn't last very long." With a mischievous expression, she then asked the two of them, "What did you say your name was?"

"Jennings, Mr. and Mrs. Jennings," replied Hitchcock. He had croaked the reply, his throat feeling constricted, as though there were a noose slowly tightening around his neck.

Phoebe Allerton said nothing during the next few uncomfortable moments, and then leaned forward. "Madeleine might not be at her best today."

"I assure you we'll be very gentle and circumspect," said Hitchcock.

"We had a circus pitched nearby all day yesterday." The tips of Hitchcock's fingers were tingling. "They gave a performance in the afternoon. Not much of an attendance. But, amazingly enough, Madeleine swathed herself in veils and

184

we went to see them. Somehow we got separated, and when I found Madeleine again, I could see she had been upset by something. Probably by the freaks, because I found her coming out of their tent, and it's a good thing too I found her then because she was feeling faint. I got her into my car and brought her home. She didn't say a word on the way back, but she was upset. Shut herself up in the house and hasn't even been out in the garden to my knowledge. Said she hadn't when I phoned her this morning and asked if she'd see you two as a special favor to Cousin Jane."

"She knows Cousin Jane, of course," said Hitchcock.

"Oh, yes. On cold winter nights they used to get together when Jane came to visit me and compare betrayals. Jane doesn't visit so much anymore now that she's gone into trade, so to speak."

Nancy Adair spoke again. "When do you suppose we can meet Miss Lockwood? We're a bit pressed for time."

"Young woman," said Phoebe Allerton, sharply revealing a new side of herself usually reserved for tradespeople, "impatience is not a virtue." She stood up. "We can go now. I saw Madeleine at her window peeping out at us when you arrived, so she knows you're here. I've given her enough time to prepare herself." She quickly amended that to "compose herself." She led the way outside with tiny darting movements, and Hitchcock briefly feared she might take wing and the introduction to Madeleine Lockwood would be lost to them forever. But no, she marched them out of her gate and across the road to the imposing house with the thatched roof. They walked in silence.

Of course she knows who I am, thought Hitchcock. Jane Farquhar, being the worldly one, must have recognized me. Jane Farquhar, spy, of all ridiculous casting. Certainly Miss Allerton knows who I am . . . that remark about Lockwood taking direction. But none of this was in Regner's scenario. But then, that piece of work was terribly sketchy at best, with holes, as Alma, *my darling Alma*, had reminded him, big enough to drive hearses through. Holes, which to fill in it was patently up to Hitchcock. Well, they were being filled in, all right.

His eyes darted to Nancy Adair, who walked ahead of him. Who are you *really*, Miss Adair? You led us to Jane Farquhar when there were at least half a dozen equally as inviting bed and breakfast establishments that you chose to pass over. That look on your face when Miss Allerton told us about the circus, I didn't miss that. I saw you bite your lower lip and I heard you clear your throat, and if you only had a glimpse of the scenario, which gave you the location of the church in King's Cross, why should the mention of the circus cause such unrest?

The circus broke camp and departed yesterday. They can't be far from here. Circuses travel slowly, especially itinerant ones. Cotton candy and popcorn and bangers on a roll. A locked wrought-iron gate kept civilization at bay from Madeleine Lockwood. Miss Allerton had found a large key in her handbag that unlocked the gate. She motioned them inside and then relocked it. They followed her up a short path to the front door, and again Miss Allerton found the proper key. She unlocked the door and motioned them in, then shut the door and said, "Wait here."

The hallway in which they waited faced a grand, winding staircase that led to the three upper floors. The furnishings, Hitchcock decided, were early Miss Havisham, straight out of *Great Expectations*. He looked at the ceiling expecting to see cobwebs and was not disappointed. Nancy Adair asked Hitchcock if he found the musty odor of old age and decay less offensive than that of cigarette smoke, but Hitchcock ignored the question. He was watching Phoebe Allerton ascending the impressive staircase in search of their hostess. Portraits hung along the staircase, and Hitchcock moved closer for a better look in the dim light. Nancy Adair realized she was shivering in this foreboding atmosphere and looked for somewhere to sit, but there were no accommodations.

"These things must be worth a bloody fortune," said Hitchcock. One of the portraits was a John Singer Sargent. Another was by Mary Cassatt. The Whistler had to be worth a pretty penny too.

"How nice! You like my gallery!"

Startled by the sudden sound of a strange voice, Hitchcock turned to the head of the staircase, and there stood an apparition that had to be Madeleine Lockwood. Phoebe Allerton stood a few feet behind her, clutching her handbag tightly.

"Your gallery is most impressive," said Hitchcock, as Nancy Adair came up behind him for a better look at the apparition.

Madeleine Lockwood, they knew, had once been a great beauty. Time had not been kind, but she had obviously made Spartan efforts to defeat time at its dirty work. Her face was heavily rouged, lipsticked, and mascara'd. Piled atop her head was a ratty red wig of a color to defy the sunrise. From her ears dangled a pair of heavy emerald earrings. Around her neck she wore a black choker, an obvious camouflage for the wrinkles. There was no way to camouflage her wattles. She wore a heavily brocaded hostess gown more suitable to an evening party forty years ago. A pearl necklace and several pins and brooches adorned her. Her hands were covered in black lace gloves and she was wielding a feathered fan. If she'd appeared at the circus in this getup yesterday, thought Hitchcock, she must have caused one hell of a sensation. She was descending the staircase slowly, followed by Phoebe Allerton. Miss Lockwood paused at each portrait and identified the subject as she fanned herself lightly.

"This is Le Comte du Ferrante. He was beheaded in 1912 for disclosing state secrets to the Croatians. A very poor businessman. The Croatians never paid well." She came down a few more steps and then paused. "This is Dimitri Razumov, purported to be one of Rasputin's lovers. At the time of the Russian Revolution, he tried to sell out the new government to the Americans, but they weren't interested. Dimitri faced a firing squad, but without a blindfold, bless him. And here we have Adriana Borgesi, one of the unsung heroines of espionage. She escaped to Switzerland from Italy when Il Duce came to power, and he sent a hit squad to track her down and assassinate her. But she was too smart for them. Friends spirited her out of Switzerland into Holland, where a tramp steamer took her to Canada." She walked down the stairs slowly. "From Canada she went to Hollywood. I am told she is doing quite well playing bits and extras in the movies." She laughed a dry little laugh. "Knowing Adriana, she's probably peddling secrets from studio to studio. She was a very wicked little minx." Miss Lockwood held a gloved hand out to Hitchcock. Entering into the spirit of her game, Hitchcock kissed her hand lightly. She said, "I can always tell class, Mr. Jennings." She looked at Nancy Adair who thought she caught a whimsical look in the woman's eyes and wondered why it was there. "How nice to meet you, Mrs. Jennings."

"How kind of you to receive us," said Nancy Adair, while Hitchcock awarded her full marks for a charming display of civility.

Madeleine Lockwood led the way into a drawing room.

The windows were heavily draped, and at Miss Lockwood's command, Phoebe Allerton fluttered about letting in daylight. Here again they were in the midst of an antiquarian monstrosity, one that Hitchcock would relish describing to Alma then they were reunited. Miss Lockwood indicated a sofa for them to sit on while she sat opposite them in a throne chair that Hitchcock suspected was either Adam or Hepplewhite. She imperiously exiled Phoebe Allerton to the kitchen to prepare tea, and the old woman slunk out of the room with her shoulders slumped.

"I wasn't going to see you," said Miss Lockwood in a voice so totally unmelodic, Hitchcock couldn't much imagine her enchanting an audience in a music hall.

"Thank you for changing your mind," said Hitchcock.

"It was Phoebe who was most persuasive. You're supposedly writing a book about espionage." She smiled, baring her false teeth. "Why are you really here?"

Hitchcock plunged in. He told her rapidly and concisely about Regner's manuscript. It was obvious she too knew Hitchcock's true identity, and he could see the only way to gain her cooperation was to level with her. When he finished, she struck a pose, her chin resting in her open palm.

She finally spoke. "So I too am a character in this rather strange chronicle." She sighed a very weary sigh. "I show up in some of the strangest places. I don't recall ever meeting any Fredrick Regner, though God knows I've encountered many a kraut spy in my day, as I'm sure you know."

"Yes. Jane Farquhar told us a bit about you."

"That fat mouth." She sighed again. "Spying isn't what it used to be. In the good old days we had charisma and ambience. Even a fat-rumped pig like Mata Hari had a soupçon of finesse. I mean when you were betrayed by that wench, it was classy, if you know what I mean. By the way, we can drop the charade of Jennings, right? You *are* Alfred Hitchcock, *n'est ce pas?*"

"I am indeed, and I trust, on this occasion, you will keep my secret."

"You've no problem with me. But Farquhar, she'd warn Eskimos about impending heat waves. Can you imagine the damn fool spent months in that place they had Nijinsky incarcerated trying to persuade him to become a spy and train in coding messages? She had this idea messages could be choreographed and danced all over the place." Hitchcock didn't think it was that bad an idea at all and filed it away for future consideration. She turned to Nancy Adair and asked sharply, "Who are you? You're not his wife. Who are you?"

At first taken by surprise by the sudden attack, Nancy quickly recovered and said, "I'm Nancy Adair. I'm a reporter, a free-lance reporter. I'm helping Mr. Hitchcock."

"I'd like you to help Phoebe in the kitchen."

"But you see I'm—"

"My dear Miss Adair." Miss Lockwood had sliced into Nancy Adair's attempt at an explanation like a fanatical vivisectionist. "I know Phoebe can use help. Phoebe, as I'm sure you've been told, can be very helpful to others, as she is to me. But on her own, she is frequently known to need help. I'm sure you've heard the clatter coming from the kitchen." Hitchcock had heard nothing, assuming the kitchen, like the kitchens in all stately homes such as this one, was somewhere well to the back of the house. "Phoebe needs help. Through that door there, down the hall, turn right at the Tintoretto, and there's the kitchen." Nancy Adair stared at the woman, and Hitchcock knew that in a battle of wills, Miss Lockwood would prevail. He also knew he'd get nothing from the old spy until Nancy was out of the room. It was quite obvious the old lady either disliked or distrusted Nancy. Miss Lockwood's eyes pierced into Nancy Adair's like some infernal rays, and Nancy suddenly jumped to her feet and left the room. Hitchcock started to say something, but Miss Lockwood waved him quiet with a gesture, then she tiptoed stealthily to the door through which Nancy had exited. She listened at the door and then swiftly flung it open, expecting no doubt to find Nancy Adair crouched and eavesdropping. Nancy Adair was not there. Miss Lockwood gently closed the door and returned to her throne chair. "Who is she?" she asked.

"My dear, what she's told you is what she's told me." Hitchcock related the events of the previous two days and Miss Lockwood struck the pose again, chin propped up by the palm of her hand.

"There's something about her I neither like nor trust. I'm very good at sizing up women; it was a woman who betrayed Rufus and me. I'd warned Rufus about her, but oh, no, not Rufus, no woman would betray him, certainly not his faithful and loyal wife. Not Miranda. *Medusa!*" she spat the name. "Medusa with a hairdo straight out of a snake pit. Can you believe it, she's with him still, while I linger here, alone, unwanted, unnecessary . . . a frozen asset," she added with a pitiful dry sob. She fanned herself for a while and then said, "I think it must be quite obvious to you by now that this Fredrick Regner is himself a secret operator."

"Quite obvious. But I'm rather flattered he chose me for his outlet, albeit putting my poor Alma in danger."

"I saw your film *The Thirty-Nine Steps*." She sounded as though she hadn't much liked it.

"I had no idea you occasionally broke this sequestration to catch a movie."

"Yesterday I went to the circus, but we'll come back to

191

that later. I'll tell you why I stole into the village to see your movie. It was Rufus phoning and telling me to."

Good for Rufus, thought Hitchcock. He said, "You keep in touch with Rufus?"

"Of course we're in touch. Why do you think we're in Regner's scenario? Let's go back to your film. It said it was based on the John Buchan book, but it bore little relationship to it other than the fact there was a spy ring at the center of the story. Well, let me tell you what disturbed Rufus about your movie and made him urge me to see it. In your film, your villain is missing a part of the little finger of his left hand." She leaned forward. "Did you know then that Rufus is also missing a part of his little finger?"

Hitchcock was genuinely surprised. "I've never heard of your Rufus until this morning, when Miss Farquhar mentioned him, but she didn't say a name then. *Now* I know his name is Rufus."

"I was madly in love with Rufus. I still am. I owe all this"—she indicated her surroundings—"to Rufus."

"He decorated?"

"Of course not!" Then she smiled. "I see you have a wicked sense of humor." She eyed him from head to foot, and Hitchcock began to wonder if she was about to attempt to seduce him. "You're not bad-looking, you know. I used to be partial to fat men. Rufus was once fat, but with him it was all muscle. Time, I'm told, has taken its toll. I haven't seen him for years, although we're in constant touch. I've been told he's now quite gaunt and quite thin."

"Who is Rufus?" asked Hitchcock.

"Why, he's Sir Rufus Derwent. How many Rufuses have you heard of? You're a cinema man, you research true stories, don't you? Don't you remember the Rufus Derwent scandal?"

Hitchcock clapped a hand to his head. "Of course! It was 1920, wasn't it?"

"Miranda betrayed us! We were coining a fortune selling secrets abroad, but *she*, the emaciated jealous bitch, had to throw a spanner into the works! My poor darling was court-martialed from the army, and only the tacit intervention of Buckingham Palace rescued the two of us from hanging. Now we're both exiles in our own country, I here in Medwin, he and Medusa in Harborshire!"

Harborshire. Hitchcock recalled his notes. *The answer might lie in Harborshire.* "Where in Harborshire is he to be found?"

She smiled enigmatically. "Are you ready for this? His home is situated on a cliff overlooking the Channel. It can be reached from the road below by a long set of stairs leading upward to the house." She folded her hands in her lap while still clasping the feather fan between them. "There are exactly thirty-nine steps leading up to the house." Hitchcock's mouth was open. "The house is called The Thirty-Nine Steps. Now how's *that* for coincidence!"

"Miss Lockwood," said Hitchcock, "it boggles the mind."

"It certainly boggled Rufus when he saw your film. To be perfectly fair about it, Rufus suspected it was Buchan, the author of the book, who would have had this information. I told him he should sue, what with the steps and the missing pinky, but he said God no, it would mean dredging up the scandal again and fresh publicity and—oh, well, here we are."

Here we are, but where are we? wondered Hitchcock. "Miss Allerton says something happened at the circus yesterday to disturb you. Was it something you're willing to discuss?"

"I had my fortune told by an old gypsy woman." She lifted her head proudly and bravely told him. "She said I would die soon."

"What an awful thing to predict to a person!" Hitchcock was truly indignant.

"She saw it in my palm. I rarely remove my gloves, but she was terribly convincing. I don't mind. Dying doesn't frighten me. Life's been much more frightening. It still is." She lowered her voice almost to a whisper. "Life is dangerous for people like you and me, Alfred Hitchcock. Regner's manuscript, the information you say you carry in your head, is very dangerous and let me tell you why."

"I'm grateful for all favors," said Hitchcock as she motioned him closer to him. He left the settee and found a stool which he placed at her feet and sat on it.

"You're doing their work for them. They're very clever that way."

"What do you mean?"

"They're searching for a double agent."

"Surely someone must know his identity. How would he be paid off?"

"Don't be thick, Mr. Hitchcock. Through secret bank accounts in strange little countries and exotic islands; they're all over the place. Through trusted intermediaries. You have been sent on this journey through the device of the Regner scenario in hopes that along the way someone will slip and inadvertently provide you with the clue that will lead you to the quarry. He did fine for both the Germans and the British until they realized he was betraying them to each other; now he's an even greater danger. I suspect he's more of a danger to the Nazis than he is to us because they have terrible plans for the future, plans too ugly and too hideous to contemplate without seeking the solace of a church to pray in. And here

194

you are, Mr. Hitchcock, here you are, assigned to draw in a face where only a blank exists. You're not doing too badly, you know. I'm sure I'm being a great help."

"You're absolutely wonderful."

"Really?" She was fingering her pearls. "I don't suppose it would be too ridiculous to consider making a return. Not to the musical stage, music halls barely exist. But since films have been talking, I notice there seems to be a dearth of good actresses of my age and stature—what few films I've seen, that is. What do you think, Mr. Hitchcock, that is, if I survive that gypsy's prediction?"

"I don't think it's beyond consideration," said Hitchcock affably. "There's a part in my next film, *The Lady Vanishes* . . ."

"I hope that's not prophetic."

". . . which calls for a little old lady who just happens to be a spy."

"Really? Wouldn't that be typecasting?"

"I always favor types. They add such flavor to my ridiculous plots and take the audience's mind off the incongruities. I call them my MacGuffins." She questioned the MacGuffin and he explained it.

"How very clever." She had a faraway look and then said, "In truth, so many of us in this field are MacGuffins."

Hitchcock got back to the business at hand. "This gypsy woman at the circus. Is she part of the network? Is she a spy?"

"The circus is called the Pechter Circus. It's continental, and for continental you can read German, although the staff is somewhat serendipitous. There are French and Greek and smattering of Italian and Spanish performers." She paused. "They were a bit upset yesterday. They were missing their knife thrower." Hitchcock blanched. "He'd gone to London a few days earlier on an errand and his return was overdue." Hitchcock reminded her of the bread knife thrown at him in the basement of the church in King's Cross. "Well, you most certainly had a fortuitously narrow escape if that was him. You'll find the circus today at Lingate, which is twenty miles up the Channel coast en route to Harborshire."

"Isn't there a naval installation there? I seem to recall doing a reconnoiter there as a possible location for *Secret Agent*, but there was some problem gaining government clearance."

She smiled the enigmatic smile again. "You're learning, Mr. Hitchcock, you're learning. They've been playing the coastal cities for weeks, especially those where there are installations."

"You've been wonderfully helpful. I didn't expect this. Dare I ask why?" Hitchcock held her hand, and she squeezed his warmly in return.

"I'm an old lady. Rufus is an old man. Our time is almost past, finished. We're both so unhappy. We both wish to put paid to all this, but we're trapped. Yes, Mr. Hitchcock, we're still spying. Once it gets in the blood, it's like most social diseases, incurable. But please, don't worry about me. Gypsy woman or no gypsy woman, whatever will be will be; *que sera*, right?"

"I must remember that," said Hitchcock, "*que sera*, whatever will be will be. They're awfully slow with the tea."

"I planned that with Phoebe upstairs, in case I decided not to trust your blond self-styled accomplice. And I don't trust her. I must caution you, Mr. Hitchcock, there's something unreal about her."

"I don't much like her myself, but I'm stuck with her. I

196

can't think of a way to be shot of her. Although I must say, having her chauffeuring me about has been rather handy."

Miss Lockwood whispered in his ear, "Chauffeurs have been known to misdirect. I'm sure I can trust you to do the misdirecting when she begins questioning you as to what you managed to learn from me."

"You can trust me, my dear Madeleine Lockwood," said Hitchcock with a twinkle, "I told you I'm a master at creating MacGuffins."

The door behind them opened, and Phoebe Allerton entered wheeling the tea cart, followed by Nancy Adair, whose face foreshadowed a tempest. "Tea!" twittered Miss Allerton.

Miss Lockwood boomed, "What kept you?"

Thirteen

Sir Arthur Willing was a stickler for continuity. Digression disturbed him, as did any other form of wasting time. As a result, he was able to understand Basil Cole's passion for tidiness. Their conference after the departure of Detective Superintendent Jennings and Nigel Pack had proved satisfying and gratifying to both parties, like a meeting of potential lovers who'd finally made it into bed and discovered the affair could probably work. It amazed Sir Arthur that in the twelve or more years he'd been associated with Nigel and Basil, they'd never socialized. They'd never gone to the theater or to a movie or to a cricket match or breakfasted or lunched or supped unless it was in the line of duty. Sir Arthur had been to dine with the Packs and found the wife, Violet, a bit of a wet noodle, but even then, the evening's conversation was monopolized by talk of the threat of the Bolsheviks and the suspicion that Colonel DeBasil's Monte Carlo Ballet was a hotbed of spies. (Their investigation proved it to be a hotbed of second-rate dancers.)

Basil Cole's fifteen-minute discourse on tidiness, equally logical and impassioned, had most impressed Sir Arthur. He had often dwelt on what there might lie in Basil's life other than British Intelligence and was delighted at last to be presented with a clue: tidiness.

"You're quite right, Basil. There are too many strings left untied, but it's that kind of case. We're not quite sure where we're going, so we can't gather in the threads until we're sure they're ready to be woven into the pattern. A bit florid all this, but it's the best way I can explain it. Am I getting across to you?"

"Oh, quite," said Basil, adding vaguely, "I suppose."

"I thought it was understood that what we're searching for is a spy who is serving two masters, us and them, whose identity is certainly unknown to us and now I'm quite certain is also unknown to them."

"The man must be a genius to be able to work both sides against each other without revealing his identity." Basil was impressed with this anonymous adversary who was obviously a sporting man.

"It's not the first case of its kind. There were others, there probably are others, and the Lord knows there will be others. They're simply brilliant craftsmen in espionage with this unique ability to create networks to serve them. Fredrick Regner, in his own way, was brilliant enough to come up with his theory and put it down on paper in the form of his scenario. And then, when he realized it was the sort of story that needed to be married to the Hitchcocks, he decided to go ahead with it." Sir Arthur puffed on his pipe and stared out the window at the fogless day, watching a barrow of flowers being trundled along the road, probably destined for Green Park. "Unfortunately, the idea's been leaked to the Germans, and they're equally anxious to learn the villain's identity. You see, Basil, he's getting too dangerous. He knows more than either side meant him to know. We have an idea he's about the defect to the Russians, and then we'll all be in the good old shtook."

"You mean go live in Russia forever?"

Sir Arthur regarded him quizzically. "What is forever? Who knows for sure if he'd need to cross the border? Don't you read your newspapers, young man?"

"Of course I do, sir," said Basil, refraining from elucidating that he scanned headlines, read the sports scores, occasionally looked to see what new films were opening in the West End, and, time permitting, attacked the crossword.

"Have you been reading between the lines lately?"

"I don't quite get your meaning."

"The dangerous innuendo in dispatches received from abroad, especially those from correspondents on the continent. There'll be a war, Basil, and this will be the most terrible war of all." Basil's palms were damp, and he rubbed them on his trousers. "Hitler wants the world, he's a very greedy little man. And, mark my words, he'll swallow up a large helping of it. A lot of it will be handed to him on a silver platter by the appeasers who are too stupid to understand they too lie in his path of destruction. He wants France and Poland and Czechoslovakia and the Netherlands. And he wants us."

"England? Great Britain?"

"The Commonwealth. All of it. He won't do things by halves."

"Certainly not for our cuisine."

Sir Arthur chuckled. "That's a good one. 'Not for our cuisine.' I like that. Must tell it to the boys at the club. Ah well, so much for levity. The sober fact is that he'll soon be on the march, we know that. He's watching us with the sly cunning of a cat tracking a dickey bird. When Edward abdicates, Hitler will woo him . . ."

Basil paled. "Abdicate? You know this for a fact?"

"The man's a pussy willow. No balls. He says he will do this unless he is permitted to marry Wallis Simpson and make her his queen. Can you imagine the two of them enthroned side by side?" He raged, "There's more logic and substance in Mother Goose!" He was beginning to wonder why there was no word from the person assigned to pick up Hitchcock's trail in Medwin, now made feasible thanks to Miss Farquhar's information. "There are devilish things going on in Germany right now; information has been smuggled to us at great risk. Regner knows for a fact that the Germans are constructing a network of internment camps where they mean to destroy millions of Jews. There is one already in operation at Dachau, and that's only ten miles outside of Munich. Hitler's reign of terror is underway; you can see it yourself with the refugees pouring into the country, poor buggers. What do we do with them? We're still suffering from the Depression. The economy is a disaster— and tell me, Basil, what's your impression of Violet Pack?"

The non sequitur didn't throw Basil. It was a ploy used frequently by Sir Arthur, and Basil was always on the alert for them. They tripped up Nigel Pack usually, but not Basil. "Well, she's not exactly my cup of tea, sir."

"Come to think of it, what *is* your cup of tea? You seem to lead such a circumspect life, isn't that rather tiresome?"

Basil's face reddened. "I'm afraid, sir, I'm not much interested in cups of tea. I'm devoted to the firm."

"I'm delighted for the firm." He wondered if Basil was homosexual, as he had wondered on occasion in the past, but refrained from expressing his curiosity. Basil was a good man, and good men were hard to find, as dear American Sophie Tucker had sung in her recent engagement at the Palladium. "Now what about Violet Pack?"

"Well, frankly, sir, I don't quite know what to say. She's never come up in our conversation before."

"Never had the opportunity. We so rarely get to natter on our own this way." Sir Arthur smiled warmly. "It's quite cozy. We must do it more often. It's this way. Nigel being one of my favorite people, as you well know. . . ."

"Yes, sir." Teacher's pet, Basil referred to him in private, but not with venom.

"He's been with us a bit longer than you have, and his performance has been exemplary, and continues to be. But I've been harboring the suspicion that all's not well with them. Has he said anything to you?"

"No, sir."

"Not even a hint?"

"Not a trace."

"Well, what do you talk about when you're together?"

"The firm, mostly."

"You mean at lunch and tea and over a drink, it's always shop talk?"

"It is, mostly, sir."

"How boring." He was buzzed and picked up the phone. "Yes? Put him through. Now what's going on, Herbert? Where are you? Still in Medwin?" He looked at his wristwatch. "They must be getting more from the old girl than I thought they would. You're keeping well hidden, right? Good. Can't have them recognizing you. Speak to you later." He hung up the phone and said, "Shop talk."

"Sorry about that, sir. I say, who's Herbert? That's a new one on me."

Sir Arthur leaned on the desk and removed the pipe from his mouth. "Basil, I'm afraid that's one thread that has to be left hanging untidily."

It was more of a lunch than a simple tea that Phoebe Allerton had prepared for them, and Hitchcock plunged into it with trencherman gusto. It was as though he had every intention of expanding all five feet six inches of himself to a fraction of bursting point. Miss Lockwood, declaring she had no appetite, had gone to the piano and, to Hitchcock's delight and Nancy Adair's despair, given them a concert. Her voice was reedy, unsteady, and determined. Her piano playing was haphazard at best, her left hand seeming to favor the black keys. She opened with "I Dreamt I Dwelt in Marble Halls" and then segued into "After the Ball," which brought tears to Phoebe Allerton's eyes. Hitchcock wasn't sure whether this was due to sentiment or despair. Nancy Adair had whispered to him it was time they got going, but he shushed her as he bit into a rather tasty sandwich of chopped eggs and anchovy paste. When Miss Lockwood started ragtiming, "I'll Be Down to Getcha in a Taxi, Honey . . ." Hitchcock agreed with Nancy Adair that it was time to go. Miss Lockwood arose from the piano bench and went to

Hitchcock and took his arm, guiding him and Nancy to the hallway.

"On to Lingate, then, is it?"

"Lingate?" asked Nancy Adair and Hitchcock gave her a look.

"I'll explain in the car," said Hitchcock; then he turned to Madeleine Lockwood with a warm smile. "You have been an absolute delight, Madeleine Lockwood."

"Well, of course, my dear, my voice isn't quite in a class with Jessie Matthews', but in its days, I'm sure you realize, it brought many an audience to its feet in ovation after ovation. You can well imagine why I was invited to sing before most of the crowned heads of Europe. Lily Langtry hated my guts, but then, I was young, prettier, slimmer . . ."

". . . and nosier," added Hitchcock.

Miss Lockwood tee-hee'd and swatted Hitchcock with her feather fan. "You wicked man." He kissed her cheek. "How nice! The touch of a man's lips. It's been a memory for too long. Well, now, here's the door." Phoebe Allerton held it open. "And you must be on your way." She now held Hitchcock by the hand and squeezed it gently by way of warning. "The best of luck."

"I shall be in touch with you very soon," he said, and she appreciated the sincerity in his voice. He thanked Phoebe Allerton and promised to read her manuscript of *Blood and Gore* provided she managed to complete the writing before the next solstice. The women stood in the doorway watching Hitchcock and Nancy Adair as they passed through the gate and crossed the road to their car. When the car pulled away, a black sedan pulled out of a side road and from a safe distance followed them.

"They're being tailed," said Miss Lockwood out of the

side of her mouth to Phoebe. "I hope it's one of the good guys. Oh, well, kismet is kismet, and never the twain shall meet." Phoebe followed her back to the drawing room. "And now, Miss Phoebe Allerton, what was all that crap about that book you're writing?"

"We'll be needing petrol soon," said Nancy Adair. "How far is this Lingate?"

Hitchcock was studying the map. "I'd gauge it at about thirty miles farther along the coast. It's on the way to Harborshire."

"What did the old lady tell you?"

"When?"

"When she so unsubtly exiled me to the kitchen."

"Well, actually, she asked if she might audition for me," he replied drolly.

"If that twenty minutes of caterwauling was an audition, she should have been strangled at birth."

"Don't be uncharitable. It doesn't become you." He wondered what did. Nancy Adair was hardly a scintillating companion. The exterior blonde did not quite match the interior moodiness. Hitchcock now realized what had been gnawing at him ever since he had reluctantly teamed up with the woman. The facade was not only false, it was all wrong. She was a blonde without a blonde personality. He was hard put exactly to define the blonde personality, but he would later give as an example that Sylvia Sidney, the brooding brunette he'd just directed in *Sabotage*, could never be a blonde because her personality was too dark.

"Your personality's too dark," said Hitchcock, surprised to hear the words suddenly erupting.

"What's that?" asked Nancy, bewildered.

"Your personality is dark," persevered Hitchcock, realizing there was no turning back. It wasn't the first time he'd been betrayed by his subconscious, and it certainly wouldn't be the last. "Your exterior is blonde, but your interior is dark."

"What a lot of eyewash!"

"No. What a lot of hair dye."

"So what? So I dye my hair? Who needs such a foolish conversation at a time like this?" There was that strange lilt again, that strange flow upward and then downward as she spoke, a pattern that more comfortably belonged to a continental woman.

"I know nothing about you. Where do you come from?"

"South Africa."

Like hell you do, thought Hitchcock. "Have you ever lived on the continent?" he asked, his eyes staring straight ahead through the windshield.

"Listen, Mr. Alfred Hitchcock, I'm the one who should be interviewing you. I'm the journalist, not you."

"You know so much about me. I know so little about you. I'm uncomfortable when disadvantaged. Are your parents alive?"

"I don't want to talk about my parents. I want to talk about Madeleine Lockwood. What did she tell you when you were alone with her?"

Hitchcock folded his arms, narrowed his eyes, and spoke between clenched teeth. "You'll not get a bleeding word out of me until you give me the courtesy of answering my questions."

They drove along in an uncomfortable silence. Hitchcock was angry and resolute, and Nancy Adair didn't quite know how to deal with it. She finally said, trying to sound friendly, "Petulance doesn't become you."

206

"There's a petrol station on our right," he said, "in case you haven't noticed." She pulled in, and five minutes later, after the tank's thirst had been assuaged, they were back on the road heading toward Lingate. Hitchcock asked, "Have you ever met Frederick Regner or Hans Meyer?"

She snorted. "Oh, come now. I never heard their names until yesterday. Where would I have met either of them?"

"Somewhere in the past," he added dryly, "assuming you have a past."

"I'm more concerned at the moment with the future. What are we going to do in Lingate?"

Hitchcock, to himself, admitted defeat. There was no use trying to spar with the woman. The enigma was impenetrable. "We're going to the circus." Now he looked at her, and there was no expression of childish delight on her face. "I take it you don't like circuses."

"I don't like the way you have turned against me. I thought we were friends. We made a bargain. I'm helping you in return for a story and now you tell me nothing and I feel lost and I don't like it."

"You're not lost, you're on the road to Lingate."

"Spare me your whimsy, Mr. Hitchcock; what we are involved in is serious business. Don't you realize we too might be targets for the murderer? Well, don't you?" He said nothing. "What happened to Madeleine Lockwood to make her feel faint at the circus yesterday?" He said nothing. "Didn't she tell you? Didn't she tell you anything? Why else is she in Regner's scenario?"

Hitchcock sighed. He decided to placate her somewhat. It might relieve the nagging. "An old gypsy woman at the circus told Miss Lockwood she didn't have long to live."

"Ha! You don't have to look in her palm to tell her that!

You just look at her and you know any day now she'll be dust!"

"How do you know she looked in her palm and not in a crystal ball?"

"How do you mean, how do I know? I don't know at all! I said looked in her palm because it's the first thing I thought of. What else did she tell you?"

"There's no need to shout."

"I'm sorry. I didn't realize I'd raised my voice."

"She told me their knife thrower had gone missing."

"Knife thrower! Ah! I see! You think he was the man in the basement of the church."

"Oh, indubitably."

"Did Miss Lockwood think this too?"

"Well, she didn't disagree."

"What else did you talk about?"

"The good old days."

"What good old days?"

"When spying was an honorable profession."

"You are making fun of me."

"No, I was just putting a little irony in the fire. Actually, I'm beginning to realize a subtle point in which I've failed in my spy films."

"Oh, yes? And what is that?"

"My spies were all suave and ladies and gentlemen. No such thing. Spies are very foolish people."

"That's what *you* think. Shame on you. Look how clever they're being with you."

"That's because it's been written for them. They're playing parts like my actors. No, spies are the failures of the species. They turn to the profession of betrayal because they're totally incapable of gainful recognition. Look at foolish Miss Lockwood. She was obviously a mess as a professional singer and was probably a very woeful child. So she was easily seduced by the glamour of espionage—"

"And the financial gain," interposed Nancy.

"Hers is from the lover, my dear, and not gained by professional acumen."

"And what about this lover? Who was he?"

"I don't know." It was so easy to lie to her, and Hitchcock reveled in the deception. What an improvement his viewpoint of spies and spying would be in *The Lady Vanishes*, he thought with satisfaction. Alma would be so pleased. Alma. He must get to a telephone, reach Jennings. He had to know what progress there was in the search for Alma. Maybe she'd been found; the thought consoled him a bit. Maybe all was well. Maybe, a word he usually loathed and rarely used.

Sir Arthur Willing's man at the wheel of the black sedan felt relieved. When they'd pulled into the petrol station, the sudden swerve had taken him unawares and he cursed himself for that. When alone on an assignment his mind tended to wander, and that was bad, but no professional operator is perfect, that's why so many are apprehended. Surprised by the sudden swerve, he was forced to continue driving, leaving them behind him, but with luck, he found a shoulder in the road where he could park and ponder his road map until they appeared again. For a moment, he dwelt with a sinking feeling on the thought they might have reversed and gone back and he lost them. When after five minutes they hadn't appeared, he entertained the option of turning back in search of them. But the gods were good. Nancy and Hitchcock drove past, and in the brief glimpse he caught of them over the rim of the road map which he had positioned to mask his face, he saw what looked like a coolness between them.

That bitch. That loathsome bitch. He put the car into gear and resumed the pursuit. How he loathed Nancy Adair.

He hummed, *La-la-la-la . . . la-la-la . . .*

Fourteen

At lunch, which they frequently took together, Basil Cole directed his attention from his shepherd's pie to Nigel Pack, who was picking with disinterest at a soggy salad. "I say, Nigel, is there something troubling you?"

"Hmmm? What? Oh, troubling me? No more than usual. What took place at your confrontation with the old man?" Then he added quickly, "Of course, if it was a private matter . . ."

"Well, actually"—he wished there were less slimy grease oozing out of his food—"we discussed tidiness." He elucidated for Nigel, who looked as though he thought he was being subjected to a leg pull, and when his discourse was over, Nigel agreed with him about the proliferation of loose ends.

"He let anything drop that I should know about?"

"Like what?"

"Like about this case. Hitchcock."

"Oh, well, actually, his trail's been picked up. Forgive me, old chap, meant to tell you earlier, but it slipped my mind. He and the girl were in Medwin at the Lockwood person's place. Nigel?"

"Yes?" Nigel was thinking his ham didn't look like ham. He wondered if it wasn't silverside. He pushed the sliver of meat to one side on his plate and carefully sectioned a slice of tomato.

"Have we a Herbert in the firm?"

"Herbert who?"

"Just Herbert."

"First name or last name?"

"Don't know. I can't recall any Herbert."

"Maybe he's a new recruit. Why do you ask?"

"Herbert is tailing Hitchcock and the girl."

"Why didn't you ask the old man?"

"I did. And old sly puss said apologetically that that too was to remain an untidy loose end."

"Well, then, we'll just have to leave it there, won't we?"

"How are things at home?"

"Why do you ask?"

"Oh, I don't know. You haven't mentioned Violet lately."

"There are times when Violet is unmentionable."

"I see; it's like that, is it?"

"It's like nothing, actually." He pushed his plate away and took a sip of his coffee. "Foul food, this. Why do we eat in pubs? Why don't we go to a decent restaurant occasionally?"

"It's too expensive, that's why. Oh, well, someday, when our ships come in."

"That depends on who's navigating. Want some cake? I feel like some ginger cake."

"No, thanks. You go ahead." Nigel got up and Basil watched him as he swivel-hipped his way through the luncheon crush to the food display. *There are times when Violet is unmentionable.* Old sly puss indeed. Very astute old sly puss. That's why he's in charge and we aren't.

Alma hadn't eaten much lunch, and Brunhilde commented as she removed the folding table which she had placed earlier in front of Alma in the drawing room, "Cook favors people who belong to the Clean Plate Club."

So there's a cook, thought Alma. That meant there were three she knew of on the premises now that Blinky was gone. It was nice to know that the man with the tic had the opportunity every so often to blow his own horn. "I don't have much appetite," said Alma. "My apologies to the cook."

"I'm the cook."

So there were still only two on the premises, Brunhilde and Dempsey. "Oh. Well, then, my apologies. I say, are there any newspapers about?"

"There's nothing about you in them."

"I was thinking of my husband."

"Nothing about him either."

Strange, thought Alma; how very strange.

Brunhilde said, "There's a wireless in that wall panel near the bar, if you want to listen to it. The wall panel slides back. Just give it a nudge."

"Thank you." When Brunhilde had left, Alma crossed to the wall panel, nudged it, and the wireless materialized. She switched it on and came in at the end of the news break. A symphonic concert was announced, and Alma sat in a chair and tried to enjoy it, but her mind was elsewhere. She was back in Munich when they were shooting *The Pleasure Garden*. She was seeing Rudolf Wagner at the piano, and she was standing over him as he played his haunting little melody. Her face screwed up, she was trying to remember something, and then it came to her: the man with the disfigured face suddenly appearing from behind the scenery and then as suddenly disappearing again. The face. The murder. The melody. She switched off the wireless and crossed to the piano.

Do mi fa sol . . . sol fa sol.

She picked out the tune with her index finger. She didn't hear Brunhilde returning.

La-la-la-la . . . la-la-la . . .

"Pretty little tune, that," said Brunhilde, startling Alma, who turned and saw the big woman wielding a carpet sweeper.

"Yes, it is pretty. Do you know it?"

"Never heard it before in my life," was the reply Alma got, and Alma was thinking, Brunhilde, you lie.

Peter Dowerty stood at the opposite side of Jennings' desk, staring down at his superior, who was speaking on the phone to Sir Arthur Willing. He said an occasional "I see" or "That's good" or sometimes a noncomittal "Um," and then thanked Sir Arthur and hung up. Jennings told Dowerty, "They're at the circus, Hitchcock and the woman." He sat back in his swivel chair. "A village named Lingate."

"Don't know it, sir."

"Didn't expect you would. What's your problem? You look a bit anxious."

214

"It's Angus McKellin's da. He's been on to me from Glasgow. He wants Angus shipped home right away."

"I've ordered the autopsy. It's a matter of form."

'I told his father there'd have to be an autopsy and he told me where to shove it."

"Sounds as if we could use the old boy here."

"He didn't have kind words for us, Mr. Jennings."

"So few people do, Dowerty, so few people do." He sighed and then said, "You can make arrangements to ship the body. It'll be ready to travel by around five o'clock or so."

It'll be ready to travel, thought Dowerty as he left the office, ready to travel. He thought of his mother when he told her he was intending to join the force and remembered her admonishing words, "I don't want you coming home in a pine box. If you're planning on coming home in a pine box, don't come home at all. Why can't you be a ribbon clerk like your brother Percy?" Because it's seeing Percy as a ribbon clerk that drove me to a more masculine pursuit, that's why, Mum. He wondered if Jennings would object to his passing the hat to raise the money for a wreath for Angus McKellin.

Before reaching the circus, Hitch phoned Jennings and detailed his progress. He learned the false Lemuel Peach had been knifed to death. Poetic justice, thought Hitchcock.

"Be careful, be very careful," warned Jennings.

Hitchcock assured him he would, hung up, and rejoined Nancy Adair. Almost immediately, they found the circus in a meadow at the other end of Lingate. There was to be one performance only, and that wasn't due to start for another hour, but people were beginning to arrive. To Hitchcock, the one-ring tent looked somewhat shaky, and the adjoining tent that housed the freaks looked even shakier. There was a line of kiosks and wagons offering games and refreshments, and spielers were barking their wares. For some strange reason, the small circus orchestra, drum, piano, pipe organ, two trumpets, and a saxophone player, were all in blackface, like members of a minstrel show. They were placed on a platform at the entrance to the main tent and would move inside just before the performance began. They weren't very good, but they were loud and were playing the circus staple, "The March of The Gladiators."

"Does this bring back your childhood?" Hitchcock asked Nancy, assuming there was a childhood to bring back, whether she wanted it retrieved or not.

"I never went to the circus," said Nancy, her nose wrinkling with distaste at the odor coming from the animal compound. "What a terrible smell. Where are we going?"

"I thought I'd have my fortune told." He was pointing to a sign over a tepee that read, MADAME LAVINIA—FORTUNES TOLD—SIXPENCE.

"And what am I to do while you're having your fortune told?"

"You're a reporter, my dear. Snoop around and find a story. Look at the handsome bloke over there in the costume of an American Indian. Don't you think he's a sight for squaw eyes?"

Herbert, the man tailing Hitchcock and Nancy Adair, parked the black sedan so that it couldn't be blocked by another vehicle. He had watched Hitchcock and the woman as Hitchcock bought tickets of admission, and then had adjusted his large dark glasses. After a quick look of reassurance in the rearview mirror, he'd pulled his black cap down around his head and then left the car to follow his subjects. From the sparseness of the locals in attendance, Herbert could see Lingate would not be a profitable engagement for the Pechter Circus. Hitchcock and the woman walked slowly toward a tepee that featured a fortune-teller. Nearby a man dressed as an American Indian was hawking souvenirs. Here Hitchcock and the woman separated, Hitchcock entering the tepee and the woman crossing over to the "Indian," presumably to examine his wares. Herbert positioned himself so that he could watch both the tepee and Nancy Adair.

Inside the tepee, Hitchcock could see it was much more spacious than it looked from outside. There were a table with two chairs and a beaded curtain that partitioned the tepee in two. From behind the curtain he could hear a woman's sultry voice humming "Falling in Love Again."

"Hello!" cried Hitchcock.

The curtains parted melodiously and the gypsy woman entered. She was neither old, as Madeleine Lockwood had described her, nor was she a gypsy, suspected Hitchcock, but there was a marvelous look to her, seductive, tempting, her upper lip curling as she examined him with interest. Her head was covered by a bright-red bandanna; around her neck hung a variety of necklaces. Bracelets jangled when she moved her hands, and there were rings for all ten fingers. She wore a multicolored blouse and a red skirt that reached down to her ankles, and her belt appeared to be made from chain mail. She was bizarre and exotic and heavily perfumed, and Hitchcock hoped there was a voice to match.

"I am Madame Lavinia. I see the past, the present, and the future." With hands on hips, she sauntered toward the table with a slinky movement that offered other promises for the future. The voice was perfect—husky, melodic, low-pitched. "Place your sixpence on the table and sit down." Hitchcock did as he was told. She sat opposite him and pushed the coin to one side. "Let me see your left hand,

217

please." He placed his left hand on the table, palm upward. "The left hand is the dreamer. Did you know this?" She took his hand in her right hand and, with her left index finger, began tracing the lines of the palm, the touch of her fingernail sending a tingle up Hitchcock's spine such as he hadn't felt since his wedding night.

"I don't have too much to do with my left hand," said Hitchcock in a voice he didn't recognize.

"Oh, yes, you do. You dream a great deal. Look. Here and here and here." The fingernail hopped from line to line. "Fantasy dominates your life. You must be an artist or a writer. Yes, it's very plain to me. You are a professional person. Place your right hand next to the left, palm upward." Again he did as he was told. "Very sweaty." He rubbed the hand on his trousers and then placed it back in position. She stared hard at his right palm, as though it might be a valuable piece of jewelry. He wouldn't have been the least bit surprised if she had whipped out a jeweler's loupe and screwed it into her eye to give the palm a more accurate assessment. "The right hand is reality, it mirrors what you really are." She squeezed the flesh below the thumb. "Yes, you are very talented. When you have learned to channel your gifts, you will go very far in your profession."

"And what is my profession?" asked Hitchcock smoothly.

"Have you forgotten so soon?" Her voice and her eyes mocked him.

"Of course not. But you're the fortune-teller and I've paid my sixpence."

"You expect too much for such a pittance."

"If the fee is inadequate, you should raise your prices."

"I should raise my sights, but that's another story." She was lighting a Turkish cigarette, having found cigarettes and

218

matches in a large pocket hidden in the voluminous folds of her skirt. She went back to this right hand. "You could have a long life if you are very careful."

"Meaning?" It was Hitchcock's turn for mockery.

"Your weight will impair your health. Go on a diet."

"And other than that?"

"You're a player in a very dangerous game."

"You haven't seen that in my palm."

"Oh, yes. It's in your palm. Right here, see?"

Hitchcock's eyes didn't leave her face. "Yesterday, in Medwin, you predicted the impending death of a friend of mine."

"Did I?" She leaned back in her seat. "Death is inevitable, so it's easily predictable. I am always patronized by old ladies and old men. They're the ones who least wish to die. Most of them want to go on forever, God knows why."

"This old lady said you sounded very definite. Perhaps you remember her. She wore a very garish red wig."

"I remember her." She blew a smoke ring that settled briefly over Hitchcock's head like an uneasy halo. "She had a companion who looked like a frightened bird. Have you come all the way here to chide me for the indelicacy of my prediction?"

"Not at all. I'm on my way to Harborshire, but when I saw the circus, it brought back pleasant childhood memories, so I decided to stop off and visit. Have we met before?"

"I don't think so. Perhaps." She shrugged. "Perhaps in another world, another life. In one of my incarnations I was an Egyptian princess."

"How many incarnations have you had? All that the traffic can bear, I suppose?"

The mocking smile was back. "Perhaps you saw me in Munich many years ago."

"How did you know I was in Munich? It's not printed on either of my palms."

"Mr. Hitchcock, sparring verbally can be so wearying. We met in Munich one night; you and your wife were with Fritz Lang and his wife Thea. I was with Hans Albers, the actor. It was a very brief introduction. I was a mere child then and looked very pale and very washed out."

"Your name wouldn't happen to be Rosie Wagner, would it?"

"I hope not. It's such an ordinary name. No, my name is really Lavinia. My friends call me Lola. I was with Albers because I was hoping he would help me with a movie career. But since I wasn't easily seducible . . . then . . . nothing much came of that night except a much-needed meal. I'm sure you don't remember me at all."

"I met so many people in Munich, they become one large blur when I try to think back. But you're quite memorable now."

"What else would you like to know about the future?"

"I'd like to know the identity of a two-headed spy."

"So would a lot of people."

"Who do you work for?"

Her eyes widened with mock astonishment. "But I work right here for the Pechter Circus. Where they go, I pitch my tepee."

"How long have you been with the circus?" His arms were folded, and he no longer found her glamorous.

"Not very long. Does it matter?"

"I understand you've lost your knife thrower."

"I haven't lost anyone. But yes, the knife thrower is missing."

"He's dead."

"So? You also have mystical powers?"

"No, I have facts, received from Scotland Yard. Nicholas Haver was stabbed to death in the basement of the church in King's Cross, shortly after he tried to kill me."

"I'm sorry to hear this about Nicholas. He had a marvelous act."

"You can tell his agent he is no longer available."

"You've already told his wife." She was lighting another cigarette.

Hitchcock scratched his chin. "I'm terribly sorry. I didn't know. I didn't mean to shock you."

"I'm not shocked," she said matter-of-factly, "I read his palm before he went to London. I warned him not to go. His insurance is in order."

"How very cold-blooded you are."

"Mr. Hitchcock," she said softly, after exhaling two slip-streams of smoke from her nostrils, "only the cold-blooded survive, and I am a survivor." Gracefully, she arose and walked to the beaded curtain. She swept the curtain aside and turned to Hitchcock, making a tableau of sinister beauty he would not soon forget. "Let me tell you this. My predictions have been ninety percent accurate. Be very careful, Mr. Hitchcock. Be very very careful." She moved, and the curtain dropped behind her. Hitchcock hurried out of the tepee.

"Be very very careful of what?" demanded Nancy Adair, with whom Hitchcock almost collided.

"You've been eavesdropping," he accused, very displeased.

"I was doing no such thing. I was tired of waiting for you and I came to get you and I overheard. It's getting late. We should be moving on."

"Hello," came a piping little boy's voice.

Hitchcock looked behind him. He saw a small boy, or

what appeared to be a small boy, dressed in a white shift that fell to his thighs, revealing bare knees and feet. On each shoulder was pasted a wing, and on his back Hitchcock could see a shaft of arrows. In his right hand, the boy held a bow. "Hello. Where did you come from?"

"Over there." He pointed in the general direction of the tents. "My name is Cupid."

"Ah! That explains your costume!" He turned on Nancy Adair. "Will you please stop tugging at my sleeve!" He returned his attention to Cupid. "And how are things going in the romance department?"

"Not so good today. I haven't shot anyone yet. Have you seen the freaks?"

Hitchcock studied Cupid's face. Was he a small boy or was he a small man who looked like a small boy? he wondered. "No, I haven't seen the freaks." The circus orchestra was blasting away, and the attendance seemed to have increased a bit since Hitchcock's session in the tepee.

"You can't go to the circus without seeing the freaks. There's no extra charge." He took Hitchcock's hand and held it in an iron grip. "Come with me. I'll show you the freaks. They're my friends."

Nancy Adair's voice reached an unnatural pitch. "Let's get out of here! There's no time to see freaks or anything else!"

Cupid tightened his grip. "We seem to have no choice," said Hitchcock. "You can wait here if you like." She chose to follow them.

Herbert, eating a frankfurter and roll, munched slowly and thoughtfully. Instinctively, he patted his hidden holster. When the three disappeared into the freak tent, Herbert turned his attention briefly to the blackfaced musicians. Then he looked at his wristwatch. The performance in the main tent was scheduled to begin in twenty minutes. He hoped Hitchcock wasn't planning to catch it. There were just a few hours of daylight left. He didn't like driving at night. The frankfurter tasted awful. He flipped it into a trash can and returned his attention to the freak tent.

Inside the tent, Cupid said to Hitchcock, as Nancy Adair glowered at him, "Look!" He now released his grip on Hitchcock's hand and was making an expansive gesture to include all the strange specimens on display. "Aren't they wonderful?"

"Indeed they are," agreed Hitchcock, as his eyes traveled from the pinheaded girl to the bearded lady to the India rubber man, whose body was twisted in a figure eight. Then he studied Alberta, the half-man-half-woman, the woman half winking at him and the man half poking the woman half while growling out of the masculine side of the mouth. A roustabout in a bellowing roar announced the show in the main tent would begin in fifteen minutes, and the tent began to empty of its sparse audience.

"Hitchcock," urged Nancy Adair, "we've seen enough. Let's go."

"You haven't met my mother!" piped Cupid. "Come!" He held Hitchcock's hand again in his viselike grip and tugged him forward. "Momma! Momma! Meet my new friend!"

The Siamese twins stepped forward in unison. They were joined at the side. The sign over their stage read HELGA AND LISL—THE SIAMESE TWINS. Helga shouted to Cupid, "Stop pulling that man like that! Behave yourself!"

Hitchcock's jaw dropped, and Nancy Adair gasped. Hitchcock found his voice. "So this is your mother."

"Yes, I'm his mother," said Helga, one hand on her one hip, "and it wasn't easy. This is my sister, Lisl." Lisl didn't

223

seem any too friendly and did not acknowledge Hitchcock's greeting. "Lisl is in a very bad mood. She's just heard some very bad news. A good friend of ours was murdered." Slowly, the Siamese twins were descending the stairs from the stage. "I believe you know about this, yes?" Her accent was strong and Germanic, and Hitchcock had the sinking feeling that when and if the others spoke, they too would favor him with a Teutonic lilt.

"If you mean Nicholas Haver, yes; I told Madame Lavinia."

"Let's get out of here," hissed Nancy Adair in his ear. "We're alone with them. I don't like it in here. These people are dangerous." They were backing away toward the tent flap. Cupid tried to grab Hitchcock's hand again, but Hitchcock pushed it away.

From the left, an ugly voice said, "You were responsible for his death." It was the bearded lady who spoke. Hitchcock suspected the bearded lady was a bearded man, but this was no time to try to prove his theory right.

"I was not," said Hitchcock, trying to mask the rising panic. They were almost at the exit, and Hitchcock hurried Nancy toward it. He half expected to see Cupid drawing an arrow at them but instead saw the freaks had stopped in their tracks, no longer following them with menace.

In the entrance stood the roustabout who was dressed as an American Indian. He shouted at Cupid and the freaks, "Get back, you sons of bitches, are you out of your minds? Get back! You! Frieda!" He was shouting at the Bearded Lady, who, Hitchcock now saw, was holding a weapon that looked like a truncheon. "Don't make any trouble, Frieda." Perhaps, thought Hitchcock, Frieda was a "she" after all, but from the way she held the weapon, definitely not a lady. "Go put your beard up in curlers! The rest of you get to your tents. Go on. You, you little bastard"—the roustabout was addressing Cupid, who bravely was standing his ground— "go get ready for the Wild West Show." Hitchcock could see the orchestra as he charged out of the freak tent with a firm grip on Nancy Adair's hand.

"What's been happening? What's been going on? What happened with you and Madame Lavinia?" Nancy Adair was babbling away, her tongue running amok. They were passing the bandstand, and Hitchcock suddenly stood frozen, staring ahead at one of the musicians. "Now what? Now what's wrong?"

"That man, that man playing the saxophone! That musician with the tic under his left eye! He abducted my wife! That's him! Police! Get the police!"

"Hitchcock, control yourself!" shouted Nancy.

But Hitchcock had lost all control of himself. People had come running, and the man with the tic was trying to shove his way off the bandstand. "Stop that man!" shouted Hitchcock. "Stop that man!"

An arrow came whizzing past Hitchcock's ear and imbedded itself in Blinky's chest. He dropped the saxophone and for a moment, he was astonished and disoriented. His black makeup was mixing with perspiration and smearing. His tic was going wild like a semaphore in distress. Then he began flailing his arms as he began to fall backward against the set of trap drums. People were shouting and screaming and running in all directions. Roustabouts were hurrying from all corners of the circus ground.

Hitchcock was behaving like a madman, and Nancy Adair slapped his face. "You fat fool!" she screamed at him. "We've got to get out of here before the police come! Hurry! This way!" She pulled him by the hand as they ran, half stumbling, jostling their way through the crowd that was gathering, running past a man with dark glasses and a black cap on his head who had reached for his gun but with relief shoved it back in the holster when he caught sight of Hitchcock and Nancy Adair tearing toward their car. Herbert ran to his and got behind the wheel as Nancy steered her car in high gear back to the road.

"That was him," sobbed Hitchcock, "that was him. The man who kidnapped Alma! That was him!"

"Control yourself, for God's sake! He's dead now probably. That arrow looked as though it went straight into his heart."

Hitchcock wiped his wet face with his handkerchief. "That arrow! Do you suppose that child killed him? But *why*? Why would they want to kill one of their own?"

Nancy said quietly, hands tight on the steering wheel, eyes glued to the road ahead of her, "Perhaps he wasn't one of their own." She waited while the thought sank in, and then she added, "And you gave him away."

Fifteen

Hitchcock stared at the palms of his hands as they sped along the road to Harborshire. *Perhaps he wasn't one of them and I gave him away.* But if he wasn't one of them, what was he doing with those thugs that attacked me and abducted Alma? And of all things, to be playing a saxophone in blackface. His sudden outburst of laughter took Nancy Adair by surprise and unnerved her. Was he losing his reason, she wondered, and if he was, how would she deal with it?

"What's wrong with you?" she shouted. "What is it?"

"I'm a bloody fool, that's what it is. The man with the tic. The blackface. The musician. It was in my last film, *Young And Innocent*, except in that one the man with the tic played the drums! Is it possible that life can be imitating art?"

"Coincidence, that's all."

"Contrivance, I prefer to think, but will God forgive me if I've been the cause of an innocent man's death?" But he couldn't erase the memory of the man struggling with Alma.

"I'm going to try and reach Harborshire by nightfall. Let's not stop for any unnecessary reasons."

"I'm not hungry, if that's what you're getting at. I should be, but I'm not. I've no appetite at all." He stared at the palms of his hands again. "Madame Lavinia. She set the freaks against us. She's Nicholas Haver's widow. Remember? The imitation Lemuel Peach, the vicar. She said we met in Munich back in 1925, but I don't recall that at all. I thought at first she meant she was Rosie Wagner, but she wasn't. Rosie was an unkneaded lump of dough, as plain and as unappetizing as an unbaked biscuit. Lavinia was something else. You have the strangest expression. Regrets, Miss Adair, regrets?"

She was staring with alarm at the rearview mirror.

"What's happening?" asked Hitchcock.

"I'm not sure. There's a lorry gaining on us. I haven't noticed it before."

"Well, move over and let him pass! Isn't that the courtesy of the road?"

"I don't think this lorry driver is interested in courtesy. I think he's only interested in us."

With an effort, Hitchcock twisted in his seat and looked out the rear window. A large red lorry was gaining on them. As it swerved, he could read the lettering on the side, PECHTER CIRCUS.

"It's a circus lorry! And I can see the man at the wheel. It's him! The one dressed as an Indian! What the hell's he trying to do? Let him pass, damn it, let him pass!"

"He doesn't want to pass! He wants to run us off the road!"

In the black sedan, Herbert was voicing a string of oaths. He had courteously let the red lorry pass him until he read the name of the circus and then realized Hitchcock and the woman were in trouble. But it didn't make sense. No one should want Hitchcock dead. But perhaps the woman. Nancy Adair. His foot on the accelerator had it pushed to the limit, but the lorry was obviously equipped with a sophisticated engine. He cursed again louder.

Nancy struggled to keep control of the steering wheel while Hitchcock waved a fist at the lorry driver. The lorry kept hitting the back of their car, the only surcease occurring when he was forced to pull in behind them to avoid colliding with cars coming from the opposite direction.

"Try pulling into a driveway!" cried Hitchcock. "There's one coming up ahead! Do you see it?"

"Yes, yes, I see it!" The car jarred violently as they were again hit from behind.

She swerved sharply into the driveway. It was overgrown with weeds and foliage, badly rutted; driver and passenger were jolted and bounced as though they had landed in a cement mixer. A few feet ahead of them was what looked like an abandoned granary, a now sorry-looking wooden edifice with its doors hanging from rusty hinges. The lorry shot past the driveway; possibly the maniac at the wheel had missed seeing Nancy's maneuver, which had taken place around a curve in the road that briefly obscured his vision.

"Look out!" shouted Hitchcock as Nancy, having difficulty in decelerating the speed of the car, crashed past the worm-eaten doors into the building. A rope hoist hung from beams overhead, once used to raise the grain to the storage bins above. Bearing down on the brakes, Nancy finally brought the car to a halt under the hoist. Both turned to look out the back window and with relief saw no sign of the circus lorry.

And then the ground began to give way beneath the car.

"We're sinking into a pit!" cried Nancy as she wrenched open her door and flung herself out of the car. Clumsily, Hitchcock groped for his door handle. The car dropped farther into the pit.

"I'm trapped!" cried Hitchcock.

"I'll get help!" shouted Nancy and ran out to the road.

Hitchcock sat quietly, beads of perspiration trickling down his brow. If he sat still, he cautioned himself, if he tried not to move, perhaps the car would settle where it was. And if it didn't settle, how far down would it plunge? he wondered. How deep were the pits in granaries? Deep. Very deep. The car moaned, and the floor groaned, and Hitchcock felt the car slipping slowly farther into the abyss beneath him. *Our father who art in heaven . . .*

Herbert saw Nancy come running out of the driveway. He also saw what she didn't see. The circus lorry had reversed and was heading backward. The door opened and the roustabout in his Indian suit jumped down and chased after Nancy. Herbert slowed down. The roustabout caught Nancy around the waist and rudely lifted her off her feet, carrying the screaming, struggling woman back to the lorry. Herbert didn't seem in the least bit interested in rushing to her rescue. Once Nancy had been shoved into the front seat of the lorry, the roustabout got in, and with an agonizing grinding of gears, the lorry went tearing away. Herbert steered into the driveway and parked while sizing up Hitchcock's predicament.

Nigel Pack had come home for a change of clothing. It looked as if another all-night session was ahead of him with the firm. There'd be no rest for the weary until the Hitchcock case was satisfactorily resolved. He had tried phoning Violet to tell her he'd be home, but there was no reply. Out shopping again, probably, decided Nigel, and what for now? She'd sent a birthday gift to her father earlier in the week, and they'd had another of their knockdown drag-outs earlier that morning about her profligate spending of money on unnecessaries. He thought that problem had been settled then.

After slamming the front door shut behind him he shouted, "Violet!" followed by a louder *"Violet?"* He went to their bedroom. Her closet door was open. Immediately he realized her overnight bag was gone. The stupid bitch! I distinctly forbade her going to her parents' to celebrate her father's birthday. The stupid, willful bitch! He crossed to his own closet and flung open the door and then began undressing.

Stupid fucking bitch, I'll do her for this.

". . . Hallowed be thy name . . ."
"Mr. Hitchcock?"
Rescue!
"Mr. Hitchcock, do you hear me?"
"Yes!" cried Hitchcock.
"Do your best to remain calm and do not panic. Listen to me, follow instructions carefully, and I should have you out of there in just a few moments. Ready?"
"Yes!" He was afraid to speak, afraid to do anything for fear that any sound, any movement might send the car

231

deeper into the pit. He heard a cranking noise of machinery desperately in need of oiling.

"I am lowering the hoist. I have tested it. It's still in workable condition. While I'm doing this, I want you to open your car door very gently. I know there's not too much space there, but there should be more than enough for you to tie the rope around your waist, gently move out of the car, and leave the rest to me."

Hitchcock blinked his eyes as gently, very gently, he found the door handle and maneuvered it open. The car rocked slowly. Hitchcock wet his lips and slowly pushed the car door open as the rope appeared. He reached for it carefully, fingers extended, hungry for its touch, hungrier than a lover in need of a caress. He felt the rope and then slowly worked his hand around it until it was firmly in his grasp. He pulled the rope in and like an oversized woman struggling into a girdle, passed the rope around his waist. At last, he had it firmly tied.

"How are you doing?" asked his rescuer, the voice very warm and comforting, very masculine and decidedly with a trace of a continental accent.

"I'm ready," said Hitchcock.

The car moved slightly.

His rescuer said, "Now move out of the car quickly and when you do, grasp the rope with both your hands as tightly as possible."

Hitchcock said, "I'm not very athletic."

"I'm not asking you to do a back flip. I just want you to hold on tightly to the rope and leave the rest to me."

How self-assured the voice sounded, like a hack writer reciting a plot he'd freshly plagiarized.

He'd called him by name! *Mr. Hitchcock*. The man

knew him. Dear God, what if he was one of *them;* what, God help him, if he was the man in the Indian suit?

The floor groaned beneath the car.

The hell with it, thought Hitchcock; if he was the enemy, he'd leave me to plunge to a certain doom. Mustering courage and strength, both freshly minted by a strong will to live and be reunited with his wife and child, Hitchcock moved out of the car. It was a tight squeeze, but he made it. As he grasped the rope for dear life, the car shuddered and the floor beneath it gave way. Hitchcock shut his eyes tightly, waiting for the worst. The car must have plunged at least a hundred feet downward. The noise of its destruction was ear- and heart-shattering, the black clouds of dust it sent upward almost blinding Hitchcock. He could hear his rescuer coughing and prayed it didn't cause him to lose his grip on the hoist's manual handle.

When the dust settled, the man shouted, "Are you all right?"

"Pull me up!"

For several moments nothing happened. A touch of fear began to envelop Hitchcock in its awful embrace. Then the cranking sound blissfully kissed Hitchcock's ears, and he felt himself slowly rising. It was a slow, tortuous procedure. Overhead, the beam to which the hoist was attached was agonizing under Hitchcock's weight. Dust in slow trickles began to descend from the beam. Herbert looked up and saw the beam showing signs of a crack. Whistling nervously between his teeth, he looked down and saw Hitchcock was just a few feet from safety. He continued cranking, his feet dug solidly into the earth. He could hear Hitchcock breathing heavily. He could also hear the wooden beam beginning to crack. He had Hitchcock almost over the top and out of the pit.

The beam, he realized, could break in two in any moment, sending Hitchcock plunging to his death. He came to a quick decision. He abandoned the crank and leapt toward Hitchcock, grabbing him tightly around both wrists. Hitchcock yelled when he felt the rope slacken, but Herbert was in excellent shape. He pulled Hitchcock to safety and the fat man lay on his back with his eyes closed, gasping for breath while managing to whisper, "Thank you, thank you."

The beam cracked and the hoist plunged into the pit, causing the old granary to tremble as though it had been hit by an earthquake. Herbert quickly helped Hitchcock to his feet and guided him outside to his car. Hitchcock leaned against the car, still gasping for breath.

"Take it easy, old man," said Herbert.

Hitchcock exhaled a huge sigh of relief and then turned to his rescuer. "Oh, my God," he said. "Oh, my God!" Herbert had left his dark glasses and black cap on the car seat when he went to Hitchcock's rescue. "You," said Hitchcock softly, his eyes blinking, his heart pounding, "it's you."

Herbert was the man with the disfigured face, the man who had been skulking about the studio in Munich, the man who had argued with Anna Grieban in the restaurant the night she was murdered. "Ah! So you haven't forgotten me," said Herbert wryly. "My name, Mr. Hitchcock, is Herbert Grieban, and I think we'd better get the hell out of here." He held the car door open for Hitchcock, and after he was settled, Herbert shut the door and went around the other side and got in behind the wheel. The engine purred and then roared, and they pulled out of the driveway. Behind them, with a great crash that must have aroused the countryside, the old granary collapsed into a magnificent wreck.

Hitchcock turned and looked out the back window. "Pity," he said softly, "that would have made a magnificent shot." He settled more comfortably and watched as Herbert placed the sunglasses back on his face and then put the cap back on his head. "I wish to thank you again, Mr. Grieban. You're a very brave fellow." Grieban, he thought. Anna Grieban. Of course. He and Alma had conjectured correctly. He had been Anna's husband. "You're Anna Grieban's husband."

"Widower."

"Yes. That was an unfortunate tragedy."

"She was very careless. And so was your Nancy Adair."

Nancy Adair! "Good Lord!" exclaimed Hitchcock, "I've clean forgotten about her! Have you any idea where she's disappeared to?"

"I do indeed," he said with a smile that must have enchanted the ladies before the awful accident to his face. "She was abducted. I saw her being taken somewhat reluctantly into the circus lorry that was trying to run you off the road."

"Why? Was he trying to catch us, thinking we were responsible for the murder of the man with the tic? Oh, sorry. You don't know what I'm talking about."

"Oh, yes, I do. I was at the circus. I saw the murder. The evil little midget is quite a marksman."

"Then it *was* Cupid who did it!"

"Unfortunately for Oscar, an unloving cupid."

"Who's Oscar?"

"The victim. The man with the tic."

"Friend of yours?"

"A nodding acquaintance. We're both in the employ of British Intelligence. That is, I still am. Poor Oscar, he was a magnificent musician but a very chancy operator. That tic was always dangerous, a dead giveaway." He chuckled. "No pun intended."

"Then why wasn't he retired?"

"He was too good in the field. Anyway, sadly enough, this was to be his last assignment. He'd had an offer to join Ray Noble's Orchestra. Oh, well, another victim of the fickle finger of fate."

"In this case, the fickle arrow. Where are you taking me?" asked Hitchcock.

"To Harborshire," announced Herbert.

"You know all about me, I assume. This awful mess I'm in."

"I've been on your tail since Medwin, thanks to Miss Farquhar."

"You know Miss Farquhar?"

"Oh, God, yes. Bigmouth and I have known each other since the war. I was interned after being captured and that's where my face was botched up, not that there was much one could do with it after the shell exploded in front of me. Miss Farquhar was my nurse. It was she who recruited me."

"Imagine," said Hitchcock with awe, "imagine recruiting such easily recognizable people as a man with a tic and a man with a . . . a . . ."

"Shattered face."

"Please do forgive me."

"Why? It's not your face that's shattered. Why not recruit us? Is it any worse then recruiting a woman like Miss Farquhar who suffers from diarrhea of the mouth? Does May 7, 1915, mean anything to you?"

Hitchcock thought for a moment. "I'm afraid not. Hard for me to think. I'm still recovering from my narrow scrape with death."

"That is the date of the sinking of the *Lusitania*."

"Indeed? So what?"

"Miss Farquhar."

236

"Miss *Farquhar*? You mean *she* caused . . ."

". . . that ghastly tragedy. Blabbed away over drinks with Sir Rufus Derwent, who promptly sold the information to the Germans, and of course you know now that this was the cause of his downfall."

"Dear God, if this information were made public today . . ."

"Nobody would believe it."

"Marvelous idea for a movie. I'm filing it away for future consideration."

"You know, Mr. Hitchcock, spying is not the romantic adventure you depict in your films. It's very tiresome work. Days and weeks can go by when nothing happens. That's why it requires people of infinite patience. People like our poor lamented Oscar and myself. I'm a very patient man. My poor wife was impatient, so she's dead and I'm alive. That's why Rudolf Wagner is dead. He was impatient. When he created his magnificent and so far unbreakable code . . . *La-la-la-la . . . la-la-la . . .* recognize that?"

Hitchcock groaned. "It's as implanted in my memory as 'God Save the King.'"

"It's why Rudolf was murdered. The Germans wanted that code, so did England and the Americans and the Russians."

"That simple little melody? How did they all know of its existence?"

"By a very complicated process understood only by those of us experienced in espionage. Believe me when I tell you that when a new product comes on the market, word swiftly gets around and countries send their emissaries to do the bidding. At times it gets a little rough. Agents tend to knock each other off in their anxiety to get there, as they say in America, the firstest with the mostest. So you see, there

237

was Rudolf Wagner at the studio tinkling away, giving a sample of his wares to anyone in his vicinity who was in the market to purchase. What wasn't known, you see, was that I had already won the prize. I was the highest bidder for England. We concluded the deal that day your wife saw me hiding behind the scenery. Unfortunately for you and your wife, Mr. Hitchcock, it was thought in the field that *you* were spies in on the bidding because Mrs. Hitchcock fell so in love with the melody!"

"Well, I'll be damned!"

"You almost were."

"It was also assumed that Anna was in on the deal. Which is why she was murdered. Frankly, if the opposition hadn't killed her, I would have had to do the job myself."

Hitchcock said, "The argument in the restaurant."

"Precisely. Anna was living a dog's life. Very poor, so often hungry, so often between jobs. When she thought I was dead, she turned to the streets, but she was such an inadequate whore. Or so I was told. Anyway, she was thinking of selling out to the Russians, who in '25 were beginning to strengthen their espionage activities now that they had a better cash flow. She suspected Wagner had sold the code to me and tried to prise it out of me. Of course I insisted I didn't own it yet, but she got hysterical and we argued. Impatience. It can be deadlier than a terminal disease. Anyway, she's dead, and then Rudolf was murdered for having sold the code to me and not to the fatherland, like a good patriot ought to have."

"So they thought we were spies! What a typical Hitchcock situation!" Herbert had turned on the headlights. Hitchcock's stomach grumbled.

"Why else do you think you were being wooed so arduously by Fritz Lang's wife, Thea von Harbou?"

The film of memory in Hitchcock's mind was winding backward. He and Alma were in the restaurant with the Langs, and Thea who was trying to persuade him to remain in Germany with promises of a great future in their film industry. "So that's what it was all about that night."

"Poor Lang. How he despised his wife. Well, he's safe now in Hollywood."

"And she?"

"Oh, she's a very good Nazi. Still writing film scripts. Still heil-Hitlering it all over the place, an aging cockatoo."

"The circus is a nest of German spies, isn't it?"

Herbert chuckled. "So the penny's dropped at last."

Hitchcock was very disgruntled. "Well, if that is so, why aren't they rounded up and imprisoned?"

"In the first place, it's heavily infiltrated with our own people. And there are others with the circus who are quite innocent of its clandestine operation, you must understand."

"Of course."

"Poor Oscar was freshly placed there yesterday. We were a long time getting him into the orchestra. Anyway, why they aren't exposed? We keep hoping they'll lead us to the man who heads this whole network in Great Britain. Otherwise, they're no great threat to our security."

Hitchcock exploded. "But they've been touring the coast where there are naval installations!"

"That's right. But they see only what we permit them to see. They'll be rounded up soon, though, let me tell you. They'll soon be of no value to us whatsoever."

"Why was the man in the lorry sent after us?"

"To catch Nancy Adair." He chuckled. "And they've got her."

"Well, I must say, if she's in a precarious predicament, I'm quite sorry for her, but I don't quite see what the prob-

239

lem is other than the fact that I think she's a bit of a fraud."
He thought again, and the blood rushed to his face. "Well, I
am the damnedest fool in the world! Of course she's a fraud!
Trying to tell me she was South African when I knew she
was continental. The continental lilt in her speech was impossible to disguise despite her perfect English. Is she a
Russian spy?"

"No, she's with the Nazis. We should stop for some dinner. I'm getting very hungry."

"She's with the Nazis! Then she was assigned to me because they thought I was a spy. And Alma was kidnapped for
the same reason."

"Mr. Hitchcock . . . by the way, may I call you Alfred?"

"Call me idiot." He paused. "Call me Hitch. Only Alma
calls me Alfred, and that's only when she's about to pick a
fight."

"Hitch, the answer to Nancy Adair is right under your
nose. You've known her for years, or at least you met her
years ago."

Hitchcock emitted a yelp of self-anger. "You're not telling me Nancy Adair is Rosie Wagner!"

"That's right. Rosie Wagner. Rosie murdered her father
and my wife. Few would have guessed the shy little mouse
was a ferocious tigress. Now she's in trouble with her own
people. She was supposed to have murdered you."

Sixteen

"Herbert," said Hitchcock, "my blood has just gone cold."

"Her people are stupid. They should have sent her out to pasture when she suffered her breakdown, remorse over killing her father, though she professed to despise him. Still, that should have been the warning right there. In espionage, sentiment is the Achilles heel. But Rosie's lover convinced them she'd continue to be an asset once she was fully recovered and assigned to the field. Actually, she's done some very nice work for them these past ten years, and I say that begrudgingly."

"Who was Rosie's lover? She was so unattractive a girl."

"She kept herself deliberately looking homely. It was a good facade. Just like Nancy Adair became a good facade.

241

But underneath that mouse's exterior there seethed a sexual volcano. Didn't you lay her last night at Miss Farquhar's?"

"Good God, no! I could never be unfaithful to Alma!"

"Probably that's what delayed her killing you. Had you fucked her and been inadequate, she'd have cut your gizzards out."

"Really, Herbert, this is most embarrassing."

"So you're a man of the cinema, but not a man of the world."

"I'm a good husband, a good father, a good Catholic"— and he drew himself up—"and a perfectly magnificent director."

"Nancy Adair has fallen in love with you." He heard Hitchcock's intake of breath. "That's why she couldn't kill you."

"How do you know this? Or are you just taking a wild shot?"

"Oh, no. When you had your palm read or whatever you were doing with the knife thrower's widow, I kept my eye on Adair. She spoke to the man in the Indian costume, and I went over to his stall ostensibly to inspect the junk he was hawking. They spoke in German, so it was easy for me. I caught snatches and what I could piece together is that he was chewing her out and she said she couldn't, that someone else would have to do it. When she saw you coming out of the tent, and she ran to you, it was to hurry you away from the circus."

"She did try to do that, I must give her that. But it was Cupid who intervened!"

"Deliberately. He was sent to lure you to the freak tent. They had taken it upon themselves to kill you, but the Indian-suited person didn't want you murdered on the premises, for obvious reasons. That monster of a midget took it in his own hands to kill you, but he was a lousy shot."

Hitchcock's eyes widened. "Are you telling me the arrow that killed your Oscar was meant for *me*?"

"That's right." Hitchcock's mouth was agape as Herbert emitted his familiar chuckle. "Anybody who can miss a target like you has to have his eyes examined."

"You know," said Hitchcock quietly, "I recall the sound of that arrow whistling past my ear."

"I'm sure you did. Then of course, when you set up that hue and cry, Nancy had to get the two of you the hell out of there as quickly as possible. There was danger at the circus, and she wasn't about to face a police interrogation because— this above all you must keep in mind—she was still out to save her own skin."

"And now they've got her. Do you suppose they'll kill her?"

"Perhaps yes. Perhaps no."

"None of this was in Regner's scenario. Not any of it." He thought for a moment. "My God, was Fredrick Regner Rosie's lover?"

Herbert laughed. "No, Hitch. Her lover was Hans Meyer."

Hitchcock slumped against the door. "I would never have suspected he was a spy. The casting was all wrong. That's why I've been so hesitant about using him in *The Lady Vanishes*. That's the title of the film I've got in preparation." He added with a weary sigh, "If I ever get to making it." His stomach grumbled again and he wished a country inn with good solid British cuisine would magically materialize. Then his mind flashed back to the cottage and Martin Mueller's murder. "Of course!" he exclaimed.

"Of course what?" Herbert shot him a sidelong glance of inquiry.

"Nancy Adair must have murdered Martin Mueller!" His adrenaline was bubbling. "It couldn't have been Hans Meyer; he was in the house with us all the time."

"She also murdered Nicholas Haver, the false Lemuel Peach."

"She's a fast girl with a knife. Oh, my God. I feel faint. I was *that* close to being murdered. She could have done me in last night at Miss Farquhar's!"

"Oh, no, then she'd have had to kill Miss Farquhar too, because Minnie Mouth . . . as we sometimes refer to Miss Farquhar . . . could have exposed her immediately to the police. Anyway, she knew about Farquhar and chose her house for the safety she figured it offered. No, Nancy Adair could have pulled over to a lonely side of the road at some point and dispatched you then."

"We were at a lonely side of the road when we parked the night of the fog. She could have killed me then."

"By then, we must assume, she was smitten. You see, Hitchcock, Nancy Adair has one vice known only to a select few. She is what is known as a chubby chaser. She dotes on fat men, they're her secret passion."

"Thank God I've delayed dieting. So when do we eat?"

"We're not too far from Harborshire. There must be an inn nearby. Wait! What's that up ahead?"

Hitchcock peered through the windshield. "It's an inn. The sign promises good food and wine. Dinner's on me."

"Oh, no. Dinner's on the British government. I'm on overtime."

Half an hour later, both were cutting into their roast chicken. Over preliminary Scotches and sodas, Hitchcock learned Alma was being guarded in a safe house in Mayfair run by the firm. Oscar, whom Hitchcock had seen over-powering her, had infiltrated the group set up to abduct Alma and to hold her as a hostage, as Hitchcock had de-duced, to trade for their safety. At the time, both sides wanted Hitchcock to lead them to the master spy through Regner's manuscript, which was stolen from their apartment by Nancy Adair. It was Hans Meyer who had impersonated Regner on the phone, luring the Hitchcocks away from their flat while Nancy had the opportunity to use a skeleton key and steal the scenario.

"I thought she knew too much about the progression of the scenario when she caught up with me in King's Cross," Hitchcock commented.

"Anyway," said Herbert, "It was arranged that Oscar would meet up with our own people in Regent's Park, and that's how your wife was rescued."

Now with their meal in front of them, they ate in si-lence, savoring each mouthful of food. Over coffee, Hitch-cock watched as Herbert lit a cigar and leaned back contentedly, the picture more of a successful businessman dining with an associate than of a professional spy nearing the end of his mission.

"What are you thinking about, Hitch?"

"I was thinking of a good night's sleep."

"Not here, I'm afraid. Look out the window on your right."

Hitch saw the red circus lorry parked on the opposite side of the road. The van was unoccupied. Hitchcock said to Herbert, "Tenacious bugger, isn't he? How do you suppose he traced us here?"

"He hasn't." Herbert was staring into the adjoining lounge. "He's at the bar having a sandwich and a beer. He's changed into coveralls."

"Do you think he's seen us?"

"He might, through the bar mirror, once he stops wolfing his food. His manners are execrable." His dark glasses had slipped down his nose and he pushed them back. They were sitting in a secluded corner, selected by Herbert, who was sensitive to reactions to his disfigured face, especially in a public dining room. On this occasion, there was only another table occupied, by what Hitchcock would later describe as two gentlewomen engrossed in mediocre food and excellent gossip. Their voices carried.

"I think we should settle the bill now," intoned Hitchcock gravely, "and then we should try to escape his attention by leaving the back way." He signaled to the publican.

"Supposing there isn't a back way." Herbert flicked ash gently into a tray.

"There has to be a back way. There always is in spy thrillers. I always have them. They're such a comfort."

While waiting to be presented with the bill, Herbert said, "You're a remarkable man, Hitch."

"No, I'm not. I'm a very timid man in a very intimidating situation. I suppose, if I were so inclined, I could demand you take me back to London at once. But I can't do that now. Not because I'm particularly brave, because I'm not, but because we're coming to the end of the trail, and I have to know how the story ends. I can't back away from the story now. I wouldn't forgive myself, and in a sense, I don't think Alma would either." He didn't dare turn around to see if the danger still lurked at the bar.

Herbert read his mind. "He's still there. He's just been served another beer."

Hitchcock shifted in his seat. "Herbert, I didn't really kill the detective, did I? I mean, awakening with a bloodied knife in my hand . . ."

246

"Of course you didn't. Timid men don't plunge knives in the backs of rescuers. Timid men stand to one side and cower and make strange noises. I've seen them in the war and I've seen them in whorehouses. Hans Meyer murdered Angus McKellin."

"Then it *was* him on the intercom!"

"Of course. How else could they get into your house? Oscar told us all this after delivering your wife to our safe house. Hans hid behind the staircase leading to the floor above you. After the others left and the detective, who had been coshed at the kiosk across the street from you, revived and went running to your apartment, Hans came in after him and killed him with the knife you were holding. Or maybe Hans was already in the apartment when McKellin found him there and Hans killed him."

"And he's still at large?"

"Very much so."

"And where's Fredrick Regner?"

"He's safe."

"Is he really ill?"

"He's dying. The Nazis apprehended him last year. They held him in a hospital established for the purpose of systematically destroying their enemies. I will not describe to you what horrible brutality was inflicted on him. After we ransomed him—and a very expensive negotiation it was—he spent three months in a sanatorium in Switzerland. Some repairs were effective. Others, unfortunately, were not. But he's a good soldier. He persisted with the scenario and we brought him here so he could continue to participate. It was his wish and we owed him that."

The publican brought the bill, and Herbert paid. "I say," Hitchcock asked the publican, "is there a back way out?"

The publican was no stranger to odd requests. "If it's the WC you want, we've got indoor plumbing."

"Well, actually it isn't. My friend here"—he indicated Herbert—"is trying to avoid someone at your bar."

"Bill collector?" asked the publican.

"Nothing that simple," said Hitchcock. "You see, my friend is having an affair with that man's wife and that man has threatened to kill him if he ever runs into him."

The publican looked at Herbert with undisguised admiration. "So it's like that, is it? Well, then, just follow me." He led them to the kitchen, which, had they toured it prior to eating, would have convinced them to depart without ordering. The back of the inn was piled with overflowing trash cans around which a mangy dog snuffled. The publican kicked the dog, which yelped and then scurried away.

"Thank you very kindly," said Hitchcock, restraining an urge to kick the publican, and he and Herbert hurried away.

In the bar, the man had caught a glimpse of the publican leading Hitchcock and Herbert to the rear exit. His glass of beer, which was at his lips, became stationary as his hand froze and his eyes pierced the departing figures he recognized in the bar mirror. He put the glass on the bar, picked up his coins, and hurried out.

Herbert gunned the motor and they were on their way as the man in coveralls emerged from the inn and trotted to the red lorry. Herbert saw him through the rearview mirror. "He's on to us," he said grimly.

"Can we outrun him?" Hitchcock wondered why his voice had gone up a pitch.

"Let us now pray." He hunched over the wheel while his foot pressed down on the accelerator. "We're almost into Harborshire. Somewhere in the village, I will drop you, if it's at all possible without his seeing it."

"No. We're in this together. You saved me. You're my rescuer." His eyes were glued to the rearview mirror. "Haven't you heard that famous Chinese adage? A rescued man's life belongs to his savior."

"Sorry, Hitch, but I'm not in the market for fresh possessions. I travel light." The lorry wasn't gaining on them, but he had them well in sight. "When I drop you, you go in search of Sir Rufus Derwent. He's the final link in this chain. He must be the connection to the man we want."

"Supposing Sir Rufus is our man?"

"Well, then, then we've got him, haven't we?"

"But he's not, is he? You would have picked him up long ago."

"Sir Rufus lives very high on the hog." They could see the lights of Harborshire ahead of them.

"Why not, he has considerable wealth, hasn't he? Look at what he's spent on Madeleine Lockwood."

"That was old money, when money had value. Most of it went when the markets collapsed in '29. He had a very hard time of it back then. And then suddenly and conveniently, at the time the Nazis came into power three years ago, Sir Rufus had a fresh infusion of wealth. Extraordinary, no?"

"What Alma would refer to as the short arm of coincidence. I think we've lost him."

"I'm going to make a turn into the Channel Road. It's the outskirts of the village. You'll have to make your way to Sir Rufus' on your own. You remember it is called The Thirty-Nine Steps."

"How could I ever forget? Now listen, Herbert, what about you, what are you going to do?"

"Get rid of the son of a bitch." The car skidded to a halt. "Get out! Quickly!" Hitchcock hadn't moved that fast since menaced by a field mouse at the cottage. He lost himself in

249

an alleyway as Herbert disappeared in a noxious cloud of exhaust fumes. Hitchcock stayed hidden until the circus lorry passed him. He whispered a prayer of deliverance for Herbert Grieban, and then set about looking for Sir Rufus Derwent's villa.

There was a precipitous and dangerous drop from the Channel Road to the rocks below. Angry waves crashed against the rocks, sending walls of saline foam upward like roaring rockets, which just as quickly crashed back down against the rocks, only to be sent back up. The wind whistled and blew, and although the sky was clear and star-studded, Herbert wondered if there was a freak storm coming in from the sea. The lorry had found him, and Herbert had decided how to rid himself of the enemy. They were now leaving the Harborshire area, where the road spiraled and curved upward and narrowed. There had been little traffic coming from the opposite direction. Herbert deliberately decelerated and allowed the lorry to come up behind him. The fish took the bait, and the lorry gained on Herbert like a hungry shark sighting plankton. The road was wet and slippery here and Herbert felt his tires go into a skid. The lorry was just a few feet behind him, ready to hit him from behind and send him crashing into the road's wooden guardrails to a certain fiery death on the rocks below. Herbert risked the one chance that could spare him. He braked abruptly while swerving to the right. The lorry hit him on the left and went into a skid. The lorry hit the guardrails, shattering the wood, and went plunging over the edge. Herbert sat patiently for a few seconds. He heard the hideous crash and then the explosion and then the reflection of the flames of the burning lorry. Herbert sighed, lit a cigar, and sat quietly puffing, waiting for his jangled nerves to calm down. Then he would find a phone and report to London, after which he would go in search of Alfred Hitchcock. All in all, it had been quite an unusual day.

It was an uphill climb from the Channel Road to the center of Harborshire, and Hitchcock, of course, wasn't in shape for it. The almost full moon helped light his way, the village being notoriously short of adequate streetlights. He knew it was an artist's colony and at one time had been celebrated for its oysters, these having mysteriously disappeared when erosions along the coast destroyed their beds. The houses he had passed were picturesque and best described as quaint if undistinguished. Harborshire thrived in the summer, and Hitchcock could see the natives were wrestling with freshly painted exteriors to give the village its famous summer color. Thoroughly exhausted and winded, he reached the village square and settled onto a bench. He faced a statue of a man he did not recognize and wondered if it had been erected in the memory of an unknown artist. The wind was rising, and so was Hitchcock's anxiety. He hoped Herbert had safely eluded the circus lorry. He hoped there was someone about who could direct him to The Thirty-Nine Steps. He wished he didn't look and feel as grotty as he did, his clothes a shabby shambles, especially after the incident in the granary. He adjusted his hat in the dark, hoping it might give him a dashing, devil-may-care look, but in his heart he knew that a devil-may-care look would be forever elusive with his girth. He dwelt on the previous forty-eight hours and the realization that so much had befallen him in so brief a span of time. The cast of characters he had encountered formed a kaleidoscope designed by a demented choreographer. He saw Alma and Hans and the corpse of Martin Mueller. There were Nancy Adair and

Detective Superintendent Jennings and the corpse of Angus McKellin. Oscar with his tic and a knife being thrown at Hitchcock and then the menacing buskers. Miss Farquhar doing a gavotte with her cousin, Miss Allerton, and Madeleine Lockwood singing "There'll Be a Hot Time in the Old Town Tonight," which he assumed she must have attacked and destroyed at some time in her career. Miss Lockwood was rudely nudged aside by a man wearing an American Indian suit, who in turn gave way to a midget named Cupid surrounded by Siamese twins and a pinheaded woman and a bearded lady. . . . A hand fell heavily on his shoulder and Hitchcock cried out with surprise and fright.

"Didn't mean to startle you, sir. But you were talking to yourself." It was a young constable with a look of concern. Little did he know that constables of any age filled Hitchcock with fear.

Hitchcock stood up. "I frequently talk to myself. It's the only time I get intelligent answers."

"I haven't seen you before, have I?" He held his truncheon in front of him with both hands, as though it were a trapeze and he were thinking of performing.

"No, you haven't. I've never been here before." Control, you damn fool, control. Stop being so nervous, you'll make him suspicious.

"Where are you staying?" He towered over Hitchcock, as most people did.

Hitchcock thought quickly. "Well, actually, I'm expected at Sir Rufus Derwent's."

"Oh. You too."

"Me too what?"

"The party."

"The party?"

252

"Aren't you going to the party?"

"At Sir Rufus'?"

"Where else would there be one tonight?"

"I haven't the vaguest idea. I'm not very social."

The policeman was studying Hitchcock with what seemed an unpleasant curiosity. "If you're expected at The Thirty-Nine Steps, then you're here to celebrate his birthday."

"Oh, of course!" Hitchcock grinned. So did the constable. Hitchcock felt better. "The party."

"Thought you'd be going to the party, dressed the way you are."

Hitchcock considered striking him, then realized he looked like a tramp, and that was absolutely fitting for his mission. "It's a masquerade party, of course."

"Where's your mask?"

"Oh, dear," said Hitchcock, looking like a naughty cherub, "I knew I'd forgotten something." He pursed his lips and then said. "That's why I was talking to myself. I was trying to remember what I'd forgotten. Like Sir Arthur Sullivan looking for his lost chord."

"Oh? Is he about too?"

The young man was obviously not heavy in the brains department. Hitchcock decided that if he had any brains, he'd be dangerous. "Could you direct me to The Thirty-Nine Steps? It appears I've lost my way."

"Certainly, sir." He used the truncheon as a pointer. "You continue diagonally across the square, just past the statue ahead, and you come to the Mason's Lane. You follow the Lane to the very top. . . ."

"Uphill?" The constable nodded, and Hitchcock's heart sank.

"At the top, you turn left and walk about one hundred

yards. There you'll come to a flight of wooden steps, thirty-nine of them. You climb to the top of them . . ." Hitchcock wished he had an alpenstock. ". . . and there is the villa. You can't miss it. You can see it from below, especially tonight. You'll hear the orchestra and see the reflections of the fairy lights strung along the branches of the trees outside. Everybody's there. Sir Rufus' birthday is a yearly event."

"I'm sure it's as much fun as Guy Fawkes Day."

"You guessed right. There'll be a bonfire too. It's always lit just before midnight. Mind how you go. Mason's Lane isn't very well lighted."

"I'll watch my step," said Hitchcock, with sincerity. He thanked the constable and went in search of Sir Rufus Derwent and The Thirty-Nine Steps.

It was a familiar gathering in Sir Arthur Willing's office—Jennings, Basil Cole, and Nigel Pack. Sir Arthur Willing was replacing the phone in its cradle and turned to the others, who looked at him expectantly.

"They're in Harborshire. Unfortunately, they've been separated." He repeated Herbert's report on the affair of the circus lorry. "Hitchcock is on his own."

Basil Cole said, "Surely Mr. Grieban will catch up with him."

Sir Arthur said, "That's what he was intending to do." He told them of the near miss in the granary. "Amazing bloke, Hitchcock. Absolutely amazing. Grieban offered him an out at dinner, but damned if he took it. I'm glad we put our money on him. Basil, order up some coffee and sandwiches, will you, like a good fellow? Cheer up, Nigel, it can't be too long now."

"Oh, I'm fine, sir. I'll be better after some coffee." Nigel Pack altered the expression on his face.

"And now, Mr. Jennings. What's going on with your jailful of freaks?"

"It's the Siamese twins, Sir Arthur, Helga and Lisl. Helga's the mother of the midget. A ferocious woman. She's not getting along with Lisl. Lisl loudly professes her innocence, says she wasn't mixed up in any espionage shenanigans but had to go along because obviously she had no choice. They keep cursing each other and slapping each other about. It's an absolutely bizarre sight. What happen's to Lisl if she's proven innocent and Helga is found guilty?"

"How the hell should I know?" replied Sir Arthur, as he lit up his pipe. "I'm not King Solomon."

Alma Hitchcock was curious. After dinner, she had asked of Dempsey and Brunhilde that she at least be permitted to walk about the secluded garden. They acquiesced and Brunhilde accompanied her. Alma said to Brunhilde, "I suppose you're worried I might cry for help?"

"Why should you cry for help? You are safe here. And if you did"—she held up a beefy hand—"I'd clap this over your mouth."

Alma looked up at the sky and wondered where Hitch was. She hoped he too, somewhere, might be looking at the sky and wondering about her. She asked Brunhilde, "Whose room is that?"

"What room?"

"The one directly up there." Alma pointed. "Where the light's just gone on." Dempsey appeared in the window and drew the curtains. "Another prisoner?"

"'Prisoner' is such a harsh word," said Brunhilde. She

255

had a sweater draped across her shoulders and drew it closer. It was chilly. Alma had been provided with a shawl but was oblivious to the chill. "You are a guest."

"And who's the guest up there?" asked Alma.

"There's no other guest."

"I know you're not deaf. I heard the cry just now. You must have heard it too."

"Very well, I suppose your knowing will do no harm. They didn't say I shouldn't tell you." 'They,' thought Alma, which 'They'? "It's a sick man. A very sick man. He's dying."

"Why isn't he in hospital?"

"He goes in the morning." The man cried out again.

"Poor soul, he's in such agony," said Alma. "I've had some nursing experience, perhaps I can be of some help."

"What could you do? He is given all sorts of sedation and it doesn't help. He's been through hell, that man has. Bloody Nazis."

Bloody Nazis. Alma felt very cheerful at last. She said to Brunhilde, "You're with British Intelligence, aren't you?" Brunhilde said nothing. "Why am I kept here? Why can't I go home?"

"Because, Mrs. Hitchcock, home is still not safe. It is for your own good that you're here. Your husband knows you're here."

"Then he's all right?" asked Alma eagerly.

"Let us hope so." And Alma wasn't all that cheerful anymore. Another cry from the bedroom.

"Please take me to him. It might help if I sat beside him and just held his hand."

Brunhilde thought for a moment, and then led Alma back into the house and to the sick man's bedroom. They ran into Dempsey as he was emerging. From a look he got from Brunhilde, he did not try to bar their way. Alma preceded

Brunhilde into the room. It was lit by a solitary lamp near the bed. On the table she saw a variety of medicinal bottles, vials of pills, a syringe, and a basin filled with water and a sponge. On the bed was a form covered by a thin blanket. Skeletal fingers twisted the edge of the blanket, and from the mouth came a series of heartrending moans. The man was emaciated and his body shrunken. Alma wished he wanted death as eagerly as Death wanted him. There was a chair next to the bed. Alma moved it closer to the dying man and sat down.

There was something familiar about him. She studied the emaciated face and tried to imagine him as a hale and healthy person. His eyes fluttered open as though he had sensed her presence, and his eyes focused at her face. The lips moved but no words formed. Dear God, she thought, he's smiling. He seems to think he knows me.

She leaned forward. "Hello. How do you feel?" Stupid question that, she knew, but what eloquence is there reserved for the dying?

He whispered and she leaned closer to catch his words. "I wish . . . Hitler . . . felt . . . the way . . . I . . . do . . . Alma . . ."

And now she recognized him and cried out, "Oh, my dear, my dear Freddy, what have they done to you?"

Seventeen

Hitchcock counted the thirty-nine steps slowly. He could hear the music coming from the birthday celebration and see the reflection of the fairy lights. The closer he came to the top, the faster his heart beat. Not from the exertion of the climb but from the apprehension of what lay before him. As he climbed the steps he thought of Herbert Grieban and prayed he had outwitted and out-maneuvered the madman at the wheel of the circus lorry. As he reached the top of the stairs, the orchestra was swinging away with "Over My Shoulder," which Jessie Matthews had introduced in her most recent film, and he wished the dancing and singing star was there to greet him. He wished any familiar face was there to greet him, and to his surprise and utter astonishment, there they were, moving in and out of the house carrying drinks and plates of food.

He saw several Adolf Hitlers and the Marx Brothers, and there were at least three Noel Cowards. A Mussolini was dancing crazily on the grass with Joan of Arc, and through the open French windows leading to the villa's ballroom, Hitchcock saw the orchestra led by a cadaverous young man sporting an ill-fitting toupee that looked like a golf mound. As Hitchcock mingled with the cleverly masked and costumed crowd, he marveled at the ingenuity of some of the guests in the ballroom. There were Greta Garbo and Marlene Dietrich and Winston Churchill and Clark Gable. Beyond them at the sumptuous buffet was a hopeful but inadequate Tarzan in a loincloth revealing a body sadly in need of muscles, with a Jane sadly in need of a bosom. A Russian czar fumbled clumsily at a two-step with a Chinese empress, and before him were two oddities, a man wearing a costume festooned with thumbs and a woman in a costume decorated with ears, their eyes covered with harlequin masks.

"Hello!" said the man cheerily to Hitchcock, "I'm all thumbs. This is my girlfriend, she's all ears. And what are you?"

"I'm all in," responded Hitchcock truthfully.

"Oh, he's all in! Isn't he heavenly?" said All-Thumbs to All-Ears.

All-Ears extended a spindly hand and said, "I'm Rosemary. Everyone remembers me. Tee-hee."

Hitchcock wondered who among those present was his host. "I suppose you're thirsting to know my name."

All-Ears tee-hee'd again. "You're reading my mind!"

"It's an easy read," said Hitchcock. "My name is Alfred."

"He's Alfred the Great!" said All-Thumbs. "Isn't that what you are? Aren't you Alfred the Great?"

"Actually," said Hitchcock, thinking that if these young-sters were the future, the Commonwealth was doomed, "I'm quite magnificent."

"I think you're utterly captivating, tee-hee," said All-Ears. "You don't have a drink! Where's your drink?"

"If you could direct me to the bar," suggested Alfred. They pointed him toward a room just past the orchestra, which was now betraying Cole Porter with "Just One of Those Things." The crush of masqueraders was a solid wall of human flesh. Very gently, Hitchcock made his way through the wall, smiling affably and even chatting or re-sponding when spoken to.

"Oh, darling," shouted Garbo to Mussolini. "Have you seen my husband?"

"Yes, darling, just a few minutes ago!"

"Where was he?"

"In despair."

A Tallulah Bankhead put her arm through his, halting his progress. "I say, whoever you are"—her voice was hus-kier than Bankhead's—"engage me in conversation. Quickly, darling. I'm trying to shake that boor coming up behind me." Coming up behind her was Abraham Lincoln. Hitch-cock thought it amazing—not only did the Americans domi-nate our film industry, they dominated our masquerade balls.

"Is he anyone you know?" asked Hitchcock, wishing her grip would ease up.

"Yes, he's my lover. Tomorrow he gets the old heave-ho. Doesn't spend a farthing to amuse me. He's tighter than the bark on a tree." Abraham Lincoln kept walking right past them.

"I think he's gone in search of greener pastures," com-mented Hitchcock.

"It doesn't matter, darling," she said, releasing her grip on Hitchcock and adjusting her mask, "our affair's been one long smirk. Who are you, darling; is that a mask or is that your face?"

"It's my face, which on occasion has been a mask. Now if you'll excuse me." He left the tiresome lady and continued his pilgrimage to the bar. How, he wondered, do I go about unmasking Sir Rufus? Probably, he decided, by just asking somebody if they know his costume. He reached the bar and, after much signaling, won the attention of a bartender and got himself a Scotch and soda. At his elbow, Little Bo-Peep materialized. She asked for and received a ginger ale, and then, resting her crook against the bar, raised her drink in a toast to Hitchcock and took a long swallow.

"By Christ, I needed that," said Bo-Peep. Both the voice and the half of her face that was not hidden by a mask told Hitchcock Bo-Peep was long past *Mother Goose* stories and well into middle age. She continued unprompted, "What a bore this party is. Let me tell you, Columbus was wrong. The world is flat. And so's this ginger ale. What's that you're drinking?" He told her. "I shouldn't, but I shall. Bartender!" While her Scotch and soda was being mixed, she asked Hitchcock. "We haven't met before, have we?"

"I don't know. Who are you?"

"I feel like the Spirit of Christmas Past, but in real life I'm Angelica Thornwell."

The way she stood looking at him, Hitchcock was expecting a clap of thunder. "I'm Alfred," he said.

She lifted her mask revealing her eyes, pale-gray eyes that told him she was capable of seeing more than one wished to expose. "Don't you recognize my name? Angelica Thornwell. The novelist."

"Ah! Of course!" He was totally insincere.

"I write murder mysteries!"

"Of course!" Mystery novelists bored him. They were usually so intense.

"Haven't you read me?" Her mouth was working like a snapping turtle.

"I don't read much fiction," he lied gracefully.

"Well, shame on you! I've written over twenty best-sellers in the past twenty years." She retrieved her crook and held it like a scepter as she led Hitchcock away from the bar. "Time has been terribly kind to me. The critics haven't. But bugger them, I'm terribly rich. There, see out there through the window." Hitchcock looked out the window. In the distance, perched on a cliff overlooking the Channel, was an oversized, pretentious, ugly villa. "My books have paid for that! Isn't it magnificent? That's my estate. My husband named it in honor of my books. 'Farfetched.'"

"I must meet your husband," said Hitchcock.

"Horatio is not here. He abhors parties. He especially abhors Rufus' parties. In fact, he thoroughly detests Rufus." She leaned into him conspiratorially. "I'm sure you know all about Rufus and the scandal that brought him down."

"I've heard rumors," replied Hitchcock blandly.

"Horatio says the Derwent family motto should be 'Dishonor Before Death.' Quite outspoken, my Horatio. Undoubtedly busy with his hobby."

"Which is?"

"Butterflies. And what do you do?"

"I don't have hobbies."

"I mean professionally, you silly." She poked him with the crook, which she maneuvered with the ease of a conductor wielding a baton.

And now, decided Hitchcock, for the moment of truth. "I direct films."

"Moving pictures?" She looked as though she had just found her straying sheep.

"Talkies."

"What did you say your name was?" Hitchcock decided if she came any closer, she'd soon be behind him.

"I only told you my first name, which is Alfred. The entire name is Alfred Hitchcock. Have you heard of *me*?"

"I most certainly have! You've rejected *all* of my novels for filming! You terrible man, you!"

"You mustn't blame me. You must blame my readers." You must blame Alma, who in my estimation will be forever blameless.

"Perhaps you'll like my new one. It's coming off the press next month. It's about a girl in distress who takes a job as a tutor to a young girl who resides in a strange Victorian gothic mansion near the moors with her father who's named Portchester, and what the girl tutor whose name is Janette doesn't know is that Portchester's mad wife is kept chained up in the attic behind an iron door administered to by a faithful woman servant who it turns out is as deranged as she is and—how does that strike you?" She paused to take a breath while waiting for Hitchcock to digest the thumbnail plot she'd just recited.

"It strikes me with a feeling of déjà vu," said Hitchcock solemnly.

"In what sense déjà vu?" The challenge in her voice was ominous.

"My dear woman" said Hitchcock, wondering if perhaps she'd been having him on, "you have just told me the plot of *Jane Eyre!*"

Her face screwed up unpleasantly. "Jane *Who*? *My* book is titled *Janette in Jeopardy*. I see you're not interested in this one either. How can a person of such poor judgment succeed in the film business? I suppose you married into it. You'll excuse me. I think I see my lover beckoning."

She swept past him with a snort of indignation, and Hitchcock watched her heading toward an Adolf Hitler who appeared to be mesmerizing her with his index finger.

"Quite tiresome, isn't she?" The voice belonged to a woman of breeding.

Hitchcock turned and confronted the Empress Joséphine. He assumed it was Joséphine, as opposed to Eugénie or Carlotta, because at her side stood Napoleon Bonaparte. Neither of them wore a mask and both were quite elderly, albeit handsome. "Do forgive us. We couldn't help overhearing you. Angelica's voice could fell an oak. How do you do, Mr. Hitchcock? What brings you to Harborshire?" The Empress Joséphine favored him with a whimsical smile.

"I'm looking for a gentleman who is missing a part of the little finger of his left hand."

Napoleon raised his left hand. "You mean like mine?"

"How do you do, Sir Rufus?" He turned to the Empress Joséphine. "And this, I assume, is Lady Miranda?" She nodded her head. "And the object prodding my stomach I gather is a gun."

"A very small gun," said Sir Rufus. "It's been in the family for years, handed down from generation to generation, like a recipe for mince pie."

The orchestra was playing "The Very Thought of You," and Hitchcock was thinking of Alma and Patricia and then briefly of Herbert Grieban. In an amazingly controlled voice, he said, "Surely you don't intend to shoot me here."

"Good heavens, no!" exclaimed Lady Miranda. "I've just had the floors polished. Kindly precede us into the hallway. I assure you, it is to your benefit to make no fuss. We have many friends here."

"Most of them, I assume, impersonating Mr. Hitler."

"Aren't you clever? Rufus, isn't Mr. Hitchcock clever?"

"Oh, indeed. I wish he was batting his wicket for us instead of the opposition." He prodded Hitchcock with the gun. Hitchcock turned and slowly made his way through the guests toward the hall, Rufus and Miranda directly behind him.

"Daddy? Mummy? Where are you off to?" They were joined by Shirley Temple holding an oversized lollipop that she occasionally licked obscenely. Her curls hung down in tired tassels, and her candy-striped little girls' dress revealed a pair of incredibly shapely legs.

"We were just going upstairs to our rooms for a quiet chat, darling," said Lady Miranda. "Do keep an eye on the party for us."

"Hello," said the woman to Hitchcock, "I've seen your face somewhere." The bulb lit. "I know! In *Picturegoer* magazine! You're a film director!"

"I am Alfred Hitchcock," he announced, prudently refraining from adding he was in a spot of trouble.

"Oh, yes, the thriller person. I'm *their* daughter, Violet Pack."

"How do you do, Miss Pack."

"It's Mrs. Pack, though God knows I wish it wasn't. What's that you've got there, Daddy?" She saw the gun. "Oh. Well, then, I'll see to the guests." She danced away, licking her lollipop, and Sir Rufus nudged Hitchcock with the gun. Arriving in the hallway, Lady Miranda signaled to a footman, and as Hitchcock led the way up the stairs, she gave some instructions to the footman that Hitchcock did not overhear. Then Lady Miranda joined Hitchcock and her husband, gently lifting her skirt so as not to trip on it as she ascended.

At the head of the stairs, Sir Rufus directed Hitchcock to his left. "There, on your right, the blue door." Hitchcock grasped the knob and opened the door. Seated on a chair against the wall facing him was Nancy Adair.

"One runs into the strangest people at parties," said Hitchcock.

"I'm sorry, Hitch. I'm so sorry," she said. Hitchcock heard the door shut behind him. The gun was no longer in his back. Sir Rufus and Lady Miranda had moved away. "I thought you were dead. I thought I'd left you to die."

Hitchcock said, "It was a tight situation, but I managed to wiggle out of it."

"You won't wiggle out of this one," said a familiar voice behind him.

Hitchcock turned and looked. Hans Meyer was seated in an easy chair against a floor-length wall mirror. Hitchcock could see himself reflected in the mirror, along with Nancy Adair and Lady Miranda, who had sat down on a settee, and Sir Rufus, who stood with his back against the door aiming the gun at Hitchcock. It if weren't for the gun in Sir Rufus' hand, it could have been a tableau more appropriate to a Noel Coward drawing-room comedy.

"Well, Hans, I gather you've been quite busy. I guess you won't find the time to appear in my film."

Hans Meyer laughed. "I have to hand it to you, Hitch." Hitchcock now resented the familiarity coming from him. "You're really quite marvelous. I was almost willing to bet you wouldn't show up tonight. I was sure that by now you'd have turned tail and given yourself up to the police."

"But there was no need to. I know the police know I'm innocent. They know you murdered that poor wretched detective." He turned to Nancy Adair. "And as for *you*, Rosie Wagner, you are most certainly a mean-spirited woman. All

266

those murders you've committed! I can assure you, murdering is a phase one never outgrows."

"Oh, Hitch," she sobbed, "I wish we had met under other circumstances. I could have made you so happy."

"Crippen's very words to the wife he murdered. Well, Sir Rufus, you know why I'm here."

"Indeed I do. A futile quest. I'd never betray my people."

"That's not the way I've heard it told. I must say you're a shameful lot, throwing in with a nation that is doomed to defeat in its futile attempt to hasten history."

"You are very naive, Hitch," said Hans. "Today we are only Germany. But tomorrow the world."

There was a knock at the door. Rufus crossed to it, switched his gun from his right hand to his left, and admitted Violet carrying a tray with a glass of milk. Lady Miranda addressed her sharply. "What are you doing here? Where's the footman?"

"His feet hurt, so I brought Mr. Hitchcock's milk." Sir Rufus shut the door and returned the gun to his right hand.

"I don't drink milk," said Hitchcock, his eyes riveted to the glass of milk, as Violet approached him slowly.

"You'll drink this one," said Lady Miranda. "There'll be no gunshots heard tonight. Come along, Mr. Hitchcock, don't dally. It's quite a painless death." Violet stopped a few feet away from Hitchcock. Their eyes met. Hers were tormented eyes, and he felt she was trying to convey something to him, or perhaps in desperation he was grasping at straws. He had to stall what to them must be the inevitable. He had one hope and one hope only, and that was Herbert Grieban. If Grieban had eluded the lorry, Hitchcock knew he would make his way to The Thirty-Nine Steps. Hitchcock had no intention of handing them his life as though it were a stick of chewing gum.

He said to Violet, "Surely, Mrs. Pack, you don't wish to be a party to murder. Don't you all realize that whether or not I gain the information I'm after, you will all be rounded up and taken into custody?"

"We won't be here," said Lady Miranda. "There's a boat waiting in the Channel. It shall take us abroad, where we'll be quite safe."

"You see, Mr. Hitchcock," said Sir Rufus, "we've been offered a fresh start in life. Perhaps you think us too old, but we don't. Mr. Hitler has promised us Transylvania, and that's where Miranda and I shall rule. Violet will come too; won't you, Violet? Of course not with Nigel. Nigel is Violet's husband, and he doesn't like us. He's so stuffy about the notoriety connected with us. Poor fool, had he known it, he would never have married Violet when he did, ten years ago. She was a secretary at British Intelligence. She took the name Violet Danvers, changing her name for obvious reasons." He chuckled. "Well, let me tell you, when Nigel discovered he'd married into the Derwents, well, now, there was a proper dust-up. Our son-in-law is an aide to Sir Arthur Willing. How's *that* for a joke, Mr. Hitchcock?"

"Nigel Pack," said Hitchcock, "then he's the one, isn't he?" Violet laughed. "I've got it. Of course. That's how he's made use of you. That's how he's been one jump ahead of British Intelligence, because he's a part of the firm!" He watched as Hans Meyer and Rufus and Miranda exchanged glances. Nancy Adair's eyes were fixed on the glass of milk, and Violet Pack's eyes never left Hitchcock.

"Mr. Hitchcock," insisted Lady Miranda, "be a good little boy and drink your milk."

Hitchcock heard a crashing noise behind him. Nancy

Adair screamed and leapt to her feet. Hans Meyer reached into his inner jacket pocket and produced a revolver, and a bullet whistled past Hitchcock's head. Hitchcock leapt behind the chair so newly abandoned by Nancy Adair and saw Herbert Grieban kneeling on one knee between the parts of the shattered door that lead to a balcony. Herbert was not alone. There were two plainclothesmen with him; Hitchcock would later learn they were part of a group of British Intelligence stationed in the area. Hitchcock could hear the bedroom door being kicked open as Sir Rufus drew a bead on Herbert. Herbert's gun barked, and Sir Rufus dropped his gun, clutched his stomach, and fell dead to the floor.

"Rufus!" screeched Lady Miranda, "Rufus, darling!"

Violet Pack drank the glass of milk.

The door fell open, and more men appeared. Hans Meyer, sweating with fear, dropped his gun and raised his hands. Nancy Adair was staring at Grieban with horror. Hitchcock couldn't believe what he next saw. Grieban's gun barked again and Nancy Adair's look of horror changed to one of surprise. "Hitch!" she gasped, "dear Hitch." With a beatific smile, she sank to the floor, blood appearing from a wound in her heart, and then her head hit the floor and soon she lay still.

Grieban had now advanced to Hitchcock's side. "Did you have to kill her?" asked Hitchcock as Hans Meyer and Lady Miranda were taken into custody.

"A trial would have been too costly," rasped Herbert. His eyes locked with Hitchcock's. "She was marked to die by both sides. Believe me, I have been humane."

Lady Miranda was struggling with her captor in an amazing display of strength for one who looked so frail. "My daughter! She needs me! I want to go to Violet!"

Violet Pack sat on a chair waiting for the poison to take effect.

Lady Miranda screamed. "In the bathroom! Hurry! In the medicine chest—the antidote!"

Violet's eyes beseeched Hitchcock. He went to her while Herbert sent a man into the bathroom. He took her hand; it was cold and clammy. "Not Nigel," she whispered. "It was not Nigel." Hitchcock could hear the noise of the raid going on downstairs. He wondered if they would succeed in rounding up the Adolf Hitlers. The man in the bathroom found the antidote and hurried to Violet. Her face was contorted with agony as she gasped a name to Hitchcock. Then she said, "God forgive me!" Her eyes rolled up, and Hitchcock heard her ugly death rattle as she fell into his arms. Hitchcock lifted her and carried her to the settee. Lady Miranda ululated like a banshee in hell. Hitchcock looked at Grieban.

"Violet told me the name. Who's Basil Cole?"

Eighteen

Basil Cole knew his cell well. He had held interrogations there on many occasions since joining British Intelligence. He was pleased that it had been freshly repainted. He liked the smell of fresh paint. It held the promise of a new beginning. He was almost glad he was under arrest. It tidied things up. There were no loose strings about, and if there were, Basil would weave them into their appropriate place for Sir Arthur Willing. He genuinely liked and admired Sir Arthur. After more than a decade with him, he respected the man for his fairness, his intelligence, the way he ran his department. True, Willing hadn't suspected a traitor in residence right under his nose, but then, that's how the game was frequently played. Basil Cole wasn't the firm's first traitor, nor would he be its last.

He was sorry he hadn't punched Nigel Pack in the nose

when Nigel spat in his face, but then, he had been cuckolding the man for years. Violet had been such a steady lover. Not terribly passionate, not terribly exciting, but very steady. He should have recognized she was reaching a breaking point in her unhappy marriage and the unpleasant course her mother and father had charted for themselves again. He should have recognized she could not face the inevitability of another deplorable family scandal. Her miserable marriage, which she didn't dare abrogate, so often plunged her into the depths of despair that Basil should have recognized the symptoms of her undermined and crumbling sanity.

Oh, God, he began agonizing. They'll make an example of me. They'll hang me in the press and on the radio and in the media across the world before they hang me proper. They say it's very quick. They say the penis erects and then you die. What a waste of life. What a waste of erected penis.

Hitchcock. What a peculiar man. The very idea of his insisting he owns exclusive rights to the story of my life. Here he's had death staring him in the face and all he can think about is material for a film. Basil was strutting the narrow cell from side to side. Well, why not? Why not film the story of my life? Let me think. What's a good title? *The Martyr*. Too simplistic. Oh, well, someone will come up with the proper title. Now who's to play me? Herbert Marshall? All wrong, and besides, he's got a wooden leg. James Cagney? Possibly, if they decide to cast against type. I've got it! Ronald Colman! Just as he was in *A Tale of Two Cities*.

"'Tis a far far better thing . . ."

Perfect. Well, now, that's all tidied up—now to think about my defense.

"Stroke? Oh, the poor dear! But when? This morning?" Miss Farquhar clucked her tongue, and at the other end of the wire, Miss Allerton wiped a tear from her eye. "Poor Madeleine. Which side's paralyzed? The left or the right? Or a bit of each?"

"She's dead!" wailed unhappy Miss Allerton. "She's gone to the big music hall in the sky!"

"My, my, my," said Miss Farquhar.

"Just as that gypsy woman predicted!"

"What gypsy woman?"

"The one at the Pechter Circus. Oh, dear, it's the end of an era, farewell to a woman who was a legend in her own time."

"Well, that's what *she* thought," sniffed Miss Farquhar. "So tell me, dear, who inherits?"

Lady Miranda was permitted to attend the double funeral of her husband and her daughter. She refused to stand near Nigel Pack, who was just as loath to stand next to her. He was in for a grim time with Sir Arthur Willing in the days ahead, and he hoped that he would be exonerated and restored to his position in the firm. It was the only job he knew. He couldn't think of anything else. On the other hand, he knew Hitchcock was preparing another spy film. Perhaps the man could see Nigel as his technical director. Perhaps he'd drop Hitchcock a note suggesting it. One must be a bit more aggressive these days, like Basil . . .

That son of a bitch. That traitor. Cheating on me with Violet all these years and me never guessing. All the drinks and lunches and dinners we had together. Why, he was almost a brother to me! Oh, Fate, how can you be so cruel!

Lady Miranda heard a sob, looked up through her black veil designed especially for her by Mainbocher, saw Nigel Pack crying, and in a snarl across the open graves to him, loud enough to wake the dead, cried, "Hypocrite!"

"I didn't!" Slap.

"You did!" Slap.

"Ladies! Ladies!" shouted the matron through the slit in the cell door, "you must stop hitting each other!"

"I can't stand the sight of her!" shouted Helga.

"She's a traitorous pig!" screamed Lisl.

"Well, sorry, girls," said the matron, "but I can't offer you separate cells."

Hans Meyer smiled at the newsreel cameras and waved at the women who hurled flowers at him and shouted words of encouragement. He was Britain's new matinee idol, with his continental good looks, savoir faire, and impeccable mien in the face of adversity. Candies and jellies and patés and aspics were delivered to his cell, along with thousands of love letters and offers of marriage.

"Be brave, lovey!" shouted a secretary. "I'll always wait for you!"

"Ain't he gorgeous, Vi?" a shopgirl asked a co-worker.

"A real proper gennelmun, he is," agreed Vi, "real proper. I'm sure he's innocent."

The detectives prodded Hans Meyer into the black van, and as it pulled away from the court house, the driver said to the man at his side, "Did you see her? Did you see that fat blowsy blonde blowin' kisses at 'im! That was my missus!"

Madame Lavinia studied the palm of her hand for the tenth time that day and for the tenth time slapped her palm and screamed, "You lie!"

Freddy Regner lived to see a rough cut of *The Lady Vanishes*. Hitchcock had arranged for him to be brought from the hospital to the private screening room on Wardour Street. Freddy looked better now than when Alma had last seen him in the safe house, but they knew it was only a matter of months, possibly less than that, until he would be dead. Amazingly, despite the knowledge of his mortality, he was in a constantly jovial mood. In its own way, his scenario had been a huge success. Hitchcock had made it a success. Freddy was truly happy.

"Now, Freddy," Hitchcock cautioned him, "you must remember—in this film, any resemblance to people living or dead is absolutely impossible."

Alma sat in the seat next to the one Hitchcock would occupy, her notebook in her lap, prepared to take the notes Hitchcock would give her during the hour-and-a-half screening. In front of her sat Herbert Grieban, his face swathed in bandages from newly discovered plastic-surgery treatments he was undergoing with a Harley Street specialist. The projectionist was not yet ready to roll the film, and Hitchcock sat down.

"When do the trials begin, Herbert?" asked Hitchcock.

"It will be months. Maybe years. There is so much preparation necessary. Tell me, Hitch, will I recognize the MacGuffin in this picture?"

"If you don't, I'll be terribly surprised." He shouted to the projectionist. "What's holding us up?"

"Half a mo'!" the projectionist shouted back.

Half a mo', thought Hitchcock. Oh, well. He had all the time in the world. His adventure would always be fresh in his mind. He recalled that afternoon months ago when he and Alma were reunited and, after Sir Arthur Willing was finished with him, they drove to the cottage to be alone together, and Hitchcock told Alma the entire adventure in his own interpretation. He could still hear her laughter when he finally settled back, hoarse from talking. "What are you laughing at?"

"You, you innocent. Don't you realize what you've been?"

"No, I don't. What do you mean, what I've been?"

"My darling," said Alma, taking his hand, "you've been the MacGuffin!"

Sir Arthur Willing fought hard against his recurring bouts of depression, but it was a difficult fight. Basil Cole had been like a son to him, if a bit of a prissy son, what with his passion for neatness and tidiness. Well, it was all neat and tidy for him now, with nothing in his future but the hangman's noose. Sir Arthur applied a blazing match to the tobacco in his pipe bowl and stared across his desk at Detective Superintendent Jennings. Their job was finished. The men had grown to like each other. Tonight they were dining together at Simpson's in the Strand. Now they were completing odds and ends, categorizing odd items of information, some pertinent to Basil Cole's case, others of little value but put in the file nevertheless.

"Snap out of it, Arthur," said Jennings. "You won't be made to suffer for Basil Cole, you know that."

"There are subtler ways of causing suffering, my boy. It's his deception over all these years. Why didn't I suspect? Why didn't I have a clue?"

"Why didn't anybody else?" Jennings smiled at Sir Arthur.

Sir Arthur was scratching his head. "Well, there's one thing to be grateful for."

"What's that?"

"Basil didn't turn out a queer."

*   *   *

In the projection room, the film was nearing its end. Hitchcock had given Alma very few notes. The film was good, very good. All it needed was the opening and closing titles and musical score to be ready for the exhibitors. Margaret Lockwood had made a marvelous heroine, a delicious lady in distress. Young Michael Redgrave in his first important role in films was certainly destined for a big future. Paul Lukas was a superb villain, though Hitchcock kept seeing Hans Meyer from time to time, visualizing what he might have been. And of course there was dear old May Whitty as the little old spy, the lady who vanished. And here were the final scenes, Lockwood and Redgrave arriving at British Intelligence trying to remember the little melody, the secret code the old lady had taught them in case she didn't reach London alive. They were coming down the hall heading to the office of the head of British Intelligence, but their minds were a blank. Then they opened the door to his office and at the piano sat May Whitty, and the melody she was playing still sent a shiver up the spines of the four in the projection room watching this final scene.

La-la-la-la . . . la-la-la . . .

GEORGE BAXT
His Life and Hard Times

a Monday afternoon, June 11, 1923, George Baxt was born on a
chen table in Brooklyn.

He was nine when his first published work appeared in the Brook-
Times-Union. He received between two and five dollars for each
le story or poem the paper used.

His first play was produced when he was eighteen. It lasted one
ght.

Mr. Baxt has been a propagandist for Voice of America, a press
ent, and an actor's agent. He has written extensively for stage,
een, and television. During stays in England in the fifites, he wrote
umber of films *(Circus of Horrors; Horror Hotel; Burn, Witch,
rn)* which are now staples of late night television.

His first novel, A QUEER KIND OF DEATH, was published in
66. His other novels include SWING LOW, SWEET HARRIET;
PARADE OF COCKEYED CREATURES; TOPSY AND EVIL;
" SAID THE DEMON; PROCESS OF ELIMINATION; THE
OROTHY PARKER MURDER CASE; and most recently THE
LFRED HITCHCOCK MURDER CASE.

Mr. Baxt lives in New York, is a bachelor, and is devoted to his
CR.